The Sadness of Whirlwinds

The Sadness of Whirlwinds

Short Stories

Jim Peterson

Red Hen Press | *Pasadena, CA*

Book layout by Daniela Connor

Library of Congress Cataloging-in-Publication Data

Names: Peterson, Jim, 1948– author.
Title: The sadness of whirlwinds : short stories / Jim Peterson.
Description: First edition. | Pasadena, CA : Red Hen Press, [2021]
Identifiers: LCCN 2021019137 (print) | LCCN 2021019138 (ebook) | ISBN
    9781636280097 (trade paperback) | ISBN 9781636280103 (epub)
Subjects: LCGFT: Short stories.
Classification: LCC PS3566.E7693 S23 2021 (print) | LCC PS3566.E7693
    (ebook) | DDC 813/.54—dc23
LC record available at https://lccn.loc.gov/2021019137
LC ebook record available at https://lccn.loc.gov/2021019138

The National Endowment for the Arts, the Los Angeles County Arts Commission, the Ahmanson Foundation, the Dwight Stuart Youth Fund, the Max Factor Family Foundation, the Pasadena Tournament of Roses Foundation, the Pasadena Arts & Culture Commission and the City of Pasadena Cultural Affairs Division, the City of Los Angeles Department of Cultural Affairs, the Audrey & Sydney Irmas Charitable Foundation, the Meta & George Rosenberg Foundation, the Albert and Elaine Borchard Foundation, the Adams Family Foundation, Amazon Literary Partnership, the Sam Francis Foundation, and the Mara W. Breech Foundation partially support Red Hen Press.

First Edition
Published by Red Hen Press
www.redhen.org

ACKNOWLEDGMENTS

My thanks to the following journals for publishing some of these stories in slightly different versions:

The Good Life Review: "The Belt," "Go Get the Gun"; *Los Angeles Review*: "Pablo," "Holes," "Tornadoes"; and *South Dakota Review*: "Scottness," "A Client," "Call Your Own Foul."

Additional thanks to Nicole Cloutier for our killer six-week writing retreat during which some of these stories were written.

Thanks also to Gary Dop for his helpful reading and critique of "Keeza of Lomasaya."

A big thanks to Grant Kittrell for his beautiful art on the cover and his helpful reading of "The Secret of Whirlwinds."

Final thanks to Kate Gale and Mark Cull for encouraging me to write this book.

With eternal gratitude and love,
this book is dedicated to
Harriet, Gayle, and Patricia—
beautiful, transformative whirlwinds

CONTENTS

The Observer Is the Observed

I, who have been so many men in vain, want to be one man, myself alone. From out of a whirlwind the voice of God replied: I am not, either. I dreamed the world the way you dreamed your work, my Shakespeare: one of the forms of my dream was you, who, like me, are many and one.
—Jorge Luis Borges

To really ask is to open the door to the whirlwind. The answer may annihilate the question and the questioner.
—Anne Rice

Whatever the whirlwind is doing out there, it's also doing it in here.
—A Friend

PROLOGUE

Pablo

I opened my front door to let in some light and fresh air. A small dog wandered down the center of my street. I was immediately worried about him. On impulse I grabbed my cap and some small dog treats left over from my deceased Jack Russell. This other dog poked his head in the gutter, meandered back out to the middle of the road, then over to the grassy shoulder on the other side, sniffing all the way, sometimes stopping to raise a leg and mark the spot. He appeared to me to have some Jack Russell characteristics—about fifteen pounds, jaunty gait, moist alert eyes, ears that flop forward, a white and brown patchwork coat. Clearly an independent individual.

I kept my distance. He had no collar, but otherwise he appeared to be healthy. I followed him for block after block into a part of the town I'd never explored. At busy streets, he paused just off the curb, looked both ways until a gap opened, and then he'd dart across and continue his inquiries on a less busy side street. As smart and nosey as he was, I assumed he knew I was following him, but he didn't give me any attention, not even a glance.

At last he trotted into a front yard and disappeared around a house. A car was parked out front. A small house, but carefully maintained, curtains pulled. My stomach sank. I wasn't in the habit of walking uninvited onto the grounds of strangers. I crept into the alley between houses toward the fenced backyard where the dog appeared to be going. The fence was five feet high. Did he jump over the somewhat shorter gate?

I saw the dog rolling in the grass at the feet of a woman who was sitting in a lawn chair facing away from me. I could see the long blonde hair on the back of her head and one bare foot of a crossed leg dangling in the air. I checked around to make sure no one was observing, and then I watched for a while.

The woman teased and praised the dog, and he responded to her, letting go of tiny barks I could barely hear. I opened the gate, and the latch made a distinct clink. The dog stopped his games and looked at me. The woman didn't move. I walked slowly across the yard, the dog watching, the woman silent and still, but obviously waiting. When I got close behind her, she said, "Thomas?"

"Yes," I said.

"Please sit down," she said.

I sat in the lawn chair near hers. "How did you know?" I said.

"I knew you lived in this town. I sent Pablo to look for you," she said, nodding toward the dog.

"Pablo?" I asked.

"Yes, he's a rascal just like Picasso."

"Oh," I said, "It's a good name."

"He says you were easy."

"What do you mean?" I asked.

"Easy to lure away from your home."

"That's not possible."

"Yet here you are."

"Maybe," I said.

"I named you Thomas because you doubt everything I say," she said.

Obviously she hadn't given me my name, but I let that go. She still had not looked at me, staring straight ahead, and it dawned on me she was blind.

"Can you look at me?" I asked.

"I *am* looking at you," she said, though she was still turned away from me, "I am always looking at you."

The dog barked once. "Pablo wants to check you out," she said.

"Is that what he just said?"

"That's right."

"That's fine," I said, "I'm a dog lover myself."

The dog trotted over to me, jumped in my lap and brought his curious face close to mine, looking steadily into my eyes. He gave my face a good lick. I was okay with that. Then he started sniffing around on my chest. I pulled out a treat from my shirt pocket, and he extracted it nimbly from my fingers. He jumped down and sat attentively in front of her again, munching.

"You've aged well," she said.

"Margaret?" I said, and she smiled, her awareness on me almost like the tips of fingers. I remembered her name, but nothing else.

"Don't worry," she said, "you will never remember me. That way we can begin again."

We sat quietly together for an hour. And then, slowly, we began.

You Will Never Remember Me

The Code

John hated going out to eat alone. It was okay for breakfast, maybe for lunch, but it never felt right for dinner. Not even at this family-owned Italian restaurant, Milano's, that was his favorite. Best food for the price. It was ten years to the day since his wife, Hannah, had died. He still hadn't adjusted to being alone. And it just got worse when he retired early from his job as a financial adviser. The receptionist escorted him to a tiny booth against the wall far back in the corner of the long, rectangular room. That at least was better than being on an island out in the middle. I'm already on an island, he thought, don't need to make a point of it. Before sitting down, he pretended to admire the copy of a Caravaggio that hung on the wall above his table: a vivid action scene of Christ falling in the road on the way to Calvary, carrying the cross, surrounded by the mob. What a strange subject, he thought, for a restaurant.

As usual, he had brought a paperback that he could pretend to read, or actually read if circumstances required. The same detective novel he'd read several times over the past year. Bradley, the detective, has awakened with a throbbing headache. Another late night with Molly and her pals. He wasn't sure she was worth the trouble. She had refused to come home with him, as always. But something else was trying to creep into his overactive mind. A couple at a nearby booth. The flash of a concealed revolver. An envelope passed under the table. A familiar face, Selena. What was she doing with that guy? John pulled the book out and set it on the table, just in case. He loved the bright colors of pulp fiction. A classic 1940s blonde bombshell stood startled in a beam of yellow light, red dress tight and sleek, bare arms stark against the darkness. Nearby, a man wearing a fedora and a trench coat lurked in the shadows, the ember of his cigarette glowing, illuminating the man's narrowed eyes. John appreciated the woman's shapely calves, and the way she gripped her black pocket book as if she might use it as a weapon. The title *Killer's Code* glared in blood-drenched letters. Maybe this time he would come to understand Selena just a little better, why she felt she had to save the life of such a man.

The waiter poured his glass of wine and set the Caesar salad in front of him. John opened the novel, pinned the first page back with a salt-shaker, and began to read. When he'd finished his salad, he walked the labyrinthine path to the washroom, weaving with conscious nonchalance among the tables crowded with young couples and families. He'd forgotten how noisy it could be in here on a Saturday night. When he got back, he discovered a mountainous plate of meatballs and spaghetti on his table. That's not what he ordered. Where was his veal parmesan? The waiter was not in sight. John sat down and glared at the meatballs. He couldn't remember the last time he'd eaten meatballs. He caught a glimpse of his waiter in the distance through an archway into a different room. He was pouring water, sliding chairs for the ladies, beginning to take orders for the large party, licking the tip of his pen. It might be ten minutes before he remembered to check on John.

The meatballs looked good. He was hungry. So he ate them. And as it turned out, they were outstanding, better even than his beloved veal. Far away, his waiter stood at a booth and was chatting. John realized this was a test from the Universe. To see if he could just take things as they come, not overreact. The spaghetti was great, he still had plenty of wine in his glass, and he could always read. Bradley got out of bed, got dressed, and headed to his office. There, his luscious secretary who had a thing for him had taken two messages. The first was from Shuford, his ex-partner; and the other was from Selena. He wasn't happy about hearing from either of them. And why the hell were they both calling him on the same day? Something was up.

John finished up the last meatball, the last twisted forkful of spaghetti. He stuck the bookmark into the gutter and closed his book. The start of Bradley's case would have to wait, although John, as always, was intrigued by the detective's old flame Selena. This wasn't the only detective novel he'd read repeatedly. It was as if they contained a clue to . . . *Killer's Code* was from his wife's large collection of detective novels still holding down seven shelves in a seven-foot bookcase against a wall in the living room. Over the last ten years, he'd read all of them, many of them two or three times. He wasn't sure why. He typically preferred mainstream literary novels, when he read fiction.

He finished the last sip of his wine, washed it down with a few swallows of water, and reached back to his hip pocket. This happened fairly often, that he would feel for his wallet and at first it would seem not to be there. But this time, it just kept not being there. He sat quietly for a moment. He felt around for his other pockets hoping that by some miracle he had put his wallet where he would never put it. No dice. Though the crowd was thinning out now, his waiter was still a universe away, delivering desserts, collecting credit cards, maybe trying to solve the riddle of why one of his customers had mistakenly received veal parmesan. For once, John was grateful for an inattentive waiter. But eventually he would remember John and come scurrying back to his table. Since John was a repeat customer, maybe they would allow him to go home, locate his wallet, and come back to pay. Still, that whole business was going to be embarrassing. I don't think I can face it, not tonight, John thought, on Hannah's birthday, I mean deathday, with my mind so full of the mysterious Selena. He realized that he had somehow conflated them in his mind, though they were nothing alike. Maybe it was just the wine going to his head.

He dropped his cloth napkin to the floor, looked around to make sure the coast was clear, then slipped off the edge of his chair and down into a crouch feeling for his napkin. At the last moment, he grabbed *Killer's Code* off the table and crawled completely under. He was certain no one had noticed him. No one ever noticed him. The booth was very solid and it made a nice little room under there with the tablecloth dropping down low on three sides. A safe space for him to take a little time and figure out what he was going to do next. Traffic was low back in this corner. Only an occasional pair of feet whispered by.

He tried to lie down flat, but there wasn't enough space. He reached back and touched the fourth wall. Not really a wall, but a kind of panel with a small handle. Storage? He pulled the handle sideways, and it slid easily, wheels on a track. He opened it as far as he could, then reached back with his other hand and opened it all the way. He could turn and look over his shoulder and see that it was just pitch black in there, wherever it was. He slowly shifted his feet back into the opening, stretching his legs, and encountered no obstructions. Soon half his body lay back in the darkness and the other half lay flat under the table. This was more like it. His body began to relax a little. He observed the foot traffic for a while. Then the voices of two men drew near.

"This sonofabitch walked out on us."

"You mean that old guy, he bolted?"

"That's what it looks like."

"Maybe he paid up front. You were really busy tonight."

"Without his check?"

"Oh, right. Hmmmm. Well, I didn't see him leave."

"He comes in here a lot. I'll be waiting on him."

"Ah let the old guy be."

"Martha's not gonna like it, with all the things been going on around here. Don't think she's had a good night's sleep in the last two weeks."

"What she don't know won't hurt her."

"Believe me, she knows."

"I've been on vacation. What's been going on?"

"Some guy gets in, three times now."

"No shit."

"We don't know how. Disarms the alarm. Has himself a few drinks, carries off a bottle of the good stuff, pops the safe open like it's a Tinker Bell box."

"What the fuck's that?"

"You get the point."

John could hear a vacuum cleaner not far away. Its headlight came into view, slashing back and forth. Pretty soon it would swoop under the booth. Then the tablecloth itself would be removed.

"Man, this guy was a pig."

The waiter swept the tablecloth onto the floor in a pile. John was now exposed to view if anyone wanted to look. If he were found now, the embarrassment would be multiplied many times over. He wiggled like a salamander back and back deeper into the opening, and still his feet met no resistance. When he was completely in the hole, the soles of his feet flattened against an opposing wall. He slid the door silently shut. He was lying in absolute blackness. He could not remember ever being in a place so dark. Now the voices of the two men were too muffled to understand completely. The suction noise of the vacuum drew close, bumped against the door, then receded. For a while, he could hear voices but they soon became infrequent. He wondered what was going on out there?

How long could he wait like this? There didn't seem to be any possible escape. But maybe, just maybe, when the place was completely empty, he would be able to walk out undetected. That seemed to be his only chance now. He thought about the Caravaggio hanging on the other side of the wall, just above his head. Such a vividly strange painting. The fallen Christ looks out at the viewer almost dispassionately. The energy of the ten or so other figures seems to spin around Christ as if he were the eye of a storm, which of course he was. Christ's face floated before John there in the darkness, his eyes so calm within the turmoil around him, as if he were consciously present in that dramatic moment, as if he were merely playing a role.

John wished he were just playing a role, one that would end soon and he could crawl out of his hole to resounding applause.

His back started hurting, so he slowly and as quietly as possible gathered himself into a sitting position. He listened, but he could hear nothing now on the other side. He leaned against the back wall. The darkness encircled him and made him wonder if he would ever see another human being again, if he would ever see his beloved Hannah gone so long, or maybe the dream woman, Selena, who could make him forget his life that had amounted to so little. He ran his hands along the floor like the body of a woman, but the dust was thick and rolled up under his fingertips. His hand touched the novel and he grabbed it. If he had any kind of light, he would read, hoping to find out more about Selena. The image of the woman on the cover came back to him, her frightened face the center of its own kind of storm. How could his life have come to this desperation over nothing, to such smallness? No one knew where he was or cared. Maybe his dog at home was getting hungry and wondering if his master would return before he starved. So maybe that was it, now, the final thread of his connection to self-worth, to life. He'd been good at helping people move their money around, and he'd made plenty of money himself. Enough to retire early, and then she died. Or did she die before he retired? He couldn't remember now. He watched these thoughts and others arise along with tension in his body. He made a decision not to believe his thoughts, to watch them as if they were a July Fourth parade going by.

And that seemed to work for a while. He relaxed and drifted. A scene arose, a table at a café. Hannah and Selena were there, and him too, though he was not a part of the conversation. They glanced at him from time to time. He knew they were talking about him. They laughed, reached out and touched hands in the middle of the table.

He woke up with a jolt and bumped his head against the wall. He shushed himself. The silence was so heavy it seemed to be falling to the floor like dust. How long had he been asleep? Maybe an hour? Maybe two? He waved his hands in front of his face, but couldn't see them. Maybe it was time to buy a cell phone. He'd resisted for so long, he hated to give in now. But if he had one there would be light, and he could read. He had never imagined there could be a darkness so complete. Did he even have hands? He pressed them to his face to be sure. He suddenly had the urge to force his middle fingers deep into his eyes. He slapped his hands down against his thighs and shuddered. Where did that come from? He had to get out of this place right now. What if morning came, and he were still here. He would scare the hell out of somebody if he suddenly emerged from under his booth. Surely by now it was deep into the night and everyone had left. He crawled to the door and slowly slid it open. It was dark out there too, but by comparison to his cave it was full of light, seeping in from windows far away at the front of the restaurant. He crawled out and sat for a moment under the canopy of his little table. He listened, but there wasn't a sound, except for a siren at some distance in the town and receding. He lifted the fresh tablecloth, stuck his head out and looked around. No one. Silence. He crawled out and stood up. It felt good to be on his feet again. His knees ached. His back was sore. Now what? He would just walk out the front door, get in his car, and go home.

He walked among the tables that had been so full of boisterous people a few hours before. For some reason his feet could feel the texture of the carpet right through his shoes. His ears had become so sensitive he could hear the air moving against his face. He approached the front of the building and could see through the huge window looking out on the parking lot that his car waited for him. Light from a streetlamp gleamed on his windshield. One other car waited in shadows not far away. He turned right toward the foyer, the cash register, and the glass front door. Further to his right there was a little bit of light streaming out of the entrance to the bar. Against his better judgment, he crept over to it and eased his head in, looked around. The light was coming from the backsplash of the counter behind the bar. It probably stayed on all the time, he told himself. A shadow moved slightly, and suddenly he could see the silhouette of a woman sitting at the bar. Also, the silhouette of a half-empty bottle and a glass.

"There you are," she said, sounding relieved. She picked up the glass and took a sip. He didn't know if she were talking to the glass or to him. Her voice was rich and breathy, took its time to formulate the words.

"Have a drink?" she said. "It's on me."

"Who are you?" he said.

"Come on, have a drink with me while we're waiting."

"Waiting for what?" he said.

She reached over the bar, grabbed an upside-down whiskey glass, set it down on the bar, poured two fingers worth, and slid it toward him. He stared at the glass, the whiskey swinging slightly like a hammock in a breeze. His eyes were adjusting to the light. He took a step toward her. There was something forlorn in the way she held herself. She was still mostly shadow. She put her right elbow on the bar and rested her head in the palm of her hand.

"Jesus, I'm tired," she said.

"I don't usually drink whiskey," he said.

"Consider it a special occasion. Or maybe an offer you can't refuse, considering what you've put me through."

"What do you mean?" he said. "Do we know each other?"

He took another step toward her, hoping to see her face better. Her voice was familiar, and something about the way she moved. Her hair fell down in loose strands. He suddenly remembered he'd left *Killer's Code* on the floor inside the wall. He felt lost without it. Didn't know what to do next. He would have to get it. He took a step back.

"Where do you think you're going?" she asked.

She moved forward slightly, her face still in shadow. He could make out the hollows of her eyes. Selena, he thought. Or was it his Hannah?

"WHERE do you think you're going?" she asked again.

"My book," he said.

"What?"

"Home," he said.

"Please don't go," she said, "have another drink with me."

"Haven't had the first one," he said. Sirens arose in the near distance. They would be here so quickly, he thought. Even if he made it to his car, he would never get out of the lot. For the first time he noticed that her drink was on the counter and a gun was in her hand.

"I have a right to do this, you know."

He could see her eyes now—round, intense, happy. "Yes, I know," he said.

What would Bradley do, he thought. He took one big step and closed the gap between them, expecting a shot, maybe to the heart, but it didn't come. He took her into his arms, and the barrel end of the gun pushed against his belly. As he pulled her close, between her breasts the gun turned, jammed against his sternum, pointing straight up through his chin and out the top of his head. He pressed his lips against hers, ran his finger over the gun's chamber, felt the little round nose of a .38. Her mouth gave in right away, softened, opened for him. The cool taste of whiskey. Everything deepened. The embrace, the kiss, the metal of the gun. The readiness of his death. The moment, as lights fluttered in around them, voices.

"What the fuck?" somebody said.

"Everybody just stay calm," someone else said.

A big hand took hold of his forearm, but it wasn't too insistent. Almost reassuring. "Sir," a voice close to his ear said. "Sir, please stop that, let her go."

They came out of the kiss. He didn't look at her eyes. He wasn't ready for that. She licked her lips.

"There's a gun," somebody said.

"Easy now," someone said, and a hand slid between them, took hold of the gun. "Easy," someone else said. She let them take it. Space between them again. Someone drew his hands behind his back and he felt the cuffs, heard them close and snap.

"You're lucky she didn't kill you," a man behind him said.

More space between her and him. He felt it coming, the last chance. He looked up at her. Her eyes were still intense, happy. It was an interesting face, old, but not as old as his own, he knew.

"I'm Martha," she shouted over the chaos, as the officers pulled them farther and farther apart. "Martha."

"Roy," he called to her as she disappeared into the crowd.

They took hold of him and maneuvered him out the front door and toward the lit-up police car. They pressed his head down and shoved him in. It was okay. They could do whatever they wanted. Everything was going to be okay. For the first time in a long time, he was sure.

Go Get the Gun

"Go get the gun," Angie said.

I put down the book I was reading. "What?" I said.

"The gun! Go get it. Hurry!"

I looked around the living room. Everything was quiet. I looked at my wife sitting in her favorite recliner with her favorite lamp bestowing light to the pages of a book by her favorite author. She was looking at me with big eyes over the top of the book.

"Well," she said, "what are you waiting for?"

"But I don't hear anything," I said.

"Are you going to let the fact that you are deaf keep you from protecting me?" she said.

"I'm not deaf, Angie. I'm hearing *you* just fine, for example."

"Well, *something* must be wrong with you," she said.

"I'm not going to grab the gun every time you imagine a bad guy is trying to break in."

"I'm not imagining. I heard something."

"It's those books you read," I said, "with all those deranged killers. That stuff gets into your head, Angie, and makes you paranoid."

She just glared at me. After a moment or two, she lifted her book again. At last, peace was restored. Sometimes I just had to reason with Angie.

After thirty years of marriage, I had learned that reason usually won the day.

I looked out the window just beyond where Angie was sitting. It was pitch black out there. I could hear the wind blowing in the nearby trees. That must have been what Angie heard. That must also explain why the streetlights were out, though I admit that absence of light was a bit strange. I sighed and went back to reading my own book.

I was getting into a good part when Angie said, "I want a divorce."

I looked at her and she was glaring at me again. This time her eyes were narrow and hard. "Angie," I said, "we've been together for thirty years. You do not want a divorce."

"Yes, I do," she said, "you don't take care of me anymore. You don't believe anything I say. You always have to be right. You don't even protect me anymore. A rapist could come through that door, and you would just let him have me!"

"That's a terrible thing to say," I said, "and you know it isn't true. I would gladly die for you if that's what is called for."

"Prove it," she said.

"What?" I said. "You want me to die?"

"No, I want you to go get that gun and make sure no one is trying to break in. I'm really frightened. Can't you tell?"

I took off my reading glasses and put on my far-sighted glasses. She came into better focus. Yes, I could now see that she was trembling. Her eyes were glassy with fear. "But Angie," I said, "it's dangerous to run around with a loaded gun unless you really need it," I said.

"If you don't get the gun, then I want that divorce. I'm tired of being so scared all the time."

"When are you afraid?" I asked.

"All the time!" she shouted. "I tell you and you ignore me. I'm tired of it."

"I can't believe you would leave me because I don't carry a gun around all the time," I said.

"There are other reasons," she said. "Do you want me to list them for you?"

I thought about that—my balding head, my thickening middle, my two glasses of whiskey every night, my cousin James who was always stopping by and staying for a week. Then I thought about Angie's blueberry pie, her beef stew, the long walks we took together, her warm body in the bed, her IRA that had grown substantially over the years.

I decided to get up and find the gun. Just then, I heard a crashing sound. Angie screamed but remained in her chair, holding her book against her chest as if it would protect her. I proceeded back to the bedroom where I had hidden the gun and a box of bullets buried under some of my shirts in a drawer. Angie had followed me so closely I thought we had become one four-legged creature. I could feel her breath on my neck, her voice in my ear. I carefully loaded the .38s into chambers of the revolver and snapped it shut.

Shaking, Angie gripped my arm like she might try to tear it off. As one, we slowly trundled up the hallway. We checked and secured the front door, the back door, and the side door. There was one more door, in the basement. We heard another crash, and it was definitely coming from down there. We slowly made our four-legged way down the stairs. I flipped the light switch, but the basement light had apparently burned out. Angie pulled out her cell phone and turned on its light. Everything appeared in order: the pool table, the futon, the table and chairs.

We made our way over to the door that opened onto a patio. Angie pressed her phone to a windowpane in the door, and outside we saw something on the patio thrashing. I stared and stared, trying to bring it into focus. And then I saw it. A badly wounded deer trying to stand up in a slippery pool of its own blood. It had been trying to get into our house. But why? I turned the lock and opened the door.

"Be careful," Angie said in my ear.

I carefully pushed open the screen door. Angie remembered the patio light, switched it on, and light flooded the scene. It was a doe, and her eyes were big, black circles. She thrashed, but she couldn't get up. One of her front legs was twisted and obviously broken. She was bleeding from a hole in her shoulder. The anguished guttural of fear broke from her throat. I didn't hesitate. I walked up close to her, raised my gun, and shot her once in the head. The blast carried its message across the neighborhood. She dropped to the patio bricks, spasmed a time or two, and died.

A thin trail of white smoke flowed out of her body and drifted into the trees. I had been present at other deaths, but I'd never seen anything like that before. Somewhere in the nearby woods, a hunter was probably looking for her. The wind was worse than I had realized, throwing the heads of trees around like crazed toys.

"I'm so glad you had the gun," Angie said behind me. "It was suffering terribly," she said.

I turned to her. She was crying.

"I don't want to divorce you," she said.

I didn't want to divorce her either, and said so. I realized I was crying too, trembling with a fear I couldn't name. We held on to each other for a while. Then we went back inside, leaving the deer in darkness.

I unloaded the gun and left it on the table. It could take care of itself for the rest of the night. Angie and I took care of each other.

Echo

I had learned to be sneaky. It didn't come easy to me, but I got pretty good at it. I could find places to hide it in the house and in the barn especially, there were so many little cubbyholes. She rarely caught me. I needed it to get through the day, she knew that, and so maybe she didn't really try to catch me. I'm not sure. But when she did find it, or found me holding it, then there was hell to pay. No loving, that's for sure. And I worried that maybe she would just get fed up and find herself another man. It wouldn't be hard for her. She deserved a good man.

We were in the barn working. I was picking up some droppings in the wash stall with a shovel, and she was checking on Telly, our pregnant mare. I ran an export/import business out of our house, but I often had time to help around the barn. Sarah waved me over to the aisle door. "Come look at Telly," she said.

Telly walked across her paddock straight toward us, like one of those trucks on the highway with a sign saying "Wide Load." I was surprised she could support herself on feet that seemed too close together. Her eyes were full of dull exhaustion, her head drooped low to the ground, and she could barely lug herself along.

"That thing's fixing to come," Sarah said.

"But she's got another month to go."

"I don't care, just look at her."

We walked down to the paddock and climbed over the fence. Telly kept trudging straight for us. She was too tired to act ugly today, and besides, it was Sarah coming to see her.

Sarah's only about half my size, but she's all muscle and bone and gentle confidence. The horses know she's in control right away. She ran her hand along Telly's mud-streaked back and suddenly stopped.

"Look," she said, pointing, "It's moving."

A knobby bulge surfaced and roamed the tight drum of Telly's stomach.

"Telly Belly," I said stupidly, in a sudden fit of fatherly emotion. Not to mention I'd hit the juice only ten minutes before and was feeling it.

"And looka here," Sarah said, leaning over and reaching under Telly. Her bags were tight and full. She took a step with her left hind and milk squirted from her right teat. "This thing's coming tonight," Sarah said.

I just kept quiet.

We led Telly up to the barn and put her in the big foaling stall. Sarah started milking Telly who stood for it calmly and sighed and even made that twisted-lip face with her head cocked like when you scratch her good spot.

"She was about to bust," Sarah said. "At least she'll be a little more comfortable for a while." She came out with a jar full of that yellowish milk, carried it into the tack room, and found a place for it in the freezer.

"Why are you saving it?" I asked.

"Gotta keep some of it on hand in case Telly won't let the foal nurse."

"Why wouldn't she?"

Sarah shrugged her shoulders. "Who knows? Some mares don't take to mothering right away."

I looked at Telly. She laid her ears back and bared her teeth. "You've got a point there," I said.

"We'd better go ahead and move in." Sarah reached through the bars of Telly's stall to skim the loose hay off her water bucket.

I picked up a gray piece of hoof left over from the farrier and sailed it toward the trashcan. "Don't you think we're being a little premature about this? Why don't you call the vet and ask his opinion?"

Sarah threw a glob of wet hay at me and I caught it on my ear. "I already did, Dumbass."

"Hey now," I said. "Do I ever call you names?"

Her left eyebrow lifted, arching high into her forehead, a family trait that stemmed from her mother's side revealing thoughtfulness, or sometimes anger. Her voice caught in her throat a little. "Look," she said. "I'm going to be here when the foal comes. And if it comes this early there could be trouble. If you don't want to stay, fine, you can go home." She turned, slammed a handful of wet hay into the trashcan, and walked briskly up the aisle and out the end of the barn.

I dragged down the two old wood and canvas cots from the loft, set them up in the aisle next to Telly's stall and swept off the spider webs and strands of old hay.

I drove back to the house and packed up some necessities—blankets, pillows, books, food and drink—and made it back to the barn in time to set up a lounge chair at one end of the aisle and watch a beautiful, cloud-swept sunset, thanks to daylight savings time and the longer days of late spring. Sarah came up behind me and settled her hands on my shoulders.

"You changed your mind."

"Not really," I said, taking a sip of whiskey. "Just got tired of playing the devil's advocate."

"Why do you do that?"

"Hell, I don't know. The way I was raised I guess."

"I'm glad you came back. It can get kind of lonely out here at night."

I twisted my head around to look up at her, her eyes full of that sunset, the pinkish light from low clouds deepening the tan of her face. "It can get lonely at night just about anyplace," I said. "Besides, this could be fun. Kind of like camping."

"You know," she said, massaging my neck and shoulders, "it's really beautiful out here."

I had to agree. The barn was situated at the end of a half-mile road in the middle of 150 acres of mature forest and was surrounded by several paddocks with new fencing, a dressage arena with good footing, and scattered around the property were fields with well-made cross-country obstacles. On two sides the land bordered on other horse farms that had given Sarah riding privileges, which didn't hurt her business at all. The owner of the farm had hired Sarah to manage the place: teaching, training, and boarding. As we sat there in the door of the barn, an owl called from the dark green face of woods to the east. A moment later there was an answering call from the forest to the west where the pines and oaks flamed red and gold in the last slant rays of afternoon sun. The fresh load of hay in the loft smelled as good as hot bread.

That night we set up a lamp so we could see without keeping the overhead lights on. We found some good country music on the radio and read and talked. About 10:30 Sarah snuggled up under her blanket and the next thing I knew she was snoring lightly, probably dreaming about the easy birth of a perfect stud colt. Behind her in the stall Telly stood motionless, resting her left hind leg, eyes glazed over and half closed, munching on a piece of hay, probably dreaming about the taste of pickled man-flesh.

I loved watching Telly and Sarah in competition. Telly was a sleek, sixteen hand, dark bay thoroughbred with a white star in the middle of her forehead. She had the look of a racehorse and covered the ground with long, powerful strides. A bold cross-country jumper, she took the obstacles with controlled abandon, the result of her unquestioning faith in Sarah.

Telly had always been a prima donna of sorts, and she was enjoying the ivory tower splendor of her retirement. She spent her days grazing and strolling and lying in the sun. Sometimes when the horses in a neighboring paddock got to running she'd trot along her fence line with her tail straight out behind her, neck arched, Arab-like head held high, black eyes flashing. Then she'd settle back down to grazing and swishing her long tail at flies.

If you had to go in to check on her feet or brush the dried mud off her back, it was best to be cautious. She'd lay her ears back and nod her head angrily. Then she'd stretch her head toward you baring her big, yellow teeth. She had drawn blood more than once. The best tactic was to go straight to her favorite scratching spot high on her neck just in front of the withers. If you scratched vigorously with your fingernails she'd crane her head out in front of her, twisting it back and forth, lips going loose and sloppy, ears relaxed and flopping like a pair of soft gloves. About sixty seconds of this and she'd be your good buddy long enough for you to do your job and get out. The only person that Telly never gets surly with is Sarah, but I guess that's understandable.

I laid my book down, took another drink, and listened. There was only pitch blackness outside the aisle doors. I could hear in the distance the endlessly repeating song of whippoorwills. Inside, there was a whole menagerie of sounds: the low, muffled crunching of huge molars; the rattle of an empty feed bucket; the slop and dribble of someone playing in his water; the pitter-patter of cats in the rafters; the sliding howl of a breeze in the eaves of the barn; the shuffle and groan of a horse getting up, or lying down. I took another drink and kept on listening. It was beautiful somehow, and different, and good.

The next thing I knew I awakened with my head slung over the back of the chair, strange guttural noises issuing from my gaping mouth, and three or four insects of indeterminate species circling my face. Sarah was still asleep on her side with Abba the barn cat curled up in the curve of her body. Telly was a dark statue in the dimness of her stall. I felt sick, my neck was sore as hell and I could barely turn my head in either direction. I took the low route to my cot and encountered Bill the barn mutt, a mischievous, friendly sort of fellow. He sensed my defenselessness and licked my face without mercy until I could climb up on the cot and push him feebly away. I felt exhausted and beat-up but I couldn't go back to sleep. I thought maybe I'd quit drinking for a few days. A fast for the heart and soul, not to mention the mind. The idea buzzed around inside of me all night like one of those horseflies that's smart enough to land where you can't see it.

Telly's foal didn't show up that night, or the next night, nor anytime during the next week. 'I told you so' blossomed on my tongue in the middle of every conversation I had with Sarah, but I somehow managed not to say it to her face, only to have it mumble forth during the day while I was filling an order or working up a new magazine ad. Out it would tumble and I'd giggle like an idiot, then slap myself in the face to restart my brain. I think it was working alone all day that brought on such strange behavior, or sleeping in a barn every night, or a combination of the two. I thought about doing a study of the subject.

Actually, I was beginning to like sleeping in the barn. It brought me closer to Sarah, deeper into her daily routine and concerns. The absence of TV was a plus. We talked a lot more. No lovemaking, given the awkward bedding, but this was a preoccupied time for her anyway, and she was worth the wait. And Bill and I had finally come to terms over this face-licking situation. I wouldn't smash him in the ribs with my fist if he wouldn't lick me in the face. He got the hang of it almost right away.

The only real problem was that Sarah was getting more concerned about Telly. We were into our second week of sleeping at the barn and of Telly showing the symptoms of imminent delivery. She was still dripping milk, biting at her sides, and was so uncomfortable that she hadn't lain down in days. She sometimes fell asleep standing up, front legs buckling, front end hitting the stall floor with a heavy thump, rear end stuck straight up in the air. This would startle her and she'd scramble up in a panic and run around in a huff for a while. The fact that she was still three weeks early made it all the more confusing. Sarah told me that an early foal had much less chance of survival. Finally she gave in and called the vet again, but he just said, "It'll come when it's ready. Call me if there's a problem."

With each passing day Sarah became more sensitive to Telly's condition and was no longer sleeping through the night. Every time Telly moved Sarah jumped up in her cot. One night I saw her get up, pull on her jeans, and go into the stall. Telly put her head on Sarah's shoulder to rest her neck, and they stayed like that for thirty minutes or so until Sarah's shoulder got sore. Then Sarah came out and pulled off her jeans and lay down, but an hour later she was back in the stall again. I usually stayed up pretty late myself, but once my head found the pillow, or the back of the chair as the case may be, I was pretty much gone for the night. That was one thing about me: I could sleep soundly anywhere and under almost any circumstances. I didn't even have any dreams, just blissful, blank oblivion. Of course there were always the mornings full of headache and regret, but a heavy dose of coffee and order-filling usually brought me back to myself before the 12:30 lunch alarm on my watch went off.

But I was starting to worry about Sarah. Her eyes looked more like Telly's every day, always only half open, red and teary with weariness. Her condition was affecting her work. One day she left a paddock gate open and three horses got loose and galloped around the countryside for a couple of hours before Sarah and the two girls who work for her could lure them into halters with buckets of grain. One of them strained a tendon and would be out of commission for a while. Sarah cried inconsolably for half an hour and wouldn't let anybody near her. The next day she left the water running into one of the horse's buckets and flooded the stall. The horse was relegated to a paddock for a couple of days while the stall dried out and Sarah wouldn't let anyone help her clean up the mess. She turned almost silent in her riding lessons and began to cut them short. Most of her students understood she was going through a phase of some kind and didn't make an issue of the bad lessons, just backed off and gave her some space. The ones who didn't got cussed out and scratched off her lesson schedule. When I realized that her state of mind was actually costing us money, I figured I'd better talk to her.

So one night when we had settled down with a couple of books, both of us just pretending to read, I said, "Sarah."

Only her eyes moved, looking at me now instead of the page. "What?"

"How was your day?"

That eyebrow vaulted up into her forehead. "You know, you're just about as subtle as that wart on Telly's butt."

"Whoa now," I said. "I'm just asking a simple question."

"Right," she said. "My day was great." Her eyebrow fell back into its accustomed position and her eyes moved back to her book.

"How did your horses go?"

"Fine," she said.

"Is Reginald getting any better?"

"Yes."

"What about the lessons? Did they go okay?"

She took a deep breath and exhaled heavily. "Yes," she said.

"Somebody said Andy was upset about something."

"Somebody who?" More eyebrow action.

"I don't know, just something I overheard."

"The boy's got a bad attitude. I had to give him a hard time. That's all. The usual teacher-student routine."

"There seems to be a lot of that particular routine lately."

She closed her book with a slap and put it down as if she were trying to bruise her own leg. "Are you beginning to get a little closer to the real subject of this conversation?" Her eyes were steel now, fierce.

"Why don't you go home and get a good night's sleep," I said. "I'll stay here with Telly and give you a call if anything changes."

"Sure," she said. "You sleep like a dead man. The foal would have to break out of the stall and bite you on the ass before you'd know anything had happened."

"Come on, it's not that bad."

"No, it's worse. I've heard of people that lived in a drunken stupor all their lives, but you're the only one I've ever known firsthand."

"Shit," I said. She had never spoken so directly before.

"What's the matter? Wasn't that the subject you had in mind?"

"No." I just stared at her. I could feel the heat radiating from my face and neck. We almost never argued.

"Cat got your tongue?" she asked, sort of smiling, her lips trembling.

"Yes," I said.

I stood up and walked out of the barn. It was a fine night, warm with a little breeze, the sky crowded with stars and a full moon. A lot of foals, and babies too I guess, are born on a full moon. I stayed out for a long time, just strolling between the empty paddocks at first, then onto the trails that wandered through the woods. Why is it in a world without predatory animals the woods are still frightening at night? It was the strangest thing. I feared for my life. The trees were menacing, their overreaching limbs full of intention. Even though the night sky was bright and the forest floor was more visible than usual, there was a murkiness of moon shadow that made everything intertwine and merge. I walked into a huge spider web and felt the fat spider scamper across my head and dive for safety.

When I returned to the barn, I slipped into the tack room through the outside door so I wouldn't wake Sarah. I sat down on the couch. The only sound was my own breathing, and I tried to listen to only that and not to the bizarre thoughts that were butting their way into my brain. I wanted a drink so bad I was aching down inside in places I didn't even know could hurt. But my bottle was nestled in the covers on my cot, and I didn't want to wake Sarah in case she was finally getting some sleep.

I'd only had a couple of drinks, and my walk had burned off all of the effects of those. I wondered if everybody had this same sick, hollow feeling in the pit of their stomach every night like I did when I didn't drink, or if it was just me. I felt restless, like I was supposed to be doing something, but I had no idea what it was. A TV would have helped, or a good book, but I'd left my novel on the floor beside my cot.

So I tried to just sit there, but my legs jerked with nervous energy, and my mind jumped everywhere at once, thinking about work and Sarah and Telly's foal, remembering disagreements I'd had with schoolmates fifteen years ago, getting angry again and ready to fight as if somebody was there in the room with me. I brooded like that for a couple of hours before I got tired enough to lie down and go to sleep. But there was no sweet oblivion that night. I had dreams so vivid they were like visions—each one opening into the next. Finally I got stuck in a ridiculous nightmare. I was in this one-hundred-story skyscraper—the tallest, most advanced horse barn in the world. Instead of offices there were stalls with horses in them. People dressed in breeches and boots carried around bridles and saddles. One man led his tacked-up horse out of a stall, its head rubbing against the ceiling. I followed them to an elevator. The horse had to lie down and curl into a fetal ball to fit in the cubicle. The man and I stood cramped together in a corner. The elevator went up instead of down and I jumped out at the next floor where I found Sarah standing with a tall, slender young man. He had his arm around her shoulders and they were laughing. She put her open hand casually on his stomach. I played it cool. I didn't make a scene. You can't deny people the things that they want, especially in a dream, not if you love them. But I was mad and hurt and the next dream was much worse, full of knives and terrible wounds.

I woke up at dawn with a somewhat stunned clarity of mind. But if soberness means I have to put up with strange dreams and nightmares, I'd rather be drunk. Maybe the dreams don't always come like that, just sometimes. I left by the tack room door not wanting to disturb Sarah, still not wanting to speak to her. The full moon had passed and the foal had not checked in. I drove home and got an early start on work.

Sarah showed up at the house for lunch, her T-shirt and breeches splotched with dust. She had not taken her braids down for a couple of days and her hair was pulling out of them and breaking off in places. The circles under her eyes had deepened. She dropped her pocketbook on the kitchen counter and came over to me. There was the hot smell of her sweat and horse urine from where she'd knelt in Telly's stall to milk her.

"I'm exhausted," she said, leaning against the wall.

"I can tell. Why don't you lie down for a while?"

"Too much to do."

We heated up a couple of microwave TV dinners and sat down.

"Listen," she said. "I'm sorry about last night."

"It's okay."

"No, it's not. I said some things I didn't really mean. You know I love you."

"Yes," I said. "I know."

"It's just that I'm so busy at the barn, and I can't stop worrying about Telly and her foal."

"I understand."

"You've been so good about it. I know you were trying to help last night. I just couldn't take any kind of questioning, that's all."

"It's okay. I should've known better."

"I'm probably going to be like this until this thing is over."

"Don't worry about it," I said. "Just do what you have to do."

"Okay. I will." She sat up straight and started eating.

"Good," I said.

She put her fork down again. "You're drinking more than usual. Don't you understand how much that worries me?"

"Am I? I don't think so."

"Maybe I just notice it since you're around the barn more these days. It really makes me nervous."

"Okay. I get the point. I'll work on it."

"No you won't." She picked up her fork again.

I vowed to myself to work on it, to keep my flask out of sight, to pour my drinks when no one was around.

Ten days later the foal still hadn't shown up. The vet said he'd never known a mare to show such positive signs of foaling for so long without actually doing it. He said it was a good thing that Sarah had been collecting Telly's colostrum every day because we were probably going to need it.

The day the foal finally arrived started out like all the others of the past month. Sarah got up early and tended to Telly and then the two of us ate some cereal in the tack room. I drove home to work and Sarah began her day at the barn with horses to train and students to teach while her minions cleaned stalls, swept out the barn, groomed and tacked up the next horse for her. When she came home for lunch she reported that nothing had changed. At suppertime she said that Telly was a little more agitated than usual, but she'd had so many mood swings over the past month it was hard to take anything too seriously. Sarah took a shower and ate supper and drove back to the barn. My plan was to stay home and watch some TV, then drive over to the barn later. I had a few drinks and fell asleep on the couch.

The ringing came from far away. There were the voices on TV and at first I thought it belonged to them. But they kept talking and the ringing didn't stop. I roused myself, stumbled across the room and picked up the phone.

"Her water just broke," Sarah said, her voice small and quick. "Hurry."

"I'm on my way," I said and hung up.

I pulled on a sweater and jumped into the car. The curves on the black-top came in odd places that night, and I had to use both lanes and the shoulders. The broken yellow centerline passed by me and under me and even over me it seemed, like tracers in a war movie. I finally found the turn-off and for a moment felt more secure, but that barn road swallowed me up. It was the strangest feeling. I was suddenly alone on a dusty dirt road winding through a forest that had no beginning or end. Everything behind me . . . my home, my work, the TV and my drinking . . . and everything ahead of me . . . the barn, Sarah, Telly having her foal . . . all seemed unreal to me. All that existed now and forever were the headlights that carved the road out of the darkness in front of me, the whine of my little four-cylinder engine, the rapid-fire shimmy of ruts and rocks in my hands on the wheel, the dark wall of woods on either side of me, the dry sting of road dust in my nose.

The lights at the barn popped into view. I veered into the driveway and skidded to a stop at the near end of the barn. I was panting as if I'd been sprinting instead of driving. I tried to run down the aisle to Telly's stall but my legs were mush and I kept bouncing off stall doors and blanket racks. I finally peered in through Telly's bars. The light from overhead bulbs was dim and yellowish and it took me a few seconds to get a fix on what I was seeing. Telly paced back and forth, obviously distressed, her eyes wide and blinking. She stopped every few seconds and twisted her head around to see what was happening behind her. Blossoming from her vulva just beneath the lifted tail was a whitish, translucent bubble. I could barely make out within it the shape of two forelegs pressed together, one stretched slightly more forward than the other. Sarah emerged from the other side of Telly all blonde and trim in her jeans and T-shirt and full of restrained light like an eclipse.

"Is everything okay?"

"So far," Sarah said. "You got here mighty fast."

"I didn't want to miss anything," I said, breathing hard, the focus of my vision coming and going like atmospheric interference on the TV. I looked at my watch. It was nearly 11:00. "I didn't know it was so late," I said. "I fell asleep on the couch."

"That's what I figured. You look awful."

"I'm okay. I just haven't woke up yet. Is that the way it's supposed to look?" I pointed to Telly.

"Yes," she said, "everything's normal so far. That's the amniotic sac. It'll break open later on."

"So what do we do now?"

"I hope we don't have to do anything."

"Shouldn't Telly be lying down?"

"She'll lie down when she's ready."

So we just stood there watching Telly make her rounds, sometimes stopping to wince and groan when a contraction came. The bubble slowly enlarged like a balloon, and more of the legs and the head began to show. Finally she lay down, buckling her front legs first, leaving her butt up in the air, then slowly folding her back legs until she collapsed onto her side. More of the legs and the foal's whole head slipped out, but Telly had a panicky look on her face and flopped around for maybe a minute and then scrambled back up again. The effort of standing caused the foal to be sucked back in entirely out of view. Telly started lapping the stall again and in a few minutes part of the legs and half of the head slipped back out.

Thirty minutes went by like this and we could still see only part of the legs and head. Telly was exhausted and in pain, but whenever she started to go down now she caught herself and began pacing again. When Telly stopped for a moment, Sarah went over to her and stroked her neck and talked to her. Telly looked worried and confused and pressed her face against Sarah's chest.

"Go get the phone," Sarah said.

I just stood there. What did she mean? The phone wasn't ringing.

"Bring me the phone from the tack room," she said, her voice impatient this time.

I stumbled down to the tack room and pushed the door open. It was pitch black inside. I fumbled around on the wall for the light switch and finally found it. The bright light smacked against my eyes. The phone on her desk had fifty feet of cord, most of which lay coiled up on the floor. I carried the phone out, feeding the cord through a finger loop, trying to keep it from tangling or catching.

When I got to the stall I handed the phone through the bars to Sarah, but she wouldn't take it. She'd positioned herself behind Telly who stood still for a change. Sarah took hold of the foal's legs and pulled on them, but there was very little movement.

"Call the vet," she said.

"But I won't know what to say."

"Do you want to trade places?" she asked, glancing at me with a strained smile, both hands around the foal's legs now, the sac pinching as if it might break any minute.

"No," I said. "What's the number?"

"424-4780."

"4 . . . 2 . . ." I said, repeating the numbers as I punched the buttons, but then my mind went blank. "4 . . . 2 . . ." I said again.

"424," she yelled, and I punched the other 4.

"What else?" I asked.

"4780."

"4 . . . 7 . . ." I repeated, but the old window of my mind was painted shut.

She looked over at me, and I could see it in her eyes—she knew what was happening to me. But she didn't say anything. She just repeated the numbers slowly.

"4 . . . 7 . . . 8 . . . 0."

I punched in the 80 and the number began to ring. I let it ring ten times. "Nobody answers," I said.

"Okay. I need your help."

I put the phone down in the aisle and lurched into the stall.

"Take the foal's legs," she said, "and pull when I say pull."

She pulled a halter through the stall bars and put it on Telly. Telly's back legs trembled and it seemed like they might buckle at any moment. What would I do then? I thought. I felt her body tighten in a contraction and I heard Sarah yell for me to pull. The sac was cold and slimy and it was hard to get a good grip on the legs, but I pulled as best I could and then the foal edged toward me a little.

"It moved," I yelled. Telly turned her head back to see what I was doing, but there was no viciousness in her eyes now. Sarah came around to see for herself. The sac had broken open and she peeled it away from the foal, which had squeezed out almost to its chest, revealing a pair of long legs, a neck and a head. Its hair was wet and matted, its eyes shut, and it was completely limp—a bay with a big white star just like its mother.

"I'm going to try the vet again," Sarah said, wiping her hands on her jeans. "Keep a hold on it and pull when she has another contraction."

She went outside the stall and disappeared. I held on to the foal's legs. There was this dread welling up inside me. The foal wasn't moving at all, wasn't looking around. Telly started walking off and I kept holding on, moving with her like a man behind a plow, but when she made her turn at the end of the stall I had to let go. The foal's head and tiny black hooves thumped against the wall. Telly headed back in the other direction and stopped in the middle of the stall. She was having another contraction. I repositioned myself and pulled for all I was worth, but this time the foal didn't budge. Telly walked off again, her back legs shaky, the foal flopping around behind her. I didn't know what to do. I stayed close to her and tried to help when another contraction came. I couldn't figure what was taking Sarah so long.

Finally she stepped back in. "I got him," she said. "They'd gone to a movie. He says if we could get her to lie down, things might go easier."

"It looks like it's dead," I said.

"Maybe not. It's just so damn big, and Telly's not cooperating. John said this might help." She held up a jar of K-Y Jelly. "Hold Telly's head and see if you can't keep her still."

So I held the mare's head with the halter while Sarah tried to grease the foal with jelly. She forced her hands as far inside Telly as she could, but it was extremely tight. Telly had another contraction, but Sarah couldn't get the foal to move any further.

"You try again," she said.

We switched positions. When the next contraction came I leaned back with all my weight. I thought I was going to pull the foal's legs right out of the sockets. Telly's legs buckled a little and she backpedaled toward me. For about two seconds she was going to collapse and sit down on me and the foal, but she caught herself. That's when the foal came to me about three or four inches.

"It moved," I yelled.

Sarah came around. The foal was almost halfway out now. The way it dangled there triggered a bizarre memory in me of Mussolini's body hanging by its feet above the crazed mob. When the next contraction came both of us pulled on the foal, but this time it was no deal.

"We've got to get her to lie down," Sarah said.

"Yeah, but how?"

We looked at her. She was panting heavily, in a half-eyed trance of exhaustion and pain. She couldn't remain standing much longer. We positioned ourselves with Sarah in front and me in back. I held on to the foal and kept trying as before. There was still no progress, and Telly was getting weaker every minute.

Finally, after another unproductive contraction, she started going down, back end first just as I had feared. She was going to sit like a dog, and I didn't think the foal could survive it. Sarah was pulling at Telly's head with all of her 110 pounds, trying to get her to step forward and hold up her back end, but she was no match for Telly's 1200 pounds. And neither was I. I was still holding the foal, going down with it as Telly was slowly sinking, and I felt like I was going to break it in half, or that Telly would when she sat all the way down. I let go of the foal and jumped down under the mare's haunch, trying at first to lift her with my arms, then folding down to get my shoulder under her, straining upward with all that I had. I could feel the blood vessels distending in my face and neck, the heat and weight of her settling more and more on my shoulder, my back and knees cracking, the foal's legs flopping against my right side. I heard a scream erupt from me as if it had come from someone else. I sounded like a high school girl at a horror movie.

And then something strange happened—an extremely loud pop, so loud that for a moment I could hear nothing else. Then a continuous, high-pitched tone. For a moment I lost sense of where I was and what I was doing. Suddenly I was looking down into the stall from above, my head next to the naked light bulb. Below me I could see Telly still slowly sinking to the floor, the foal's hooves sweeping the straw, Sarah still pulling with every ounce of her strength at Telly's head. And only part of me was visible beneath Telly, like the rim of a partial eclipse. From this vantage I saw clearly what I must do. I must drop to all fours and clip Telly's left leg out from under her, so that she'd go over on her side and not sit on the foal. And the instant I thought it, I was back within myself, my hand around her left back hoof forcing Telly's leg to slide out from under her in the loose straw, my back becoming the off-center fulcrum that rolled her over. I heard the heavy crunch and groan of her, and I scrambled out from under her thrashing legs. I sat against the wall, blowing just as hard as Telly was.

"Are you okay?" Sarah said.

I nodded.

"We can't stop yet." She grabbed my arm and yanked me to my feet.

At least Telly was in the proper position now, lying on her side in the straw. And the visible half of the foal was stretched out on its side facing away from her. It jerked involuntarily—a flutter of rapid breath where its chest entered the vulva. With the next contraction, we pulled together, and this time the foal slid to us substantially. Everything but the hind legs was out. We pulled again and only the back feet stayed tucked away. The foal was breathing, its eyelids twitched, its ears flopped around out of control, and it tried to raise its head. It was wet and trembled all over in the cool night air.

"Let them rest now," Sarah said.

I nodded and sat down in the straw, leaning my back against the wall. I was splotched with blood and amniotic fluid. A sharp, salty smell pervaded the air. Every muscle and bone in my body ached. But in one sense I felt better than at any other moment in my life. My mind was perfectly empty. Everything in the world was still and at peace. A moment later I heard Sarah's voice speaking with hoarse excitement to the vet. He'd stayed on the line all this time. He probably could hear a lot of the struggling, must have heard that horrific screech of mine. My throat felt like someone had scratched it with a hoof pick.

Sarah returned and stood over the foal. "It's huge," she said. When she touched it, it startled and made a little squeak. She pulled its back leg back a little and found the sheath. "It's a colt," she said happily. She rubbed him with a towel trying to get him dry and warm him up a little. Then she sat down beside Telly's head and stroked her neck. Telly's breathing had become normal again, but she was still too worn out to move. All of us just crashed where we were and took a break.

Finally, Telly stood up with a groan and stepped away from the foal. The umbilical cord stretched and broke, and the amniotic sac swung from Telly's vulva, dragging in the straw. Sarah tied it into a knot to get it out of the way. Telly strolled over to her colt making a gentle nickering sound. The colt raised its head and rolled onto its stomach. It looked like a disheveled, feeble old man rudely awakened. Telly touched her nose to its nose and began licking it in the face and eventually all over.

"He's beautiful," Sarah said.

I wasn't so sure about that, but I nodded in agreement, figuring she had a better eye for such things. I was mainly interested in the way Telly kept walking around the foal without stepping on him. Her hooves would come down just inches away from his fragile legs or his head. Her 1200 pounds could cripple him for life. Sarah noticed my concern and shook her head. "Don't worry," she said. "She knows what she's doing."

Sarah continued to work in her busy, efficient way while I sat and watched. She poured a cup of iodine over the colt's navel to help prevent infection. When Telly finally delivered the placenta with a wet slapping sound to the floor of the stall, Sarah picked it up carefully, a great gray mass of membrane, and carried it to the wash stall. Picking off bits of straw, she laid it on the concrete floor and ran a hose into the end that had broken. As the placenta filled with water, she spread it out so she could inspect every inch of it. Thick veins scrawled across its surface. She tinkered with the two horns of the placenta, which coincide with the horns of the uterus, so that the water could get into them.

"It looks good," she said. "No holes or blemishes."

"Good," I said, remembering this was a sign that the mare's internal functioning had been sound.

The colt was already attempting to stand. He'd rest for a moment after each effort, then he'd attempt to thrust his body upward into the air with a jerk, trying to pull his feet and legs under him at the same time. At first it didn't seem possible that he'd ever succeed. His legs were too long, the straw was too loose and slippery, and he was totally uncoordinated.

"Maybe we should help him," I said, stroking the soft, damp coat of his shoulders.

"He's doing just fine by himself," Sarah said, laughing. "The effort to stand is like exercise, it helps them to get stronger."

So we kept watching him, and Telly kept chewing her hay patiently in the corner. By the end of his first hour, the colt had stood on his own several times, only to fall down again after the first few steps. After a while, Sarah and I guided him to his mother's nipples. He was so tall it was hard for him to bend low enough to reach under her, and the best he could do was to dry suck her leg. But he finally found what he was looking for, learning to scrunch down to get a good angle, and began to nurse enthusiastically. Sarah thawed out and heated up some of Telly's first milk anyway. The colostrum is richest in the mare's first milk, and it would be good for the colt. We fed it to him from the middle finger of a rubber glove with a hole pricked in it. At first I had to hold his head still and direct him toward it, but once he'd gotten a taste he took hold of that flimsy finger with a real sense of purpose. Within two hours he was standing, nursing, walking and even running around confidently between naps.

Sarah looked at me. "You did good today. Might've saved this fella's life. I'm really glad you were here to help."

I grinned. "Thanks," I said. "Me too."

That stud colt is nearly a yearling now: big, strong, athletic, beautiful, and rascally as a wild dog. I love him. Sarah was having a hard time deciding on a name for him, so she asked me to take a run at it. After my out-of-body experience, I'd spent some time online researching it. I read a few books. I came across this modern religion called Eckankar based on some older religions. It has a lot of teachings about astral projection, another way to say out-of-body travel. I had told Sarah about my strange experience the day after the foal was born, and she just rolled her eyes while pulling her next ride's girth tight.

"How many had you had before you got here?" she asked.

"Not many," I said.

She planted her left foot into the stirrup and pulled herself up into the saddle. "Too many," she said, and rode out the end of the barn into bright sunlight.

At dinner a few days after that, I proposed the name "Eckankar" for the stud colt. She tilted her head, a sign she was thinking about it. She wiped her mouth with a napkin and looked at me.

"I think I like it," she said. "It sounds grand and powerful."

"And we can call him Echo," I said.

"I think you just gave him his name."

The other evening after a few drinks I walked out into his paddock. I had just sold a hundred ceramic Buddha figurines and was feeling good. The fall sky was full of cirrus clouds streaked purple and pink by the sun that was sitting fat and bright on top of the woods that surrounded us. He watched me alertly as I approached, ears pricked forward, eyes wide. His red soccer ball lay on the ground maybe thirty feet away from him. I walked over to it and kicked it straight at him. He caught it on his chest and cut loose with a magnificent buck. The way he kicked out, if anybody had been behind him they would be nothing but a sack of broken bones. We proceeded to play a game. He booted the ball in my direction and I booted it back to him. He had this crazy, playful energy, and it was contagious. We played like that for ten minutes, but one time he followed the ball after he kicked it and suddenly skidded in the dust right in front of me. He stood up on his hind legs and turned into a ten-foot-tall, wild-eyed devil. He threw a jab with his right hoof and caught me on my left hand, which I had raised to my face to protect it. I sprinted for the gate, holding my busted hand, and he chased me bucking the whole way. As I clambered over the gate, he hit it with his chest behind me. I ran into the barn and into the office where Sarah was on the phone. When she saw I was hurt she hung up and rushed over to me.

"What happened?"

I realized that I didn't want to tell her, but I had no choice. In the midst of caring for my hand silently, she looked up at me. I knew she could smell my breath. "The next time you come to the barn after drinking, I'll ban you from the place forever. I hope you're hearing me."

It wasn't anger that was coming out of her eyes, it was something else much worse in this particular moment, and it hurt my heart. I knew she meant it. She looked back at my hand. My left pinkie finger was bending in the wrong direction and already swelling up like a cucumber.

I'm a man who has floated bodiless and aware in a place that looks on this world as if it were a dream, and still I go on drinking. I have had a profound vision of peace and ecstasy, and still I go on drinking. An amazing woman manages somehow to keep loving me, and still I go on drinking. A beautiful stud colt named Echo has stood on his back legs and struck out, breaking my little finger. Now it won't fold up all the way and it won't straighten out, and I can't attempt to grip without pain. Trust me, a horse's strike can kill a man. For that reason, I accept the finger's deformity and pain as a stroke of good fortune. It could've been a lot worse. I bear my broken finger as a badge of honor. I often show it to people and tell my story. I love that horse even more than before. But if I ever get in a fight, my left jab will be seriously impaired.

Home

I'm sitting on my couch watching television. I know I should be doing something more productive with my evenings, so I watch documentaries to convince myself that I'm learning and improving my mind.

This one's about a guy who's trying to get back to the house he grew up in. His parents were murdered when he was a child, maybe five years old—that much he knows. He was adopted soon after and moved far away. As an adult, his memories of this house are like the foggy fragments of a dream: a big place with long hallways and many rooms, a large finished basement with a pool table and a bar, a second and third story, and a crow's nest up among the canopies.

The violence and trauma of the last days in his home meant that social workers deliberately kept the adoption records difficult for him to trace. They thought they were protecting him from a terrible past. His quest has led to many dead ends. Whenever he gets a new lead, he takes off time from work, or quits if he has to.

In a simulated scene with actors, he and his girlfriend are sitting on a couch in the man's Virginia apartment. Her black, curly hair falls over half her face.

"Why is this so important?" she says.

The man is thin with short red hair. His eyes are intense. "I don't know," he says, "I just feel driven to see where I came from."

In the next frame, the man is working at his computer. Finally he uncovers a good lead on a house in California. Suddenly the man and his girlfriend are standing in front of his apartment door.

"You quit your job, didn't you?" his girlfriend says.

"Yes," he says, "I may be gone a long time this time."

"Take me with you," she says, tossing her hair out of her face with a flick of her head.

"I can't," he says.

"Why not?" she asks, "I want to share this with you."

"I may find what I'm looking for, something that changes everything," he says.

"If you don't take me, I won't be here when you get back."

That day she packs her bags. He believes he loves her, and he knows he'll miss her, but letting go of things he loves is his forte. At the door, she turns and looks at him, her beautiful eyes a deepening call into a familiar world, her black hair wildly romantic. As she closes the door, he feels a thick cloud descend and block his path back to her. But another cloud within him clears, and a new path comes into view.

The next day he flies across the country. He's made arrangements to see the house which has been vacant and for sale for months. Research reveals that twenty-five years ago a husband and wife were murdered in the house. The homicide team could not find their small son. Three days later, he reappeared at the house, sitting in the crow's nest, studying the behavior of squirrels. Newspaper articles in the local paper from that time tell the whole story, but he can't read them. They say things about his parents he doesn't want to know.

He parks outside the gated entrance and walks a quarter mile on a dirt pathway cut among thick woods to the house. His eyes follow it up three stories to the crow's nest shrouded by the canopies of ancient trees. Once inside, he knows he is finally home. The previous owners remodeled, but the bones and facades are preserved.

More than events, he remembers the feelings. They loved him. His mother carried him up to the crow's nest where they watched the birds and squirrels. His father built a secret room, and when the intruders were breaking in, his father made him go there. There were terrible sounds for hours—screams and crying—and then the silence.

This son, now a grown man, stands before the old fireplace. The cameraman zooms in on the man's hand as he reaches for a brick at the highest point he can touch standing on toes, presses it, and a door in the wall opens. It's pitch black inside. He reaches in to find a switch, but he knows there is no switch, no light. He aims his flashlight at the darkness, but a voice in his head tells him not to turn it on.

He lived in that room for three days until there was nothing left. Even the silence seemed distant. The darkness of that room had befriended him, had taken forms his mind couldn't describe in words, had shown him how to let go of everything: his parents, his home, his friends, his hope. He didn't need to go back in there. He backed out and pulled the door shut. He felt the weight of so many unanswered questions. He felt the vastness of a mystery that would, nevertheless, fade into the past forever, if he would let it. And he couldn't move. Standing there, he let go of his last and best friend, his one true love—the darkness of that room.

The TV show ends soon after that. The talking heads don't have a clue. His girlfriend will not take him back. But at least he has some kind of closure.

I turn off the set in the middle of the rolling credits. I am so alone on my couch it's difficult to feel my own presence. The night outside my window is complete in its blackness. The house is so dim and silent and still it feels like it's floating in the infinite body of emptiness. Everything I love—my wife who is traveling for her work, my friends, my dog, my own work, my dreams of the future—spins away from me like old photos caught up in flames.

The Mandy and Andy Show

Saturday morning was beautiful, dry, and warm, so I put on a pair of shorts, a T-shirt, white socks and tennis shoes, packed a small backpack with a couple of books and sandwiches and beers and headed for the park only a mile or so away. The neighborhood was quiet. People had already hooked up their trailers and taken the boat to the lake, or loaded up their vans with kids and supplies and driven into the nearby mountains full of scenic overlooks with picnic tables. The fishing lakes and waterfalls would see a lot of action that day. Some of my neighbors were probably sleeping in late, getting some well-deserved rest. In any case, no one was around.

Until I spied my friend Hank working in his yard. He wore coveralls, a long-sleeved shirt, gloves, and boots. He also wore a wide-brimmed floppy hat, dark glasses, a scarf around his neck, and a white filter-mask covering his nose and mouth. He was pushing a seed-thrower, and thousands of seeds were flying around everywhere. His lawn was disappearing under layers of seeds.

"Hey Hank," I said.

He seemed startled and stopped in his tracks. He looked around until he spotted me. He waved his hand.

"Do you think maybe you got enough seeds there on your lawn?" I asked.

He looked around at his handiwork and then back at me. "You can't ever have too many seeds," he said in a voice muffled by his mask.

"Yeah, I guess you're right," I said.

"Hey, you want to come in for a drink?" he asked.

I had never known Hank to drink, day or night. "When did you start drinking?" I asked.

Hank lifted his hat and scratched the top of his head. "Last night," he said.

"Really? Anyway, this is too early for me," I said.

"It's Saturday," he said, "it's never too early on Saturday."

"For me it is," I said, feeling the cans of cold beer against my back. "Maybe I'll stop by around five or six."

"Can't," he said, "got a date with Margaret." He started pushing his seeder again in a small circle so he could still talk to me. The machine whispered rhythmically.

"What about Susan?" I said.

"Susan?"

"Yeah, Susan, your wife."

"Ohhhhh, you mean Susan. Yeah, she knows about it. No problemo."

"Where is Susan?" A stream of seeds hit my pants. I noticed ten bags of unopened seed lined up against the wall of his house.

"She's out with Rico."

"What do you mean 'out'?"

"Yeah," he said, "she's got this thing for the guy. I don't personally see it, but hot is in the eye of the beholder, right?" He laughed.

I forced out a laugh.

"So where's Mandy?" he asked.

"Who?"

"Mandy?" he said, "your wife?"

The question hit me like the crack of a whip. "Ohhhhh, you mean Mandy," I said. "She's . . . she's . . . Damnit Hank, I don't know where she is."

"Now that's weird," he said.

"She wasn't around when I got up this morning."

"Hmmmm," he said, "that's mysterious. And you haven't bothered to look for her?"

"I forgot all about her," I said, "can you believe that?"

"Just business as usual," he said.

"What?" I said.

"Hey, Fred," he said, "if you ain't coming in for a drink, then I got a lot of work to do. I want to finish this job by dark."

No grass could be seen on his lawn. Only seeds. I made tracks in them as I walked. "Okay," I said and gave him a little salute, "I'll see you around."

"Not if I see you first," he said, laughed, and headed his seed-whirling machine toward a far corner of the lawn that had fewer layers of seed piled on.

I walked down the street trying to understand what had just happened. I realized I wasn't even certain it was Hank that I'd been talking to. I never really saw his eyes. His voice was muffled and didn't really sound like Hank. Hank was an absolute teetotaler. And my name was Andy, not Fred. But the Mandy stuff, that had caught my attention. I knew she wasn't back at the house. How had I forgotten about her so completely? It didn't make any sense.

I noticed Margaret sitting in a swing on her front porch. She was reading a book. "Hey Margaret," I called out and waved.

She looked up from her book and waved. She was wearing a floppy hat and a party mask of some kind. I turned onto her brick walkway and got a little closer to see her better. "How're things going?" I asked.

"Not bad," she said. Her voice was muffled by the mask, but I could still understand her words.

"So why the mask?" I asked.

"It's none of your business," she said.

"Oh, sorry," I said.

"But since you asked, I got it at a party last night. I like it so much I decided to wear it today."

"Isn't it hot under there?" I asked.

I was wearing shorts and a T-shirt. She had on boots, long pants, a sweater that covered her arms, and that mask that looked like Hillary Clinton.

"It's perfect under here," she said. "Why don't you come sit with me for a while?" She scooted over and patted the empty space beside her on the love-swing.

"I can't," I said. "I've got to get to the park before this beer turns warm."

"Good luck with that," she said.

"Listen," I said, "have you seen Mandy today?"

"Uh oh," she said, "have you lost your wife?"

"Sort of," I said.

She laughed. "Don't you remember? Mandy has yoga on Saturday mornings."

"Oh, I forgot about that." Mandy didn't have yoga on Saturday mornings, or any other time for that matter. She hated yoga.

"Yeah," Margaret said, "with that fellow Matt. He studied for years in some yoga country. He's an absolute swoon, don't you think?"

"I've never met him or seen him," I said.

"Yeah," she said, "she's been going to his class for about a month."

"Didn't say a word to me about it," I said.

"Hey," she said, "you want to come in for a drink?"

"Too early for me. Besides, I'm on my way to the park, remember?"

"Of course I remember. What are you saying?"

"I didn't mean anything," I said.

"Well, if you aren't going to mean things, Fred, I'm getting back to my book." She raised her open book to a reading position. Her eyes behind the mask moved back and forth between me and the pages of her book. Were those Margaret's eyes? I couldn't tell for sure.

"Okay," I said, and I strolled out of her brick path and proceeded down my street.

I walked by the houses of many of my friends, but I tried hard not to see anyone, not to talk to anyone. Fifteen minutes later I got to the park.

There were a few mothers out with their little kids playing on the swing sets, sliding boards, and climbing mazes. I found an unoccupied picnic table and pulled out my beers and sandwiches. Peanut butter and jelly, and chicken salad. I was hungry. Thirsty too. The beer wasn't really cold anymore, but it still tasted good. And maybe it was helping me to sort out the events of the morning to date. One thing was clear: the woman on Margaret's porch wasn't really Margaret. Okay, I've had a little bit of a thing for Margaret for years, but she's never been even the slightest interested in me. Plus we're both married. So what was that business with her inviting me to cozy up with her on the love-swing? And then inviting me in to have a drink? It didn't make sense. She was one of Mandy's best friends. The real Margaret would never do that. And she knows me, she would never call me Fred.

While I was thinking, I heard the sound of Mandy's laugh. It was unmistakable. I spotted her at a swing set maybe fifty yards away. She and some guy were swinging together and talking, like a couple of kids. I packed up my stuff and headed their way. She was wearing some sort of cap, so I couldn't get a good look at her face, but I knew it was Mandy by the way she moved, and by the sound of her laughter, and that familiar jumpsuit she was wearing. As I drew near, the guy got out of his swing and executed a slowly unfolding headstand beautifully. They continued their conversation with him upside down. It didn't appear to make a difference to him. Or to her.

"Mandy!" I shouted to her.

Her head turned quickly toward me midsentence. I stopped for a moment to stare, then kept walking to get a better look. She was wearing the most outlandish make-up I've ever seen. She hates putting on make-up, but there it was. It was so thick it appeared to be flaking off every time she moved her head or spoke. It was pink and white and black and red. Her eyelashes were so long they stuck to her cheeks when she closed her eyes. Her luxurious blond hair was tucked up under that big hat.

"Fred," she shouted, "what are you doing here?!"

"Who are you talking to?" I shouted back.

That seemed to puzzle her. She sort of cocked her head and gave me a long look. "You," she said, "I'm talking to you."

"How would I know that?" I said, "considering Fred isn't my name. How could you forget your husband's name?"

She just stared at me with her mouth open. It was strange to see her normal colored tongue and teeth behind those bright red-painted lips.

"Is there some problem?" Matt said.

I turned and looked straight into the tips of his toes. His shoes were some sort of upscale Merrells. Little bits of wet grass clung to the sole. I let my eyes move down, or was it up, his body until I was gazing into his upside-down nose. He may be Mister Cool Yoga Man, but his snot-bearing nostrils were just like everybody else's as far as I could see. "There's no problem," I said. I realized that I could easily kick him right in his nose without exerting much effort.

"Is this guy bothering you?" Matt said.

"I don't know," Mandy said. "I don't know what he's doing. I thought he was my husband Fred, but now I'm not sure. With that mask he's wearing, I can't tell."

I wasn't wearing a mask. I felt my face to be certain. Nope. No mask. Matt refolded his body, found the ground with his feet, and suddenly sprang before me ready for action. His face was wildly painted in bright colors. He was bald as a kitchen table. Bits of grass were stuck to his very ordinary, pink-skinned scalp.

"I think you'd better leave," Matt said.

"I'm not leaving without my wife," I said.

"Is this guy your husband?" he asked Mandy.

She kept staring at me with her mouth wide open. Finally, she swallowed and said, "He could be. I'm not sure. Is that crazy?"

"Nah, that's not crazy," Matt said. He turned to me. "Okay," he said, "I guess you're off the hook."

"Thanks," I said, "but that doesn't mean you're off the hook." I took a couple steps toward him. Our noses were an inch apart. His eyes were beady and darting around. Where the paint ended, I could see the true color of his lids. His long lashes fluttered menacingly. The thick paint on his face smelled like burning plastic. "What are you doing here with my wife?" I asked.

"Talking," he said, "you might want to try that sometime."

"What the fuck does that mean?" I said. "I'm ready to kick your ass to Timbuktu."

"Go ahead and try," he said. The inch of air between us was vibrating with ecstasy. What did I just say? Vibrating with tension.

Then Mandy stepped between us and pushed us apart. Her eyes beyond the paint appeared to be really concerned. "Both of you, stop it!" she shouted. She looked at me, and her tone was pleading. "Fred, please just go home."

"I'm not Fred," I said.

"But you said you're my husband, right?"

"Yes," I said.

"Then please just go home, and I'll meet you there. Okay?"

I nodded reluctantly. I really did want to kick Matt's ass. And I think he really did want me to try. He probably knew some kind of Kung Fu from his years of living in one of those yoga countries. Maybe I would've been the one to end up in Timbuktu. Maybe that's where I already was. I picked up my backpack, pulled it onto my back, and started walking back home.

"Thank you Fred," Mandy said. But I didn't stop to look back at her. I didn't want her, or me, to turn into a pillar of salt.

The walk home took only half an hour. It went fast and I saw no one. Margaret was no longer reading on her porch. Hank was nowhere to be seen. His yard was so well seeded it probably would never again grow a blade of grass. When I got home, I slung my pack onto the hall floor. I went straight into the living room and flopped down on the couch. I was exhausted, but I didn't know why. Unless it was the confusion. I was totally and absolutely confused. I no longer had any idea what was real. I wasn't even sure who I was. I didn't like the name "Fred." "Andy" wasn't much better, but it was mine.

I looked around the room. It was so quiet I didn't want to move. I wondered if I could get away with that for a while. Nothing was moving, except the bird feeder outside the window where a little, upside-down nuthatch was having some fun. The air conditioner kicked on. The day had become hot. Mandy's wind chimes were ringing on the side porch in a soft breeze.

Then Mandy herself walked into the room. She sat down beside me on the couch. She was quiet for a moment. Then she put her hand on my thigh and said, "Where have you been?"

I looked at her. This was the Mandy I knew. No makeup. Her hair was pulled back and tied with a band so that it could flow down her back. Her eyes were cool, blue, and steady. "I went for a walk," I said.

"Why didn't you tell me? I would've gone with you."

"I wish I had," I said.

"Yeah?" she said. "How come?"

"How was yoga class?" I asked.

"What yoga class? You know I hate yoga."

"Do you know that guy Matt?" I asked.

"Yeah," she said, "I've met him. He was at the party last night."

I had to think about that. Last night was a black hole to me. I couldn't remember a thing.

"He's a good-looking guy," I said.

"Yeah, he's an alright-looking guy. Why, are you interested?"

"No," I said, "I'm not. I thought maybe you were."

"Why would you think that?"

"What about this guy Fred," I said.

"No," she said, "don't change the subject. Why are you asking me about Matt?"

"I don't know. I heard something . . ."

"On your walk . . ."

"Yes, on my walk."

"And you jumped to a conclusion."

"No," I said, "I jumped to confusion. That's different."

"I'm not having an affair with Matt. He's too young for me and he's not my type. Okay?"

"That's good news," I said. "What about this guy Fred?"

"What Fred?"

"You don't know anyone named Fred?"

She looked at the ceiling like she does when she's thinking. "The only one that comes to mind," she said, "is Fred Murphy, the pharmacist."

"Was he at the party last night?"

"Yes, he was," she said. "You ought to know, you spent most of the night matching drinks with him. I didn't know you two were such good friends."

"And you're not . . ."

"Having an affair with him? Boy, that was some walk you took. No, I'm not having an affair with anyone but you." She took my face and held it tight between her hands, looking me hard in the eyes. "Just you," she said.

I was convinced. So what had happened to me last night? Had Fred put something in my drink? And what had happened this morning? Who were those people I had spoken to? For that matter, who was I?

"What's my name?" I asked her.

She smiled. "Andy," she said. "And we are the Mandy and Andy Show, like always."

"We could just call it The Mandy Show since 'Andy' is included in your name."

"That would be misleading," she said.

"What about 'The Andy and Mandy Show'?" I asked.

"What, you want top billing?" she asked.

"Yes," I said.

"Well, you're going to have to earn it," she said, and then she planted a good one on me.

On Monday I drove down to that pharmacy. I asked one of the pharmacists at the counter if I could talk to Fred. He looked back where Fred was filling a prescription and caught his attention. He said, "This guy wants to talk to you." Fred looked at me and back at the other pharmacist and just shook his head. "He's too busy right now," the other guy said. Then Fred's eyes met mine. He seemed content with that. Finally I shouted, "I'll call you." He nodded and went back to work.

And I did call him, numerous times. He never answered. I left several messages for him. I was on the verge of becoming a stalker when, a week later, I heard that Fred had pulled up stakes and left town. I never saw him or heard of him again.

And I've never been the same since that Saturday morning walk. It's not a bad thing, this new me. Everyone I meet or see appears to be an alien. Not in any scary or creepy way. It's just that I don't feel they are who they appear to be. It's not like they're lying. They just aren't really anyone in particular, like they obviously think they are.

And the same goes for me. I don't know who I am. I don't know if I'm Hank or Margaret or Matt or Fred. Maybe I'm all of them, or none of them. Or maybe I'm just Andy, though I sure can't find any trace of that guy in me. When I look in the mirror, I have no idea who I'm actually seeing. The longer I look, the less sure I am.

Or maybe that misleading idea I had was right. Maybe I'm the "andy" inside of Mandy.

Maybe not.

The Big Mistake #2

My wife sat at the breakfast table looking out the big window into the backyard. She watched the feeders and searched in her bird book.

"I've never seen this one before," she said.

I looked up from my book in which the hero was on the verge of making a big mistake that would drive the story for another hundred pages.

"What's it look like?" I said.

"Small," she said.

"Unh huh," I said, letting my eyes fall back to the book and its hero who had turned to look at me impatiently.

"A purple head with green eyes," she said.

"No way," I said.

The hero, an antihero really, set his phone down on the arm of the couch. The tiny voice of the woman he loved squeaked out of the phone.

"Yeah," my wife said, "orange wing feathers and a red breast."

Not possible, the hero said. "Not possible," I said, repeating like a moron.

"It keeps looking at me between seeds, twitching its head back like it wants me to come out," she said.

She's pulling your leg, the hero said, taking his glasses off and cleaning them with the hem of his shirt. His love's tiny voice was screaming from the phone. He was making his big mistake.

"I'm going out to talk to him," my wife said.

"Him?" I said, but she was already through the door.

I stuck my bookmark in the gutter. The hero put his glasses back on and glared angrily at me. I shut the book and headed for the back yard. But my wife came through the door with a little bird on her finger.

"Look!" she said. Her eyes were full of happiness. The bird looked around.

"Nice digs," he said in a tiny voice that sounded like the hero's lover on the phone.

I wanted to keep looking into my wife's eyes, but the bird stole her attention. She sat back down and set him on the table. She dropped some sunflower seeds down for him.

"Thanks," he said and proceeded to stab one of them with his sharp little beak. When he'd finished the seeds, he drank some water from a small bowl my wife had brought him. Finally he sat down and took stock of things. He looked at me for the first time with his green eyes.

"Who's this?" he said.

"Oh," my wife said, "that's Jim. He's okay."

"I'm on the lam," the bird said, ruffling the purple feathers on the back of his head. "I need a place to stay for a few days."

I looked at her and shook my head. She looked away from me and back at the bird.

"Mi casa es su casa," she said.

"Great!" he said. He jumped back up to his feet. "Where do I sleep?"

"I'll show you," she said, extending her finger. He hopped aboard.

She walked back to the bedroom, and I followed. She pulled some of my shirts off the shelf and made a little nest for him on my side of the bed.

"You can sleep on the couch for a few days, can't you?" she said to me.

"I guess so," I said.

The bird jumped into his nest, sighed, and closed his eyes. My wife lay down on her side. She looked a little tired.

"Don't you have a book to read?" she said.

I walked back down the hall and into the living room. I sat down on the couch and opened my book. The hero was creeping down a dark alley with his cell phone in his hand. His lover's tiny voice was giving him directions. The full moon shone on the wet cobblestones. His thick glasses kept fogging up, but he didn't stop. He just kept on creeping forward one step at a time.

Holes

The engine just stopped like a candle in a sudden draft, and I let the car roll to the grassy shoulder. I turned the key and pressed the gas pedal, but nothing happened. I got out and stared at the old car. The mechanic had warned me it was on its last legs, that it would leave me stranded. Sure enough. The engine was still ticking under the hood, and the car seemed to be sinking into a long sleep. I picked up my book from the front seat, opened the trunk, and pulled out my skinny suitcase.

I looked out on the landscape. I could hear the wind whistling and cackling over the teeth of great sage and over the tongues of smooth boulders. Book tucked under my belt, bag swinging at my side, I began to walk. The heat pressed on my head and cooked my ears. I found a big rock, sat down, and waited. I hadn't seen a single car all day, not a single human being. A hare, a rattlesnake, a big lizard, several buzzards circling high in the clear sky, yes.

Finally I could hear the sound of an engine faraway to the east. When it came into view, it was floating on a watery mirage, a tiny speck glinting in the sun. As it got closer, I stood up and made my thumb super large, a trick I had learned from an old hobo. The car barely slowed as it came beside me, and I could see the long-haired driver looking at me. The car skidded and came to a stop just a little ways past me. I grabbed my bag, checked on my book against my belly, and ran toward what I now saw was a small white truck, noting the mangled rear fender, the rusted-out bed. The passenger-side door swung open.

"Where you going?" the man said. His hair was tangled but cut back away from his face. His beard was long and darted around on his chest.

"West," I said.

"Me too," he said, "jump in."

I climbed in. The seat was lumpy, splits in the leather repaired with shoelaces. I crammed my bag beside my feet, the floor littered with broken golf tees. If the man had been a steak, he'd have been chewy. He finagled the gear shift into first, his big hand floppy on the knob, and we started rolling. The engine sounded good. No glass in the windows, and up around third the wind pushed me back in my seat. His tattered white T-shirt flew around him like an embattled flag, showing flashes of a body so burnt by sun it was turning black. His jeans had more holes than denim. Sandals dangled from his otherwise bare feet.

"You live around here?" I said.

"Not far," he said, "you need a place to stay?"

I thought about it for a minute. When we hit 85 mph, I said, "Sure, thanks. I left my car about a mile back."

"Saw it," he said, "tomorrow I could fix it for you."

"Thanks. You look like you work outside," I said.

"Golf," he said. He flicked his head back as a signal, and I looked through the paneless rear window. On a solid part of the bed lay an old golf bag holding half a dozen clubs.

"Golf without holes," he said. "I can play anywhere."

We pulled off the paved road onto a dirt one, dust wake erasing everything behind us. Rocky bluffs rose up on both sides as the road drew us into a deep gorge. We parked in front of an old trailer. I noted a lone solar panel on the roof. On the homemade front porch, wires ran from a stationary bike into the trailer.

"Home," he said, pulling the front door open with an inviting bow. He led me to the couch. "Sleep there," he said.

I dropped my bag to the floor and pulled my book out from under my belt.

"What's that?" he said.

"My book of answers," I said.

He got a strange look on his face, then ran to a small desk and pulled a book out of the drawer. "My book of questions," he said, holding it up and shaking it as if it were a bar of gold.

We sat together on the couch and opened our books. I turned a few pages.

"Answer 37," I said: "She wanted someone to touch her."

He flipped a few pages. "Question 37," he said: "Why did she leave?"

We looked at each other. Then I turned to the middle of my book.

"Answer 443," I said: "In the distance, she heard people laughing."

He turned to the middle of his book. "Question 443," he said: "Why did she leave?"

"How many times does the book ask that question," I said.

"It comes back a lot, every week or so," he said. "Does having the answers help?" he asked.

"Depends on who you are," I said.

That night I didn't get any sleep, the answers coming to me so fast I could barely write one down before the next one came. I knew he was writing questions frantically in his little room. I could hear the pencil scratching on the page.

The next morning, before he drove me back to my car and got it running, we compared our questions and answers. "She's never coming back," he said.

"I guess not," I said.

Then we played golf. Ragged bags of ancient clubs slung over our shoulders, we climbed a switch-backing trail up the wall of the bluff to the floor of an infinite prairie. He teed up a yellow ball, took his stance, waggled his club a few times, took a slow, deliberate backswing, took a mighty downswing leaping off his feet, and struck the ball with a fierce "thwack." The ball arced against the sky for a long time and landed faraway among the sage.

"Now you," he said.

I had played a little golf as a kid. I stood over the ball, slid the face of my driver behind it. I looked out at my target, a giant sage maybe three hundred yards away. Little twisters made of sand stood up on their hind legs and ran across the complicated, barren landscape like children racing toward the face of a cliff. I looked back at the white ball waiting patiently. I took a much more controlled swing than my friend, wanting to hit the ball straight where I could find it. My shot sliced far to the east of his, disappearing into a ravine.

"Remember," he said, "there are no holes, only the distance in every direction. Once you start this round, it will never end. I've been playing the same round for about ten years now."

But I wasn't like him. All day, before we met back at his trailer, I kept seeing "holes," targets like sagebrush or boulders that I aimed for. I made sure to hit that target on the third or tenth shot, whatever it took. I couldn't help myself: I counted every shot. In my head, I kept adding up my score.

Tornados

I walked out into the front yard to trim my thorny hedge. My blades needed sharpening, but they still worked well enough. The lengths of new spring growth fell to my feet. I was careful to dodge those dangerous thorns. I danced and danced as I cut. My neighbor walked by, a retired old gentleman getting his exercise. He stopped and watched me.

"Hey," he said, "what are you doing there?"

"Can't you see I'm dancing?" I said.

He stepped into my yard and came closer. "You call that dancing?" he said.

"What's wrong with it?" I said, still cutting and dancing.

"You're not keeping the beat," he said.

"What beat?" I said.

"Here, let me show you," he said.

I stopped cutting and watched the old man begin to dance. He was tall and skinny and he reminded me of a scarecrow puppet. He did a clog step mixed with some fancy movement of his own.

"What are you dancing to?" I said.

"Don't you hear it?" the old man said.

I strained my ears to hear. A murder of crows in a magnolia tree were calling up an ancient tune with a strong beat. I started dancing. I danced and danced.

After a few minutes, the old man said, "Not like that. Like this."

I looked at his legs bowing like fledgling crepe myrtles and his feet flying like carpenter bees—wild and ordered and funny and graceful. I tried, but my feet got lost and I tripped and fell right into the pile of thorns. One of them went all the way through my forearm. It felt like the sting of a huge yellow jacket. I tried to stand up, but my head was spinning, and I fell back down. The old man kept dancing, his face covered in a big grin.

"More like this," he said, and his legs and feet got faster and faster until they disappeared. Legless, the old man floated in the air above me. His legs were in my chest now, humming like an engine.

My neighbor Rosemary appeared in her flower shift and she laughed loud and clapped her hands. Soon she was dancing too, she and the old man spinning around my front yard like a couple of tornados. Their invisible feet whirred beside my head.

"Don't kick me in the head!" I shouted, but they just laughed.

Rosemary danced right beside me. Her skirt swirled and opened above me like a vast dark tunnel, her knees two giant pistons driving a great machine. I must've passed out because I woke up in the hospital. The walls and windows and strange machinery spun around me like some kind of crazy dream.

"Welcome back," the doctor said, smiling, his face ballooning into view.

He bent over me with a pair of snippers and snipped the hooked point of the thorn. "This is gonna hurt," he said, and he yanked the rest of the thorn out of my arm. It hurt so bad it knocked me back into the tunnel with Rosemary's churning knees.

Suddenly I awoke in my front yard, lying on my back. The wind was blowing up in the canopies. Some white clouds were running away fast. The crows still made a ruckus, but it wasn't music.

I stood up slowly, braced against the maple. The old man and Rosemary were gone. My trimmer lay in a pile of thorny cuttings. My forearm was completely healed. I hobbled into my house. It was dim and cool in there.

"How's the trimming going?" Emma said. She was sitting on the couch with a book, her feet curled under her.

"I'm taking a break," I said.

"Be careful, those thorns are killers," she said.

I looked at her, I realized, for the first time in a long while. Really brought her into focus. That face. She looked at me too, and smiled.

"Tell me about it," I said, sitting down as close to her as I could.

Mr. Death, Mrs. Birth

I glanced through the window of Brau Burgers as I was walking by and saw an old friend sitting at the bar. He turned to me and hoisted his drink. I hoisted a pretend drink in the air, but that felt insufficient. I decided to go in and say hello, maybe slap him on the back. The place was crowded and I had to dodge a couple of waitresses.

When I got to the bar, a seat opened up next to my friend. I've noted there is always an empty seat next to him, no matter where I find him. He slapped me on the back before I could do it to him. He's quick, or slow, depending on the situation. A cylinder of light lowered over my friend and me, as if we were trapped together on center stage. But I could still see and hear everything going on around me. The place was really alive that night.

"Good to see you, old man," he said.

"I'm not that old."

"Old enough." He let go of a loud and raucous laugh.

He was wearing a black T-shirt that said, "Smoke'm if you got'm" on the front and "Get off my back!" on the back. An old, red, pillbox-style baseball cap sat snugly on the top of his head. Black embroidery read "The Cleveland Spiders" next to a black spider holding a baseball bat. Crazed eyes, wild grin full of teeth.

"Bartender," my friend shouted, and a young man with a towel slung over his shoulder appeared in front of him. My friend pounded the bar one time with the heel of his right hand. "Give my friend here a glass of whiskey, same as mine, you know the brand." When the young man had left, my friend turned to me. "They got the good stuff here."

"Where did you get the hat?" I asked. I couldn't take my eyes off of the spider's black eyes that gleamed with a mesmerizing emptiness.

"I took it off the head of a dying man." He raised his glass to his lips, took a sip, and just looked at me.

"I guess you aren't going to tell me that story, are you?"

He smiled over his glass. "Right," he said. "But I'll tell you the last game the Cleveland Spiders played was in 1899."

The young man reappeared and set down two shots of whiskey in cut crystal glasses. The color was dark gold. It caught strands of the scattered light and sent them back out again. My friend lifted his glass and said, "Cheers!" I raised my own, said "Cheers," and we clinked our glasses together. He knocked his back in one clean gulp, and his eyes lit up as if some great insight made of fire had come into his mind. I was afraid, I admit it, not knowing what this special brand of whiskey might be, but I knocked mine back anyway to prove my worth, set my glass on the table, and waited. At first, it was so smooth that I felt nothing different. Then, with my friend sitting there grinning at me, I felt a slowly gathering presence within me, an increasing awareness of my mortal flesh and brain and bone and organs perched on that barstool with a crowd of others swirling around me. "There," my friend said to me, pointing at my face, "there, you're getting it."

"Getting what?" I said, and he just laughed again. He had the habit of laughing longer than what was appropriate for the joke. But I wasn't going to be the one to tell him.

"Mrs. Birth is here too, you know," he said.

"Who?"

"Mrs. Birth," he said. "That's what I call her. She hates it."

"I don't blame her."

"Don't bother looking for her," he said, "you'll never find her in this mob."

"I wasn't looking for her."

"You wouldn't recognize her anyway," he said, "not at this particular time."

"Whatever you say," I said.

"Don't worry, you'll know her when you need her."

I couldn't help myself: I looked around the room. There must have been forty women in my view engaged in various forms of eating and drinking and talking and laughing and flirting and arguing and smiling and grimacing and gazing thoughtfully out the window. I could feel myself inhabiting the bones and flesh of every one of them, becoming present in all of their eyes, and in the eyes of the men around them too. I was all of them, not myself anymore, with a thousand different mindsets and different voices, and I suddenly felt I was being pulled into my own death, until I forced my eyes away from them and back to the eyes of my friend who just stared intently at me. Then he laughed and laughed until he was choking. When he had recovered, he looked at me and said, "You're starting to see her, aren't you?" And all I could do was nod my head.

"I'd leave her be if I were you," he said.

"Sounds like good advice."

"You wanna know just how exciting she is?" he asked. "When I offer to buy her a drink, all she wants is sparkling water. Can you believe that?!"

"Yeah," I said, "I get that."

"Whose side are you on?" he asked. He glanced around the room conspiratorially. "And then you know what she does?"

I shrugged my shoulders.

"She complains I'm always following her."

"Why would she think that?"

"Yeah," he said, "and then I have to straighten her out with irrefutable logic. I look right at her and I say, 'I got here at Brau Burgers before you did. I was already at the bar when I saw you walking through the door.' 'No,' she says, 'That was me seeing you walk through the door. You're always getting us confused.' And she smiles that smile. It just burns me up. Literally. It burns my scalp, which is why I'm bald and have to wear this fucking hat!" The logo image on his cap changed from a spider to a screaming face with a scalp on fire.

"Damn," I said.

"Yeah, man, it pisses me off." He shook his head and took another slug of his suddenly refilled drink. Then he fixed me with his gaze. "You know what she does?"

"No," I said.

"She's doing it right now. All day long, she's undoing all of my work. And then she has the nerve to curse me for undoing hers. Can you believe that?"

"Uhhh, uhhh," I say.

"I wish I could get away from her, just for a while, you know?"

"Why can't you?" I ask.

"Because," he said, "we're married, and she holds me to the vows every day."

"I can't imagine you married to anybody," I said.

"Seems like forever. I can barely remember the ceremony."

"Have you thought about divorce?" I asked.

"Can't go there," he said, lowering his head, swinging it like an old bull in a pasture.

"Why not? She torments you. Spoils your work."

"I know. But it's different at night when we're at home together."

"How so?" I asked.

"Well, as the evening grows darker and darker, as it deepens and deepens into silence, we undress each other, and we mingle."

"You what?" I said.

"She's the very best mingler in the universe," he said. "Pure ecstasy. I can no longer track where I end and she begins. It goes on all night. And when we wake up at dawn, we get dressed, we sit across the table watching each other drink our coffee. And then we rise up, walk out the door into the day, and start all over again, making and unmaking everything."

"Sounds exhausting," I said.

"What do you think *you're* doing every day?" he asked, and grinned.

Suddenly his face changed, his eyes growing wide. "I gotta get outta here," he said.

"Why?"

"There goes Mrs. Birth out the front door. I gotta keep her in sight. She's like a damn whirlwind, I can't keep up with her. But don't worry," he said, holding my gaze with his own, "we'll finish our business later. I'm in no hurry. I like you Mister Jimbo. And the drink's on me. Enjoy." He tossed a few ancient coins onto the bar.

Then he stood up, and his body transformed into that of a slender, muscular young man. An athlete. "Gotta be fast," he said. He scrambled out Brau Burgers and disappeared down the street.

On the bar in front of me, my glass was full of whiskey. I held it up, looked into that amber elixir, the light playing through it all warm and vibrant like a bow on a cello string. And just then I saw the woman I'd recently met enter the room. Her eyes lit up when she saw me, as did mine—the promise of mingling in the air. She sat on the stool where my friend Mr. Death had been sitting. His cone of light gave her a presence I'd never felt before. I saw myself looking out of her eyes, and felt her rising up in me and looking out of mine. I bought her a shot of this special elixir, and raised a toast to her.

The Lair of Herself

1. Scottness

Scott wasn't sure that Mathilde's would be open on a Friday evening in mid-January. As he pulled into the parking lot, he could see the lights on inside. Past the neon signage for imported beer on the windows, people were moving around. He was in luck. He ordered a Cuban sandwich and potato salad at the counter, a Pacifico, then studied the cheesecakes and pies under the glass case, thinking maybe he would take something home. Home for the month of January was the house he was renting in Chicahauk, a community on the northern end of the Outer Banks. Not many people this time of year, the house was cheap, and he could be alone.

Three of the tables in the small dining room were occupied. He found a vacant one next to a young couple. They were talking in intense but quiet tones. He hung his jacket over one of the chairs. He was about to sit down to wait for his sandwich and drink his beer when the young woman stood up beside him. He wanted to meet her eyes and smile but her back was turned to him. She wasn't exactly standing, but rather was arching backwards over her chair so that her face came to him upside down. He was looking down into her face that held a fierce grimace. Her narrow blue-gray eyes caught and then focused intently on his, or so he thought. He tried to maintain the smile he had planned to present to her. But her upside-down face—like a hidden second face that she rarely presented to the world—was too intense for him, and he turned away.

The young man had already jumped up from his chair to catch the young woman and prevented her from careening backwards into the middle of Scott's table. The young man slipped his right arm around her waist and steadied her. Scott took a step back, observing the scene—the slim young woman in jeans and blue sweatshirt, heavy curls of her red hair awash beneath her dangling head, the clean-cut young man trying to secure her—and Scott wanted to do something, but didn't know what it would be.

"Can I help you?" Scott said to the young man, who was straining to keep her upright.

"No," he said, "I've got her."

"Are you sure?" Scott said.

"Yes," the young man said, not taking his eyes off the girl, "she'll be alright in a minute."

And for a moment Scott stood within grasping range in case the young woman started to fall. Her head kept pushing back and over as her body attempted to release the massive energy flowing through it, the muscles of her throat becoming taut strands in that current. Beautiful, he thought, but immediately wondered if such a thought were perverse. He held his hands out in readiness, but he never touched her. He could feel instead some invisible band of energy around her. He wanted to touch her, to help this rather competent young man to guide her back into her seat, or maybe onto the floor where she could lie down.

Scott became dimly aware of the other people turning in their chairs to stare, but that was the least of his concerns. However she moved, however the young man maneuvered her, wherever Scott positioned himself, the woman's head tipped in his direction, her stunned eyes following him though they saw nothing, or else they did see and were drawn to him, the way the eyes of a portrait sometimes appear to follow one around a room, or the way the flame of a fire swivels to follow a camper trying to avoid the smoke. Scott could not avoid the smoke. Her eyes kept finding his, penetrating them with some cold stream of thought that had no words.

The young man's embrace was skillful, allowing her to bend and flow, until finally the current that was possessing her withdrew and dropped her body into his arms. He gently piloted her back into her seat. At last the tension receded like a tide from her body and her head dropped forward, chin on chest, eyes no longer pinned to Scott. He felt the tension go out of his own body, too, as if someone had their hand on a rheostat. The room that had been bright with her exertions had suddenly dimmed.

"It's alright," the young man said to the young woman, stroking the side of her face, gazing into her half-closed eyes.

"Is she okay?" Scott asked.

"Yeah," the young man said glancing up at Scott, "she's through it now. But thank you."

"You're welcome," Scott said, not knowing what else he could say or do. But he still felt that he should be doing something. The young man was lean, athletic, flawlessly attentive to her, and yet Scott felt that there was something else that needed to be done, and that he was the one who was supposed to do it. What was it? He sat down slowly at his table.

He realized that the entire event had taken up less than a minute, perhaps only thirty seconds or so. And yet for him, and for the woman too, he thought, it had felt like an extended era within a lifetime. A decade, a marriage, a vocation. Very strange, certainly one for the books, literally in his case, he thought, trying to laugh at the idea, at the way he was already plotting how he could work a moment like this into the novel he was currently writing.

A slender woman maybe in her fifties ran out of the employees' area, drying her hands on an apron. "Oh Marlee," she said. She had the unevenly cut short hair of a beach dweller, and a weathered rugged face. She took Marlee's head in her hands and looked into the young woman's eyes.

"Are you alright?" But Marlee was unresponsive.

"This one was worse," the young man said, "but she seems to be through it."

The two of them helped her to her feet, and for a brief moment, her head listed to the side toward Scott, and her limpid eyes fell in line with his. Please tell me, he thought to himself, that her eyes did not smile at me.

"Is there anything I can do to help?" Scott asked again, feeling the kind of redundancy that he would cut out of any paragraph he wrote. The woman turned to him and shook her head, an appreciative glint in her eyes.

"No," she said. "But thank you. We know what we're doing."

That statement shot a solid dose of silence into Scott. He nodded and turned away. And then the girl was gone, the two caretakers guiding her wobbly steps through a door into some back room and presumably to a cot or a couch where she could sleep it off.

Scott's sandwich finally appeared on his table, and he ate it slowly, ignoring the stirred-up whispering of the other diners. He bought a quarter of a cheesecake on his way out. In his car, and for the rest of the evening, he couldn't stop thinking about the experience.

Everything he knew about epileptic seizure told him that she had not seen him. But for that moment, now suspended in his mind, he had looked through all his mentally filed-away definitions and explanations, past the intense mask of her face, into a deeper place inside of her; and from there where she lay curled up in the lair of herself, she had been looking back out at him. And when he saw that she saw him, it triggered a charge of current running from the base of his spine right out the top of his head, where the strand of it separated into a high canopy of limbs in the moonlit sky, leaves swaying in a breeze from the sea.

He shook himself. What are you doing? he thought.

Even as he considered the incident now, that current sparked in his spine, making him feel hugely erect and powerful, but also as naked and exposed as any tree standing alone, as if he had been turned inside out.

It was happening again. He wanted her. But how could that be? He had been in her thwarted presence for no more than a few moments. Not a word had passed between them. For a while he had been in this phase of his life in which he fell desperately in love with women he knew nothing about and could not have. Except for the women he possessed vicariously through the male characters of his novels: beautiful of course, and magnificently flawed. He knew he had to ask himself what all of this meant about his state of mind, about his character as a man.

It didn't matter. She was gone. What were the odds he would ever see her again?

Besides, the longer he thought about it, the more times he revisited the incident, the more he knew he had seen something essential looking out of her, something not her exactly in the sense of her name and gender and work etc., and yet most ultimately her. And because she was looking from that place in herself, he was triggered into that place in himself, and for once in his life, he had seen her without judgment and without desire. He had seen her clearly for what she was, an object in his awareness, as he was an object in hers. But there was something more. Something essential.

Yes, a moment later his distorting thoughts had taken over, as always. And he had wanted her. But he had sensed, for the first time, that what he really wanted was that clear-seeing being that was both her and himself, at a level deeper than his petty Scottness. Okay, he thought, is this just more of my self-indulgent bullshit?

No, he thought. For a very brief moment he had been "seeing" itself, without delusion. His distorting thoughts could not spoil the perfection of that. But what did it mean? What was he going to do about it?

2. A Client

Arumble like thunder, and for a minute he thought it might rain, until he realized a Harley had pulled up outside. When she strode through the office door setting off the entry bell, he wished like hell he'd turned off the green neon vacancy sign. She walked like she owned the world—the kind of cockiness in a small woman that always put him on guard. Strapped into a makeshift papoose on her chest was a miniature dachshund. Something like a smile came into the woman's face except that her mouth wasn't curved right, more like a sine wave than a crescent, turned up on one side and down on the other. Was that possible? The dog's head swiveled all around, its sharp black eyes landing on everything like it was casing the place. Then the dog turned to Walt and there were two sets of eyes, one over the other, looking at him.

"Uh, can I help you?" he asked.

"No doubt," she said, her voice kind of low, but not gravelly—sandy. She pulled a black Harley skull cap off her head. Her other hand was on the counter, colorless nails trimmed short. She made a little maneuver with her head and a rope of dark brown hair tied with red and purple stays swung around her shoulder and landed on her chest beside the dog who gave it a quick sniff. She took the rope in her hands and inspected it.

"You looking for a room?" Walt asked.

"Psychic," she said, looking back at him. "I could use a good palm reading. You do palms?"

Smartass, he thought. The last thing he needed right now was a smartass. "Look," he said, "we don't take pets here." He pointed to a small sign with a dog inside a circle and a red slash mark through it. That had been Sally's idea. Make it clear, she had said.

"This ain't no pet," she said. Her face was brown from the sun, without makeup, muscular, somewhat irregular. "Ain't no regular dog neither," she said. "This here's Chaco." At the sound of its name, the dog perked up and gave her a lick on the underside of her chin.

"I'm really sorry, but we can't make exceptions."

"He don't bark. You heard him bark yet?"

"No, but . . ."

"Won't hear him, neither. Not if I tell him. This dog understands more English than my ex ever did. He never did a damn thing I told him. That's why he's in the penitentiary, which is why he's my ex. Not to mention he killed a man, over me of course. Still, I don't cotton to killing, unless it's an emergency."

"It's not just the barking," Walt said. "It's the pissing and shitting."

"Chaco never makes his substances unless I tell him it's okay, which is always outside."

"And then somebody steps in it," Walt said, "and that's another problem."

"I catch it before it hits the ground, okay? I got a system."

"And the dander—some of our clients are allergic to dog dander."

"Jesus I hate that word," she said.

"Dander?"

"Client," she said. "I hate that word."

"Oh," Walt said. Her eyes stayed stuck right on his like they had from the moment she'd walked in the door, except for when she was tending to her hair. Her brow was busy, like it was sending its own signals, crinkling up as she listened to what he was saying, but then smoothing out when she spoke.

"I don't know what else to say," he said, "except what I already said."

"Well then keep your trap closed, take my money, and give me my key—see, I got cash." She pulled a silver clip out of her tight jeans pocket, and it did indeed hold a thick fold of twenties.

"Look, there's a Quality Inn about a mile down the road."

"I can't stay in chains," she said.

The pun zinged in. Walt decided to ignore it. "Why not?" he asked.

"It's against my principles," she said. "People to them are clients." The sine wave turned into a crescent, and she gave him her first smile.

Sally stuck her head in from the apartment door. "I've got to get an early start tomorrow, babe. Map Quest says it's seven hours. I'm gonna hit the sack."

Walt looked back over his shoulder to her smiling face. Her hand hooked around the door, long red nails sharp against the white paint. "Okay hun," he said, "I'm gonna close down in a few minutes. I'll be in soon."

"I'll be asleep, but I'll see you in the morning."

"Okay," he said, and the door closed.

"She's pretty," the woman said.

"Yes, she is," he said. "And I'm gonna close up soon. So . . ."

"I've gotta stay here," she said.

"No, you don't have to."

"It's the Breezeway Court. I gotta have a breeze."

"The Quality Inn has excellent air conditioning."

"Not the same thing. I need to sit in your breezeway and feel the breeze on my skin."

Walt was getting tired—tired of this conversation, and just plain tired. He had spent a large part of the day putting down new tile in one of the bathrooms. "Okay," he said. "You can stay, but just one night, and you have to get an early start in the morning. Okay?"

"I need the room for a week," she said, "maybe two, depending on how things go." The woman leaned forward and put her forearms on the counter. Chaco naturally moved forward with her chest and both his paws plopped down on the formica. His loose lips folded up against his gums, giving him this strange little crooked grin. A low growl emanated from his throat.

"Your dog is growling at me," Walt said.

"Yep," she said. "He can always tell when a guy's hitting on me."

"But I'm not hitting on you," he said.

"Uh huh," she said.

"You need to leave now."

"Your sign says you got weekly rates," she said.

"Only when it's slow."

"How many vacant rooms you got?" she asked.

"None of your business," he said.

"Six by my count, at least," she said, "I only need one. Chaco here stays with me."

"Look, I don't know how else I can say 'no'."

"Good. I'm glad that's over with. I'll take it for one week to start. And I'll pay a hundred extra for Chaco here. That's a fair deal."

"It's not about fair, it's about policy." He hated himself right after he said it. What a stupid word, "policy." It was right in there with the word "client." There were four dark eyes staring at him expectantly—two above, two below. His own eyes moved up and down between them. What was it he saw in her eyes? It was a state of permanent amusement, permanent curiosity. As if it wasn't possible for something serious to occur. As if there was nothing in Walt's world that could knock that look off her face. Why would he want to knock it off her face? All he knew was that he did.

"You won't be sorry," she said.

What did she mean by that? He looked away, found a registration and slid it over to her. Sally would be leaving early in the morning. By the time she got back, this woman—he let his eyes drop to where she was filling out the form—this Wisper Wisper would be gone. What kind of name was that? She pushed the application back over to him. He wouldn't put her file in the cabinet, would hide it in a safe place until he decided what he wanted to do with it. The transaction was cash, so he wouldn't ever have to record it if he didn't want to.

"I want that room over there," she said. "Nobody's parked there, so I know it's vacant." She had turned and was pointing through the window of the office across the lawn and the small swimming pool to the opposite end room of the motel's horseshoe, the room closest to the road.

He gave her the key, and she gave him a little smile as she took it, their fingers touching. She and Chaco walked out the door. The bell rang like Christmas Eve. He watched her mount her Harley, a Sportster. A rich, low rumble. She rode back out to the street and turned into the far entrance where her room was.

Walt kept watching her through the window while he was locking up, flipping off the "Vacancy" sign. When she got off the bike, she set Chaco down and he ran and ran, checking everything out. She pulled a bag off the back of the bike and went into her room, leaving the door open. Every few steps, Chaco raised his leg and shot a burst of piss into the grass. Then he squatted, and stayed in that position for a long time. Walt could see the dog visibly shrinking. Maybe he'd been on that bike all day.

Wisper's silhouette crossed her window. Great, Walt thought, I'll be cleaning up behind that damn dog for the next week. That's some system she's got. Wisper came back out and pulled something else off the bike. Chaco had his own agenda, somehow pushing his way into the heart of one of the azalea bushes next to the pool. Walt stood now in the darkened office and stared out the window. Wisper stepped out of her door onto the lawn. She stretched, arching her back, hands raised above her, face looking up into the clear sky full of stars. Something was on her right hand. She followed Chaco and wherever she found one of his loaves and fishes she reached down and grabbed it, finally reversing the bag and carrying it to the exterior trashcan.

Without her leather jacket and chaps on, Walt could see why she called herself Wisper. She was slight of stature and flexible. She did some stretches. Then, a cartwheel. She flopped down in the grass. Chaco unearthed himself from one of the bushes and ran over to her and pounced on her. They wrestled and played for a few minutes, his ears flopping around like butterfly wings. Then, she scooped Chaco up and started toward her door.

When she got to the covered walkway she turned and looked directly back across to the office. Walt felt that she was looking straight into his window, the path of her eyes like a thin cool stream working its way across the lawn and between two slats of the blinds. The hackles came up on his neck, but he knew that she couldn't see him in that window from that distance with the room dark. Still, she looked as if she did see him. She and Chaco turned and walked into the room and closed the door. Walt stood there for another moment looking out the window and wondering what the hell it was that he was doing, and what the hell he thought was going to happen between himself and this woman named Wisper.

Later that night he tip-toed into his bedroom and carefully snuck under the covers on his side of the bed. Sally turned over on her side to face him.

"You didn't rent that woman a room, did you?" Her breath was hot on his ear.

"Course not," he said. "She's got a dog."

3. Call Your Own Foul

Matt pedaled his tall, black bicycle, Mr. Spock, onto a narrow path through trees toward the north end of the park. He emerged onto a concrete basketball court and practiced riding tight circles and figure eights. He loved this place. Thick trees, mostly evergreens, surrounded it so that even in winter he couldn't see through to the street or the rest of the park. Sort of an island within the larger island of the park, which was an island within the larger island of Chicahauk.

Most of the homes, almost all rentals, were vacant for the winter months. He relished the rare sighting of a permanent resident out walking her dog or just getting some exercise. He loved the aloneness of the people and the weight of the silence, with the sound of the Atlantic off in the distance. He leaned Mr. Spock against a tree and shrugged the pack off his back.

"Temperature and humidity indicate rain will not arrive until 10:00 p.m., Captain," Spock said.

"My conclusions exactly," Matt said, holding a wet finger up to the air.

He pulled his basketball out of his backpack and began to stretch. After a few minutes he started taking some shots from close in, layups and minihooks, working on the spin and his feel. Then some longer jump shots. He liked the sound of the sturdy, steel rim of the goal, when the ball dropped in clean. Basketball was his game, Captain was his name.

Even at fifty he was a good player, a scorer with a deadly three-pointer, an excellent fall away jumper on the baseline, and a good running halfhook from ten feet in.

Suddenly, he noticed a young woman, late twenties maybe, had appeared at the side of the court. She held a basketball pinned between the wrist of her right hand and her hip—her long red hair tied back into a ponytail with a rubber band. In the ocean breeze, unruly strands waved around her face. She wore a yellow sweatshirt, white shorts with red stripes down the thigh, and yellow socks with black, high-top basketball shoes—and stood so still she reminded Matt of a slender crane in the shallow water of a pond.

When her eyes caught his, she said, "You wanna play?"

Her bright, clear voice tumbled toward him down a long tunnel. "Sorry?" he said.

"Basketball?" she said, as if she were coaxing a small, shy dog.

"You mean one-on-one?"

"Make it take it," she said, her ponytail living an active life of its own behind her head, "game to eleven. Shots behind the line count two. Take it back to the three point line on exchange of possession . . ."

"Wait a minute," he said, "I haven't even said I want to play."

"Come on. It's more fun than just shooting."

"It's not that," he said. "I'm a lot bigger than you." He felt a twang of feminist guilt as the words left his mouth.

"Gimme a break," she said. "I've played with guys a lot bigger."

"You sure?"

"Duh," she said.

"Airballs don't have to be taken back," he said.

"Deal."

She flipped a quarter and he called "heads" in the air.

"Heads it is," she said, picking the coin up. "We can use your ball," she said. "Just let me get a feel for it."

While she took shots with his larger and heavier ball, he untied and retied his shoelaces. He smiled to himself. The way he could shoot, he was hard to beat in a one-on-one game.

"Call your own fouls," he said.

"Right," she said.

He brought the ball in first. Made a quick move to the right and rose up for a half-hook runner, missed, and she tracked the ball down quick, ran to the line and touched it with her right foot, turned and got a ten-foot bank shot off before he could get there. "Bang" the ball said going through the chain net. One nothing. Okay, he thought, I've got to put a little energy into this. He checked the ball to her at the top of the three-point line. She started with a nifty little crossover dribble between her legs, took an angle to the left for two steps, then rose up in the air turning to the basket as she did, hands holding the ball above her head, that photogenic release, this time not a bank shot, and "Bang" the ball said as it poured cleanly through the chain.

"When do I get a shot?" he said.

"You already had one. That's all you get. Unless you can stop me."

"Bring it on," he said, tossing the ball to her.

"Bang," said the ball flying through the net.

She won that first game eleven to three. When she went up for that fall away jumper, she floated, hung there at the top of her leap for a moment, those crane eyes keenly and yet placidly fixed on the rim, and then that release that was made in basketball heaven. And her quickness to rebounds gave her a lot of extra shots. It was as if she could tell where the ball was going before it landed on the rim. In the next game he worked harder. He closed the gap on her fall away and actually blocked a couple of them. And he started following like her shadow on the long rebounds so that she couldn't get off a quick shot. Still, she was clever and simply knew how to create space for herself. It was eight all in the second game when she put him away with three fall away jumpers in a row. "Bang, bang, bang."

"Best three out of five," he said. He was beginning to be a little tired, but he couldn't let her beat him like this.

"Why not?" she said. "I can go all day. I shoot better in the dark than I do in full daylight."

He hadn't even noticed that it was starting to get dark. "Bring it in," he said.

"Losers bring it in," she said, tossing him the ball.

He didn't like that, but he took the ball. Better not give up a chance to score. This time he went up with his long jumper and nailed it, bang, two points. She tossed him the ball and again he just went straight up with it. Bang, another two points.

"Can you keep doing that?" she asked.

"Let's find out," he said.

She tossed him the ball. He went straight up again. "Bang," said the ball.

"Six zip," he said.

"I went to school," she said.

She got the rebound and brought the ball back to the top of the key. She handed it to him, sticking closer this time. He went straight up with it again, and just as he was about to release the ball he felt a sharp jab in his belly. His shot hit the left side of the rim and bounced off. She sucked the rebound in and headed for the line.

"That was a foul!" he shouted.

She was taking it to the basket already, but finished with a casual finger roll that missed. She caught her own rebound and turned to him.

"You said we were calling our own fouls."

"Yeah, but that was obvious. You gotta call those."

"You call that a foul?"

"You hit me in the stomach."

"Okay," she said, "but we don't call touch fouls where I come from. Your ball."

She tossed it to him and again stayed close. He went up for the outsider again, but missed this time. She'd broken his rhythm. She got the rebound, but he stuck to her like gum on the seat of a chair, forcing her into a seventeen-footer.

"Bang," said the ball.

She was tough, but he was on his game now. And he kept the lead while she chipped away at it. At ten to eight his favor, he missed a hook shot that would've won the game and she got the rebound. Instead of her usual crossover, this time she tried to back him down into a post up position. But he held his ground. She leaned into him, and he could feel the ribs of her back. She couldn't weigh more than 110, he thought. She felt flexible and strong, pushing into him. Then she pinned him with her elbow and spun toward the basket, one and a half long strides across the lane, left handed reverse layup. The ball gently flew up and kissed the backboard, the lefty spin sending it back to the right and into the basket. This time the ball said "Jesus" as it rustled through the chain net. Matt just stopped and looked at her.

"Where did you learn to do that?" he asked.

"Right here," she said. "You lead ten to nine. Check the ball."

Matt tossed the ball to her. This time she posted him up again. No way she could keep doing this. He tried to reach around her to disrupt her dribble, but she had this knack of keeping the ball out of reach. She pinned him with her left elbow sharp against his side and spun to the right, her ponytail slapping his face, searing his left eye—she was suddenly beside him with an angle to the basket. She stretched her right arm out and the ball appeared in her right hand, nestled there like an egg in a nest. He reached over her right shoulder but the ball was inches out of his reach. She flipped it up and it took in the sights on the way, then smooched the backboard, took the little bit of spin she'd given it, and fell toward the basket.

"Kiss my ass," said the ball going through.

"Ten all," she said.

"Win by two?" he said.

"That's not what we agreed on."

"That's the way we always play it."

"We?"

"The guys I play with."

"Okay," she said. "Win by two."

He tossed the ball to her. When it hit her hands, she was already moving, but he was ready for her. He was getting used to her sneaky ways. She posted up on him again, and he thought he had her now. He'd seen all of her post up moves already. And he was at least a foot taller than she was. She made a quick turn into the lane, so quick that it seemed to Matt like time had been left behind—stretched like a rubber band—and was having to catch up with itself. Still, for that first instant, he was with her, until that elbow sharp as a broken board caught a middle rib on his right side. A sharp pain of shock ran along the central bone of both his front and back ribs, bolted across his heart and completed the circuit in the middle rib on the left side of his body. His middle ribs were like electrified pincers plucking his heart. He was suddenly on his back on the court, and all he could see from that vantage point was the ball already out of her hand, the black circumference lines whirling up slowly in a helix toward the backboard, the trees beyond it black lace against the gray sky.

His mind was empty in this moment, without the least sliver of a thought, as he watched the ball climbing, climbing, until it finally met the backboard and climbed another rung higher, changing trajectory to the left where it hovered for a moment as if suspended by a string over the goal. Then it fell slowly, at the rate of a feather but straight down, through the basket, whispering some word as it rustled the chain that Matt could almost make out:

"Ssshhit," it said.

The ball landed on the court without a bounce, like an obedient dog commanded to sit. His mind likewise sat down, panted slightly, waited for the world to begin again. A hand appeared before his face—slim and graceful, as if accustomed to extending itself into flight—an offering, an opportunity. He reached out with his own hand and took hold.

The Secret of Whirlwinds

1. Mister Fabulous

Straightening his tie, my husband walked into the living room where I was sitting on the couch with a book I knew I would never read. He stopped to look at me for a moment, then smiled. My husband was a successful, good-looking man. His face was Carey Grant and Robert Redford somehow combined. When he smiled, women were moved. When we first met, I was one of them.

"How is it?" he asked, nodding at the book.

"I haven't even started it," I said.

"Keep me posted. I may want to read it myself."

It was a new novel by a bestselling writer he'd picked up for me at the bookstore. The book had won a Pulitzer Prize, but I'd never heard of it or the woman author before. According to the blurbs it was about a bunch of Millennials in a city having a hard time finding independence and love. I handed the book toward him. "Go ahead," I said. "I'm not going to read it."

He looked at me the way he often did: puzzled, slightly peeved. For the last two years I had begun to realize that he and I were not in sync. He had no clue what kind of book I would like to read, though he'd been looking at the books stacked on my bedside table for years. What sometimes concerned me was that he thought he knew.

"You know I can't read it at work," he said.

"What about at lunch?"

"I'm with people at lunch. You know that."

I set the book down on the couch.

"It was a gift for you, you know."

"I know," I said.

He waited for me to say, "I'm sorry," and when I didn't, he said, "I'll see you this evening."

After he left for work, I put on my warm jacket and went for a walk. The temperature had dropped into the low thirties over the last few days, and the wind was blowing the December leaves in whirlwinds all around me. I had quit my job selling real estate a month before, and I was trying to figure out what I wanted to do with my life. After all, I was still young, I didn't have any children to take care of, so I could do anything I wanted. Still, nothing appealed to me. A lot of the jobs I might consider required further education, and the thought of going back to school, with my husband's full support, made me want to go to bed and never wake up.

I kept walking from street to street, neighborhood to neighborhood, deep in my thoughts, not paying much attention to where I was going. My husband wouldn't be home until six in the afternoon. My jacket and gloves and earmuffs were all very warm, and I was content to walk and ponder. The neighborhoods of this town are full of mature trees: oaks, elms, sycamores, redbuds, maples and hickories. And the whirlwinds of leaves that day were diverse and sturdy. They appeared all up and down the streets. One of them came up beside me and walked along with me for a while. It made me feel I wasn't all alone with my thoughts and decisions. I looked over at it, and it looked over at me. I nodded and it nodded back. And then I stared. Its eyes were red bud leaves, or seemed to be. Though those two leaves were spinning, they managed to arrive at the same place briefly in each orbit to give the illusion of flickering eyes. Its nose was a rather large oak leaf, and its mouth a string of maple leaves, all caught up in that somehow organized repetition of spinning features. It wore a cap of sycamore. It was very self-contained, throwing only a small puff of wind against my face.

"Are you going my way?" I asked, just having a joke with myself.

It smiled and said, "Indeed."

I was stunned, of course, but I didn't let that prevent me from keeping up my end of the conversation. "How do you know where I'm going when I don't even know?" I asked.

"Have you not noticed that you have been following me?" he asked.

I could tell it was a "he." His masculine voice and his powerful spin gave him away, or so I thought. "We're walking side by side," I said, "I'm not following you, nor you me."

"If you pay close attention," he said, "you'll notice that I'm just slightly ahead of you. You're so lost in your thoughts you just automatically follow me. I've led many such as you to many places."

So I gave my attention to our walking, though of course he had nothing like legs and wasn't taking steps, but rather was spinning steadily forward like a wayward top. I decided to turn left at the next corner, but as I did, I felt him moving just ahead of me to turn me. I was indeed following him. "Okay, I followed you just then," I said, "but I had already made the decision."

"Do you know where you are?" he asked.

I looked around. A middle-class neighborhood with sidewalks and a small park with swing sets at the next corner. "No," I said, "I've never seen this place before."

"Deciding is an illusion," he said. "If you were deciding, this isn't the place you would come to."

I was sure I saw the flaw in his logic, but I decided to let it be. I didn't want this conversation to go any further. "Okay," I said. "Think what you will."

"Oh, I never think," he said, "I don't have a brain. The words I speak just pass right through me. I have no idea where they come from."

I looked at him. It was true, I could see right through his "head" to the window of a house. "Well," I said, "it was nice to meet you, but I'd like to go my own way."

"No such thing as going your own way," he said. "Besides, I'm on a mission. I'm leading you to a particular place."

For the first time, I felt a little fearful. I didn't want to be captive to a whirlwind-man. It was challenging enough to be captive to an ordinary man. I stopped walking and faced him forcefully. He stopped and turned toward me. "I want you to leave me alone now," I said, "I want to go my own way."

"I cannot do that." His red bud eyes were kindly when he spoke. "I wish I could, but I just can't."

"Why not?" I asked.

"A whirlwind cannot abandon its mission, any more than a leaf can abandon hers."

"That makes absolutely no sense," I said. "You go your way, and I'll go mine."

With that, I strode away, but the whirlwind stayed right with me, continuing to lead just slightly.

I stopped again and stomped my foot. "Leave . . . me . . . alone!" I shouted. He stood before me, sheepishly shaking his head. Pure rage rose up in me, and I took a swing at him. My hand punched through leaves. I stumbled on the follow-through and passed right into the whirlwind. Suddenly, I was standing inside of him. I had disturbed the pattern of whirling leaves, but they quickly regrouped and swirled all around me. I was looking through his red bud eyes, and the world had a completely different appearance. People walking nearby were barely recognizable as humans. Their bodies were the aggressively moving pencil strokes of an artist, as if the people were constantly being redrawn. Their heads were bright gold coronas shooting out umbilical cords of light. And yet their eyes were dull and staring, almost like badges or shields.

"Maybe it's better this way," the whirlwind said, his voice sounding directly inside my head.

"Is this what we really look like?" I asked.

"It depends," he said. "It's what you look like without the distracting flak of thought."

I thought about that for a moment. "I have no idea what you're talking about," I said.

"You don't need to know," he said.

"That's exactly the kind of thing my husband would say," I said.

"Oh, I'm so sorry," he said, "I just mean that we are from different worlds."

"I think that's what my husband also means," I said.

The whirlwind didn't know how to reply to that, so he began moving up the street. My body was suspended within his and needed to make no effort to walk. Passersby paid me no attention. I was going to ask him about that, but he spoke first.

"I'm not a man," he said.

I took stock of his presence flying all around me. It was true. I had misunderstood him. He had no gender. So why did I keep thinking of him as "he"? He definitely wasn't a "she."

"So, where are we going?" I asked.

"To the Winter Carnival," he said.

"And how far is that?"

"Just another mile or two," he said. "Don't worry, you'll be home before your husband returns."

Maybe I didn't care if I was home when he got home. I realized that there were many things in my life that I was supposed to care about, but didn't.

Within the whirlwind, the world was amazing, and I discovered I had no fear of what was happening. I assumed that I had gone suddenly and totally insane, but decided I was going to study it, to understand it if I could. I had no difficulty moving my arms and legs, no difficulty looking around at the scenery. The whirlwind moved with a sense of purpose now, cutting through back yards and alleys. I just allowed everything to happen. Within the houses, I saw sometimes women and sometimes men taking care of infants and cleaning the rooms. Lots of homes were empty, their occupants off at work, the children at school or daycare. We reached the outskirts of town and in the near distance I saw a vast field that was occupied by a gigantic carnival. Its skyline was impressive, with all kinds of flying, twirling, rising and falling rides. As we got closer, I could see hundreds of booths, arcades, and edifices that held what must have been strange and wonderful demonstrations. There were perhaps thousands of cars parked in row after row as far as the eye could see. People swarmed over the carnival like ants over pizza left on the ground, and the roar of their combined voices rolled over the landscape. When we arrived at the gate, the whirlwind gently excreted me from his body.

"I can't go any farther," he said.

"Why not?"

"A whirlwind cannot enter the carnival. I become breathless there, and if I get out of breath, I die."

"Oh," I said. "So what am I supposed to do here?"

"Find the mechanical storyteller," he said.

"The what?"

"He's known as Mister Fabulous. Ask him your questions. I'll be waiting for you here," he said.

"What questions?" I asked, but he was already drifting to an open area in the enormous parking lot where other whirlwinds had gathered. I had never noticed the world of whirlwinds before. Whenever the wind is up, they are everywhere, and they are alive. Fortunately, as I approached the gate, I had regained my normal way of seeing. I don't think I could have entered the chaos of the carnival if I had kept seeing like a whirlwind. I stood in a line to pay at a bright red booth. When it was my turn, a huge clown smoking a cigar looked down at me from the booth and said, in a deep and raspy voice, "How many, Sugar?"

"Pardon?" I said.

"Tickets!" he shouted.

"Oh," I said, "just one."

"Ten bucks, Darlin," he said. He slid a ticket toward me on the counter top.

I reached into my pocket, found my wallet, and pulled out a ten. As I handed it to him, I said, "Can you direct me to Mister Fabulous?"

"Never heard of him," he said. "Move along."

I felt the person behind me pressing against my back, and so I did what I was told, and moved along. I hadn't been to a carnival like this since I was a kid. Back then I loved the rides, all except the ones that took me upside down.

This was the biggest and most extravagant carnival I had ever seen. Row after row of games of chance and games of skill. Whack-a-Mole was my favorite as a kid. I loved it when the mole popped up somewhere else. A game that was impossible to win, it seemed to me. My father loved darts and target shooting and basketball, any real game of skill. He won a lot of prizes for me. My boyfriends too, later, when I was older.

The rides towered all around me—the Tilt-a-Whirl, the Whip, the Caterpillar, the Kamikaze—I rode them all back then. Kids were screaming in joyful terror. But now I had to keep my concentration. I had no idea what Mister Fabulous would look like. I walked endlessly it seemed up and down the aisles and side trails, but I couldn't locate Mister Fabulous. I asked a couple of unoccupied carnies where he was, but neither of them had heard of him. One of them shrugged his shoulders and said, "The only thing I know is the Graviton. That's my territory. Mister Fabulous could be anywhere. This is a fucking universe." He spread his arms out wide. So I kept walking. I went down a side aisle and discovered the naked lady show. A carnie with a microphone stalked up and down telling stories of the sexual prowess of the scantily clad young woman standing in the middle of the stage. A sizeable crowd of men had gathered, all of them rapt, shouting classic encouragements to the young woman. "Take it off!" a number of them shouted. "Let me show you what it's all about!" a skinny young man with a mustache yelled.

According to the carnie up on the stage, men had jumped off the

Brooklyn Bridge, walked on beds of fire, crawled through the narrowest and deepest of caves, climbed the remotest and highest mountains, swum across the Dead Sea, just for the privilege of having a few minutes of her company. She looked like an ordinary pretty girl to me. She had to be freezing cold, but she just kept gyrating her hips and flashing her dark eyes at the crowd.

Except for the woman on stage, I couldn't see another woman anywhere. I suddenly felt outnumbered. Then my eyes spotted a familiar man in the crowd near the front, my husband whistling and calling. I looked at my watch. One p.m. He was on his lunch break, "with others," he had told me. This wasn't like him. What in the world was he doing here? I tried to work my way through the crowd to get to him, and the men, to their credit, gave me space to step through. But when I got to where he was, the crowd of men seemed to swallow him up. I called his name, but that caught the attention of the other men, and they started calling to him too, mockingly—"John! John! Where are you?"—so I stopped doing that. Then I heard his voice coming from behind me. "I could eat you for breakfast, lunch, and dinner!" It was such a stupid thing to say I couldn't believe it. I was so embarrassed for him. I fought my way back to where he was, ignoring the sleazy remarks of the men, but again the crowd enfolded him. Then I heard his voice off to my left. I was too short to see over the men, so I pushed through them blindly. "Me first!" my husband shouted. The men roared with laughter. Their energy jumped up a notch. I stopped pushing.

"What's the matter sugar?" the man next to me said, putting his arm around me. He was tall and sturdy. Looking down at me, his face was like a rock. His eyes were soft, sweet pools of water, almost pleading.

I was suddenly afraid again, standing in the midst of a hundred raucous men. I shoved his arm off me, and they made a small circle around me. I saw my husband's face a couple of rows away. Gawking at me, his eyes were soft and pleading too. I tried to work my way back out of the crowd, but they were less cooperative than before. "Where you going, pretty thing?" one of them said. Suddenly my husband grabbed my coat and spun me around. His eyes had changed, fierce now, full of rage. He shook me and shook me like a wayward child. I swung out with my right hand as hard as I could and hit him on the shoulder. The men were laughing. "Feisty, ain't she?" one of them said. The crowd pushed into us and I broke away from my husband. Finally, I worked my way out to the perimeter and turned around. But my husband had disappeared. The men were no longer interested in me. Other young women wearing almost nothing had paraded onto the stage, and now the show was about to begin. The women slipped through a door to the interior. And the men lined up at two separate booths to buy their tickets. I watched my husband take his turn and pay his money. Soon, they had all filed into the show room. I stood alone now on the lane. Thirty yards away at the end of it, the carnival roared with life. A nearby Ferris wheel torched the sky. I could see tiny bodies way up there, dangling their feet. Screams came from every direction. But it was another world here, quiet and lonely.

I didn't want to reenter that chaos. I wanted to find some safe haven where I could lie down for a while and rest and think about what I had just experienced. But I knew there was no such place in the carnival.

Suddenly I caught sight of a small, colorful booth standing in the gloom of the closed end of the lane. As I approached it, my eyes focused, and I saw the name "Mister Fabulous" in bold gold script across the top. The booth was really a large, rectangular box standing on its end. Within it, sitting under yellow lights that cut shadows across his face, was a small man dressed in a blue suit, red tie, and a black bowler hat. His orange cheeks were bright with rouge. His brilliant red lips were fixed in a slight smile. His eyes stared into space blankly. On the lower panel of the booth were words written in the same bold gold script: "Mechanical Storyteller. Insert one dollar." These machines had been a dime or a quarter when I was a child.

I looked around to make sure I was alone. The lane was empty. I could hear pounding strip-club music coming from the naked lady show, the voices of men shouting. Trailers surrounded Mister Fabulous on three sides, presumably the domiciles of carnies who were all at work somewhere out there in the carnival. I turned back to Mister Fabulous. I had him all to myself. I pulled out a dollar, smoothed it against my palm, and inserted one end into the slot. Something sucked the dollar into the machine. I heard a small cackle coming from somewhere inside. Mister Fabulous suddenly came to life with a little bit of jaunty carousel music. He smiled more broadly, tipped his bowler to me, and brought his black and white wooden eyes up to gaze directly into mine. My moment had arrived.

"Can you tell me what I should do with my life?" I asked.

Mister Fabulous slowly shook his head. "No way José," he said in a gravelly but clear voice, "I do not tell people what they should do."

"But I have questions," I said.

His eyes narrowed condescendingly and again he shook his head. "I do not answer questions," he said.

"Well, what do you do?" I asked.

"I am the mechanical storyteller," he said, "and you are the mechanical listener."

I started to say, "What does that mean?" but his voice interrupted me.

"The story will now begin." He paused for a few seconds as if to see if I was ready to listen. Then he began:

"Many people were born on the same day. Many more in the same week. Many more in the same year. Many more in the same decade. Sam fell in love with Jackie, but Jackie loved Ralph, but Ralph loved Tom, but Tom loved Sally, but Sally loved Jill, but Jill loved Steven, and so on. They formed a very long chain of lovers and beloveds. And some of them got serious and decided that the one who loved them was pretty okay and they got married. When that happened, a gap formed in the chain, and some other dangling person moved into the gap and completed the chain again. There were many such chains, and many gaps formed all the time, and many dangling people filled many gaps. Men fell in love with women and then fell out of love with them. Women fell in love with men and then fell out of love with them. Men fell in love with men, and then fell out of love with them. Women fell in love with women and then fell out of love with them. And so on. Each of them wondered what he or she was doing, what he or she *should* be doing. Sometimes when things were going well, one of them thought they knew what they should be doing. But then things would go badly, and they realized they didn't know what they should be doing. And so on. They kept falling in love and out of love. They kept making babies. More and more love chains kept forming. They all thought they knew and didn't know, knew and didn't know, what they were doing and what they were supposed to be doing. And so on. That is still happening now and everywhere. Sometimes a person just stops participating and sees what is happening. Such a person just sees it. Still the mechanical stories keep going on and on, but here and there a person sees it, steps outside the story, and stops being so mechanical. Nonmechanical people do not make emotional chains. And so on. That is my story for the day. Thank you."

The music slowed down and stopped as Mister Fabulous slumped, his eyes went dull, and the smile on his face grew slack.

"That's it?!" I shouted. "I came all this way just to listen to this crap?!" I became outraged and threw a tantrum on the spot. I let it all hang out. I shouted and screamed and became red in the face, I'm sure. I stomped the ground until my feet ached and my shoes were covered with carnival dust. Something in me was watching all of this. It wasn't like me to lose control. Exhausted, I just stood there in the empty lane wondering what to do next. The men were still shouting and cat-calling to the dancing naked women. Then I noticed a stream of red arrows flashing on the lower panel of Mister Fabulous' booth. The arrows pointed to the slot for the dollar bill.

"What," I shouted, "you want more of my money?"

The stream of red arrows just kept flashing and flashing. I pulled out another dollar and inserted it, hoping Mister Fabulous would tell me a better story, one I could use. I heard that small cackle again somewhere in the depths of the machine. Mister Fabulous came to life as before. He tipped his hat, smiled broadly, and raised his eyes to meet mine.

"You came back for more," he said. His lower wooden lip moved up and down when he spoke.

"I want to hear a better story," I said.

"My stories are neither good nor bad," he said. "I can only tell the story that comes out of me. Are you ready?" he asked.

"Yes," I said, "I'm ready."

"The story will now begin," he said. He paused for a few seconds to see if I was listening. Then he began:

"There was a woman who decided she wanted to change her life and would run with the whirlwinds who are neither men nor women. She sought them out in remote fields where they gathered like a herd of spun tops. She ran among them and spun and spun, but the debris of their bodies soon fell to the ground like spilled salt, and she was left spinning by herself under the night sky. Everywhere she went, the whirlwinds rose up, danced, and soon died. Until one day she managed to befriend a lone whirlwind who drew her into his hollow bell. She saw through the eyes of this whirlwind, and what she saw rang and rang in her mind and heart. She was stunned and amazed, feeling she had indeed entered into a new life. When the whirlwind's body of sand and trash fell to the ground around her, she wasn't sad. Her eyes remained full of the world. The more she walked into it, the more she saw different kinds of beings. Beings made mostly of water who stood upright and walked on the earth. Beings made mostly of earth who lay very still under the light of the sun and moon. Beings made mostly of fire that ate whatever they touched. Beings made mostly of air spinning tirelessly and mostly unseen in every corner of the world. That is my story for the day."

I just stared at Mister Fabulous as he once again slumped and his eyes went dead. How did he know about the whirlwind? And why didn't he say more about it? Why didn't he tell me what to do? I ran over to him and gave his booth a good kick. He came back to life and glared at me.

"I like your story," I said, "but you were supposed to show me what to do."

Mister Fabulous' eyes intensified. He leaned forward and raised his bowler in an incongruous gesture. I could see that he was starting to go bald on top.

"Fraud," I said to him quietly.

"Yes," he said, "the mechanical storyteller is a fraud."

"I need to know what to do," I said. I hated the pleading in my voice.

"The future is only a mechanical story," he said.

"How is that supposed to help me know what to do?"

He seemed to be growing weaker. He spoke in a gravelly voice that had become so soft I had to hold my ear very close to his wooden mouth. "Do whatever you want, it is not you who is doing it," he said.

Then he slumped again, and all the lights on the machine went out. Even the red arrows pointing to the money slot. The carousel music slurred to a halt. I hadn't even noticed it was still playing.

Why had I been taken to this place by the whirlwind? If Mister Fabulous had any more stories, I didn't want to hear them. The naked lady show must have ended, because the men began to file out of the House of Love laughing and high fiving. I saw my husband John among them. His eyes caught mine briefly, but he made himself small and disappeared into the carnival at the end of the lane. I had no interest in pursuing him. I was exhausted beyond understanding. I gave Mister Fabulous a sarcastic salute, walked to the end of the lane, and entered the noise and chaos of the carnival. For the first time in my life, the emptiness of all the games and rides came home to me, weighed me down. What was everyone looking for? They seemed to be having a good time, but there were loners lurking in the shadows. Some children were crying. Some adults were cursing. The games were impossible or easy to win, the prizes not worth the price of playing. I made my way back to the gate where the gigantic clown ticket seller grinned at me. He tipped his bowler hat. I ran out to the open field. It felt good to get outside of the carnival and back into the real world where the air was fresh and moving. It was December, and the days had become short. It would be dark soon. Already, the town's lights were coming on and shining in the distance like . . . I shifted my eyes. The early evening sky was full of clouds capturing the pinks and purples of last light. I found the whirlwinds playing in their field nearby. They were bobbing and whirling in such a tight-knit group that they sometimes became one large whirlwind that could do a lot of damage if it headed into town. Nobody in the nearby parking lot seemed to notice them at all. My whirlwind spotted me, separated from their games, and was soon standing next to me.

"I don't think I can walk all the way home," I said, barely able to stand, my right foot throbbing from kicking Mister Fabulous.

"No problem," he said, and he absorbed me into his body as before.

"I didn't like Mister Fabulous," I said.

"Nobody does," he said.

I wanted to stay awake, wanted to experience the world through the eyes of a whirlwind again, but I just couldn't. I must have fallen asleep. The next thing I knew, my whirlwind excreted me onto the front stoop of my home. I turned to him.

"Thank you Mister Whirlwind," I said, bowing to him.

His maple leaf mouth turned up in a smile. But he said, "I am not a man."

"I know, I know," I said, and thank God for that, I thought.

He slowly drifted to the sidewalk in front of my house. Then he unraveled before my eyes. His leaves fell into disarray onto the ground.

My husband came home from work only a few minutes later. He found me on the couch crying and crying. He sat down beside me and stroked my hair. It felt good and bad at the same time. Good and bad, good and bad. As if the suction end of an umbilical cord were stroking my head. I looked into John's handsome face.

"What's wrong, Sweetie," he asked.

"Nothing . . . I don't know."

"What have you been doing all day?"

"Walking. Just walking for hours and hours."

"But why?" he asked.

"I felt like it. I don't know. I just wanted to figure out what I should do."

"Oh, the job thing again."

"Yes. No, not exactly."

"There are no exact sciences," he said.

"Do you know how many times you've said that?" I asked.

"No. What difference does it make? It was just a . . . just a . . . an expression, I know. I'm just so tired of being mechanical, that's all," I said.

Again, a quizzical look came over John's face. "What you need is a drink," he said. "I know I need one." He rose from the couch and headed into the kitchen. I heard glasses clinking together, and ice cubes being extracted from the maker.

"I met a whirlwind," I said, not sure if it was loud enough for him to hear.

He stuck his head back into the room. "A what?"

"Never mind."

"Did you say a whirlwind?"

"I was joking," I said. His head disappeared back into the kitchen.

"I figured out something else I need to tell you," I called out to him.

He stuck his head back through the door. "What's that?" he said.

"I know that something is wrong."

"Wrong?" he said.

"Yes," I said. "Something is really, really, wrong."

"Oh, okay," he said, "let me finish with the drinks and I'll follow up on that."

John went back into the kitchen. When he came out, he was holding a drink in each hand. He was trying to smile. He stood for a moment on the other side of the coffee table. "What was it you were saying? Something is wrong?"

"Yes. And I can't keep on being the way that I have been."

He stood there for the longest time just looking at me. I was the most relaxed and the clearest in my mind that I had been in a long time, maybe ever. I smiled, but I don't think it was a smile I'd ever made before, or that he'd ever seen. He looked and looked at me, as if I were not the woman he knew, as if he were trying to get inside my head. It took him a long time before he finally set the drinks down, came around the table, and sat beside me.

"I saw you at the carnival," I said.

"What carnival? It's past the carnival season. There are no carnivals."

"I know. I know. But I saw you. And there's no going back."

He pulled back a little to see me better. He looked and looked. "I have no idea what you're talking about," he said, "I haven't been to any carnival."

"I know. It's okay."

We sat for a while, drank our drinks slowly, talked the usual small talk. I struggled to follow his words, to keep the line of conversation going. My attention kept being drawn to the painting across from me on the wall. It seemed unfamiliar, though I had selected it in collaboration with my husband. Three women in flowery, pastel summer dresses with their backs turned to the viewer, walking away slowly in a bright, vague beach land-scape of light and wind and cloud. It was pretty, but it meant nothing to me.

When he went to bed, I walked out to the front stoop and looked at the stars in the cold night sky. I peered into the darkness partially lit by streetlights, looking for my whirlwind, knowing there would never be an-other one exactly like him. I walked out into the yard and the cold breeze burned on my bare arms. I felt naked before the world.

I have enough money to live on my own for a few years, I thought. For the first time it occurred to me that the earth is a whirlwind living in a solar system that is a whirlwind living in a galaxy that is a whirlwind living in a universe that is a whirlwind. I would tell my husband that I needed to visit my family alone for Christmas. He hated our Christmas gatherings anyway with all their prayers and singing. I would never return to my house, except when my husband was not at home, and then only to retrieve a few of my things that I didn't really need.

I wandered farther out in the yard and the sky grew vast over my head. The neighborhood stretched its spider legs and yawned. I could feel them out there, millions of sexless whirlwinds made of twisted wind and loose debris rising up on the surface of the earth.

2. The Broken Voice of a Woman

Three men gather in a middle-class living room. A couch, a couple of recliners, coffee table, pole lamps well positioned for reading, imitation oriental rug, small pillows of various colors thrown around for those who want them, landscape paintings and photos of mountains and backcountry trails on the wall, big-screen TV in a corner, brick fireplace with a white, wood mantelpiece sporting a violin bow, a ceramic jar sprouting incense sticks, a colorful cup decorated with pumas, serpents, and condors.

The men are sitting in a row on the couch, giving their rapt attention to a smart phone on a stand in the middle of the coffee table. Coming from the phone are somewhat chaotic sounds: buffeting wind, the particles of a voice, a woman's voice, not quite cohering. She is asking questions to someone, to something. But so far no one has answered, at least not loud enough to be heard.

"Why didn't she video the damn thing?" Tom asks.

"I don't know," says Frank, the woman's friend. "You've seen the photographs. Isn't that enough?"

"So fake," says Charlie.

"She says that it believes videos will frighten people," Frank says.

The three men look at each other and then break out in laughter.

"Believes?" Charlie said.

"What a load of crazy crap," Tom says.

"Yeah," says Frank, "but it's interesting crap."

"*You* have to think it's interesting," says Charlie, "because you're in love. You have some skin in the game."

Suddenly, a much more forceful voice in the recording cuts in with a single word: yes. The voice could be male or female, somewhere between soprano and baritone, except that it has a slightly artificial twinge. The men lean in, focused now. The woman interviewer's voice, too broken to be understood fully, breaks in with some kind of question. And then the other voice, strong as a next-door radio station, speaks.

Okay. Some facts about Whirlwinds: I cannot lie down. I never sleep. I never get sleepy or tired. I'm completely and perfectly what I am, nothing lacking; I'm never increasing nor diminishing, though it may look that way to you. Increasing and diminishing occur in time, but there is no time for whirlwinds. I exist and yet I don't exist. When I say "I," I don't mean "me." No such thing. So, that's just a few facts for you to chew on.

Discontinuous female voice asks another question.

Whirlwinds do not ordinarily speak to humans. You're hearing this voice now because I trust you, and because it is my purpose to serve you. Humans almost never see a whirlwind as it is, and this makes communication virtually impossible. The minds of humans are too busy with thinking to see much of anything. But there are a few rare humans whose minds are empty at least part of the time, and they do see us, on occasion. You are such a person. You are open, you listen, and you see. You are trying to find ways to wake people up to the secret of Whirlwinds. So I will tell you whatever I can, whatever is coming through me. Emptiness, open space, is the spawning ground of whirlwinds and their voices. One of the important secrets of whirlwinds is that they exist to be of service to other beings. Not just to humans. But to pretty much all beings, no matter how small or how large. We are everywhere, often invisible to creature eyes. Many of us are in service to humans, guiding them to some place they would never reach without us. Sometimes they don't even know we are there, doing our work. Humans and whirlwinds have many affinities. Likewise whirlwinds and dogs, crickets, mice, whales, horses, fleas, amoebas, even atoms. Atoms are just a tiny form of whirlwind. Humans, too, are a different species of whirlwind, but humans and my species of whirlwind cannot mate because my whirlwind species has no sex. Like humans, we are attracted to each other. But any commingling we do produces only a larger whirlwind. Our reproduction occurs at the whims of the source of wind. (Pause. The straining voice of the woman interviewer is heard.) *Yes, I'll try to speak a little clearer. My voice comes out of nowhere, so I realize it is hard to know where to hold the microphone. I see you engaging with your whirlwind nature and dancing with me to stay close. My spin has to be aggressive to create enough energy to speak. I hope the spinout is not too hard on you. Is that better now? Can you hear me now?*

Garbled female voice . . .

My speech obviously doesn't come from the manipulations of wind over lips and tongue and larynx and vocal chords. But it is a manipulation of wind nevertheless, an abrasion of wind-spun particles of dust and other debris. My speech doesn't come from some imagined self inside me as it most often does with humans. I have no brain, and therefore no thoughts, and therefore no mind as such. No thoughts precede these words as they fly out of me. In other words, it isn't me speaking because there is no me. These words are being spun directly and organically out of the source of all whirlwinds.

Indecipherable female voice . . .

Well, in human time, whirlwinds usually last only a few minutes before spinning themselves out. But there are many whirlwinds that remain in human time for a whole day or even more. Everything depends on the weather and the energetic circumstances and the requirements of a whirlwind's service. Some, like hurricanes, can last for many days.

Woman's fragmented voice . . .

Yes, but we know we are not separate individuals. We know there is only one whirlwind, and it never stops spinning. And out of its spinning, our spinning arises. There is no individual identity for us. We see you being ravaged by your beliefs in such things. We know that we are destructive. Tornadoes and hurricanes are like the feet of humans crashing down on the habitats of small creatures on earth. People aren't normally aware they are destroying and killing.

In any case, they can't help it, any more than a hurricane can help being what it is. Although people can't see this fact, hurricanes are also serving. For whirlwinds, everything is always happening at once. Everything arises together, and everything depends on everything else. Like you. You arose in our midst. We are talking to you, hoping that you can show others our secrets, which are not secrets at all. They are in plain sight, but aren't being seen. If you know, for example, that you are also a whirlwind, it might change your life.

Female interviewer's badly broken voice . . .

I didn't say you have to change your life. To whirlwinds, you can't change your life. There is no one to change it and no one to be changed. Life is happening. Whirlwinds are spinning. These understandings are what make whirlwinds, comparatively large ones especially, so frightening to humans because humans are not in control of even their own spinning. And these same understandings are what make small whirlwinds so fascinating. Fascinating or frightening depending on your vantage point. We whirlwinds are like your children: thoughtless, playful, unrelenting, vividly alive. Children too are both fascinating and frightening, don't you think?

Female interviewer's patchy voice . . .

Yes, I agree, not just children, but all existing beings, whose number is beyond infinite. We whirlwinds enjoy whatever is given to us because we have no stake in it. Because we lack nothing, we want nothing. Because we have nothing, there is nothing to lose. Gathering in very remote places is how we have fun. The company of other whirlwinds is . . . ecstasy, bliss. We play and play and play, new whirlwinds bursting from earth and wind all around us.

Female interviewer's voice interrupts.

Oh, I'm sorry about that. So much time in the company of—and talking with—a whirlwind will definitely kill your batteries. I have enjoyed taking this spin with you. Until next time . . .

Female interviewer's broken voice . . . and the audio goes blank.

The three men sit in silence for a moment. Tom suddenly laughs.

"So whirlwinds are airhead philosophers? Gimme a break. You know this is a joke, right."

"If you spoke to her you would believe that she believes that she is talking to whirlwinds," says Frank, her friend. "And she has this evidence."

"You call that evidence? People who believe they are talking to whirlwinds are . . . like . . . the definition of crazy, delusional," says Charlie. "Come on, the whole thing was so fake: 'I enjoyed taking this *spin* with you?' Funny, but not even remotely convincing. I'm thinking Saturday Night Live. I can see John Belushi—no, John Candy—being the whirlwind."

"Yeah," says Tom. "I give her some credit for being . . . creative. I mean, it was fun to listen to, except what the fuck was that whirlwind thing saying? I mean I heard it, but it didn't make any sense."

"It's not supposed to make sense," says Charlie. "It's supposed to bamboozle and entertain. Right?"

"Bamboozle?" says Frank.

"Exactly. Spiritual crap," says Tom. "If that's what she's doing, making fun of that spiritual mumbo jumbo, then I say 'Bravo!' She pulled it off and she's done the world a service."

"I know her pretty well . . ."

"I bet you do . . ."

"And she's not a spiritualist. And we're friends, no sex. I trust her to tell me the truth."

"Ouch," says Tom, "that has to hurt after all the time you've put in."

"It hurts me to think about it," says Charlie.

"Exactly," says Tom. "Hey Frank, this was fun, but can I trust you to get me a beer? One for my friend here too. And let's shoot some hoops. Whaddya say? I gotta get some revenge after last time."

Frank looks at them for a moment. He shrugs his shoulders once, gets up and heads for the kitchen.

After Tom gets his revenge, Frank sits in a lawn chair in his yard. Evening is coming on, and the breeze is cool, chilling the sweat on his body slightly. It feels good. He looks through the canopies of his maple trees to the dimming sky. He wonders where she is tonight. Wonders when he'll see her again, if ever. Every week or so, she calls him or sends him an email from wherever she is. Every couple months she shows back up in town and they get together and talk for hours. He figures she's crazy as a loon, and he knows he's at least slightly pathetic, but he can't help himself. He's in love.

3. The Sadness of Whirlwinds

Frank parked his car in a remote turnout on a dirt road beside America's largest and deepest forest somewhere in Montana. It was important that the exact location not be revealed. She had made that absolutely clear to him. No one else was to know where she was, or where her rendezvous took place. The body of this forest reaches into significant parts of several states. The sun was still low in the morning sky, the dawning of a beautiful day in early September. Frank raised the hatchback of his old Subaru and began removing a few items: a backpack, which he stood upright against the bumper; a walking stick that received the same treatment; a brown, wide-brim Stetson with a raven feather in the band; a pair of sturdy hiking boots. He took off his running shoes, tossed them in the trunk, and pulled on the hiking boots, lacing them with even pressure all the way up. He closed the trunk, locked the car with his remote key, swung the backpack over his shoulders, tightening the straps snugly across his chest and waist. He hoped that no one would vandalize his car in the week he'd be in the woods.

He grabbed his walking stick that he had carved from the wood of a Paper Birch and looked toward the east where the sun rose over a dramatic ridge, its face still in deep shadow. Then he turned toward a stand of Douglas Fir, spotted the trailhead, and began to walk. Consulting topo maps he'd bought from the Park Service, he walked for hours, stopping

sometimes to run his finger along a trail. The trails branched and meandered like some of the fractal designs he'd studied in school long ago. The
destination was clearly marked on the map, and at least he was heading in
the right direction.

A few hours in, he noted the fresh print of a grizzly nearly two feet long
on the muddy edge of a creek, and soon, on a bed of grass, a pile of scat the
size of his hat and full of raspberry seeds plus a few chokeberry pits. He figured he was being watched and just kept walking. He would love to lay his
eyes on the giant, but it was better not to. Safer. He wasn't one of those hik-
ers that wore cowbells to warn the bears away. If he wanted to listen to bells
all day, he'd live in a church. Besides, he wanted to see the wildlife. Higher
up on the side of a ridge, he saw cougar tracks. He took it as an omen. Either
something terrible was going to happen, or something amazing.

As the sun grew low on the horizon, he camped for the night at a creek.
His first and most important task was to filter the creek water and fill all
of his canteens. Then, fighting the hordes of mosquitos, he lowered his
naked body into the cold, fast-moving water and allowed it to cleanse him
for maybe ten minutes. He held his nose and lay back in the stream completely submerged. When he reemerged, rubbing the water out of his eyes,
he saw two whirlwinds streaking across a flat sandy patch of ground on
the other side of the creek. He wondered if they were friends of hers. They
disappeared so quickly, he wasn't sure he'd actually seen them. When he
started becoming numb from the stinging cold, he scrambled to the bank,
grabbed his towel, kept hopping and jumping to fight off the marauders,
and pulled three layers of clothes on in record-breaking time. Still the
mosquitos munched on his ears and eyebrows.

He unzipped his tent, sprang headlong into it, and zipped the front
tightly shut. He ate some dried fruit and hefty trail mix he'd put together.
Soon the darkness was complete and he could feel the weight of it pressing
on his tent. When he'd finished eating, he stuffed his food back in the
canister and screwed the lid tight. He wrapped a scarf around his face to
discourage the biting beasts. Outside, he felt the weight of an incredible

silence. It almost seemed alive. He took a long leak in the sparse grass, hoping it would be his last one until dawn. Standing there for a moment, he gazed at the night all around him. His body hummed with a pleasurable tiredness and the tonic effects of the cold stream. He'd never seen so many stars before.

Back in his tent, he snuggled into his sleeping bag, attached a small battery-powered reading light to the back cover of the book he was reading and adjusted it to light the page. The book was entitled *The Secret of Whirlwinds*, which she had self-published a year before. She'd sold around five thousand copies on Amazon and other websites. Frank figured she'd moved a lot of them based on the title alone. And while the cover called the book nonfiction, he thought that most of its readers believed it to be fiction, so outlandish were its contents. And maybe the cover sold some copies too: on it there was a grainy photo of her standing next to a ten-foot-tall whirlwind and holding a microphone at arm's length toward it. The background was a windswept Western landscape, rim-rock country with great sage all around and a prominent ridge in the distance catching the late afternoon sun. She wore a sturdy jumpsuit, goggles, and heavy gloves. It was a dramatic image that would capture anyone's attention.

And she was a good writer: vivid, clear, direct, objective, with a graceful sense of a well-made sentence. She could tell a story, too, about her adventures in searching for whirlwinds that would hang out with her and even sometimes speak to her in philosophical terms. More photos accompanied her stories. She had borne the cost of publishing the book herself, but had made all the money back plus a couple thousand profit by now. He had met her at a launch party for her book at a local bookstore in her and Frank's hometown of Lexington, Virginia. About twenty-five people showed up. She read a section from the book describing her first conversation with a whirlwind. Simple refreshments were served afterwards. Her hometown friends and family didn't know what the hell she was doing, but they wanted to support her, and she sold ten or fifteen books that evening. Frank waited until everyone else had left for her to sign his copy. He immediately asked her out to dinner. She accepted. They talked and talked. Aside from the fact that she was plainly beautiful and direct, he had never met anyone like her before. Her face was architecturally clean showing the lines of her cheekbones and jaw, her hair short with bangs that sprouted over her forehead, and her eyes penetrating with some mysterious intent. As the relationship progressed, she made it very clear to him that she had converted to Whirlwindism and that she was in effect sexless. That had been discouraging, but he discovered that he was crazy in love with her and somehow he would manage his desire and just plain old love her. He wasn't sure he could survive that way of life for long, but he was determined to give it a try. That, at least, had been his approach so far. And this was the first time she had invited him to join her on one of her adventures. He'd read the book twice before, and he was reading it again in preparation for whatever was going to happen out here in the middle of nowhere. He caught himself falling asleep and turned the light out.

The next morning, he discovered that something had knocked his food canister around a bit, but it was none the worse for wear. His sound sleeping and the murmurs of the fast-running creek had kept him from hearing much of anything throughout the night. He figured he had another fifteen miles to go and was glad to get an early start. A couple of hours later, the trail ran beside a wide meadow. He saw what at first looked like the rotting remnants of a tree trunk, but when it rose up he knew it was a sandhill crane. He'd heard that these birds were shy, but this one stood and observed him alertly without flinching. As Frank came alongside the bird, it turned and strode along with him about thirty feet away. It must be five feet tall, Frank thought. He saw clearly its red crown, orange eyes that drew a steady bead on him, long black beak, and when it opened its beak to call, he saw its reed-like, sensitive-looking tongue. The call had some similarities with the gobble of a turkey, but had a harder edge and carried like a rifle shot echoing off the nearby cliffs. Its legs were sturdy with knobby knees, its feathers gray with brown on the neck and wing. Soon the trail turned away from the meadow and the bird stayed behind.

But Frank heard it calling for the rest of the morning. And then it, or one of its clan, appeared stretched-out in the sky above him, its mysterious and disturbing call flooding the entire landscape. For more than two hours the birds kept appearing above him on the trail as if they were ushering him away, maybe protecting their young. He decided not to take it personally. He further decided to consider it as another positive sign. And as he called up his memory of the crane as it straightened up and walked beside him, he kept seeing it as a whirlwind.

Much later in the afternoon, he saw what he was looking for. If he could navigate efficiently, he would be there before dark. When he came to the river crossing less than ninety minutes later, he knew he was getting close. This was a major landmark on the map, and the butte itself rose from woods only half a mile away, standing maybe fifteen hundred feet above the valley floor. At this point, the river was only forty yards across. He took off his backpack, set it on the bank, and removed his boots and socks, slapping at the mosquitos attacking his bare feet. He released his pair of river shoes from a carabiner on his pack and put them on. Raising his pack above his head, with boots and walking stick attached, he stepped slowly down the bank full of bird and raccoon tracks and into the river. The cold water eased the sting and itch of the welts on his feet. The current came from his right but wasn't strong enough to topple him. He leaned into it to keep his balance. At the midpoint the water was on his chest, in the armpits. Being buried in the river like that made him feel part of the country, as if all phenomena were defined by flowing. Rather than looking at the world, he was in it, looking out. Now the water was shallower as he approached the other bank. Climbing onto the narrow beach, he noted that he was tired and hungry, but the place was so beautiful he just had to sit for a minute to take it in: the river, the woods, the butte itself like a bear hulking over the valley. He pulled his socks and boots on, then stood up and gazed at the butte, running his eyes along the top edge hoping to see someone up there looking for him.

He stared and studied. The map told him there was a trail on the other side, but he would never get there and manage to climb up by dark. He had to find a quicker way. Ten minutes later and back into the woods with no trail, he found the slope. The tangle of roots and small boulders made walking difficult. He had to take every step consciously to avoid turning his ankles. He worked his way around the north face of the butte where it appeared to have more angle, more slope. He came out of the woods at the foot of the butte, and yes, he believed the degree of slant would allow him to scramble slowly to the top. He needed to get going because the dark was coming on fast. His forty-pound pack wasn't going to make it any easier. The lower slope was mostly loose rock, but in ten minutes he had reached a level with grass and trees that gave him something to grab hold of to pull himself up. Forty-five minutes later, as the sun was being sliced in half by the horizon, he reached the top. He flopped down and looked around. A scattering of small, ground-hugging junipers and thick-limbed sage. The surface mostly flat and rocky but with a few trees. In the near distance, he saw a small fire. The silhouette of a woman stood up beside it. She came running and soon had her hands on him.

"Oh my God," she said, "you made it!"

"Yep," he said.

She took his hands, pulled him to his feet, and together they walked to the fire. The backpack had become part of his body, but she found the buckles and keeps to get him free of it. It slumped to the ground like a tired soldier. He wanted to do the same.

"Come on," she said, "let's get your tent up while we still have a speck of light."

He tried to help her with the poles and the guy cords, but was so beat he could hardly move. Then she brought out a canteen and poured some water into a small bowl. She dipped a washcloth into it. "We can't bathe until tomorrow, but you need to get cleaned up a little. You don't want to get into your sleeping bag like that."

He suddenly realized he was absolutely filthy from his climb. His face was smudged, his hair full of dirt and bits of leaf and bark, his hands covered in dust and scratched up from the brambles. She helped him wash off the worst of it. The mosquitos were not so bad up here in the dry breezes.

As the sun disappeared, and the night sky opened up to them, they sat by the little fire and she told him of her adventures. Whirlwinds were approaching her now everywhere she went. They spoke freely to her because she had so completely embraced Whirlwindism. Ridge tops and mountain valleys. Once in a canoe, she saw a whirlpool forming ahead of her. It stood up from the surface as a huge waterspout. It spoke to her, but she was so frightened of being swallowed whole that she wasn't sure what it had said. She back paddled as hard as she could. When the spout had seen she was afraid, it had sunk back into the whirlpool that soon subsided, and the water grew calm again.

She asked him about his adventures, but he said his were nothing compared to hers. Still she insisted, her hands like sparks in the light of the fire. So he told her of the grizzly tracks and scat, the cougar tracks, his prodigious battles with mosquitos, and his encounter with the sandhill cranes. She said that the cranes were her favorite animals in the backcountry because she knew they were protecting her. And him too. The whirlwinds had told her so.

The next morning Frank mostly ate and drank and rested. And took in the views offered by the butte's crown that was maybe two hundred yards wide and a quarter mile long. Big enough for him to stretch his sore legs. On the eastern edge, he saw on the valley floor the curve in the river where he had crossed. He saw the narrow beach where he had looked up to this very point hoping to catch a glimpse of her. A little farther east a herd of elk browsed in a meadow. Hawks and bald eagles cruised on the intervening air. Nearby, marmots squeaked and whistled and showed themselves briefly among boulders. She joined him in his explorations at times, and at other times she disappeared and he didn't know what she was doing.

Late morning she came to him and said they needed to walk down to the creek, replenish their water, and bathe. She led him to the western side of the butte where a switchbacking trail started down the steep slope.

She laughed. "Why didn't you use this trail to come up?"

"I didn't think I had enough time to find it."

"You can easily climb this trail in the dark," she said.

"Now I see that. But then I was crazy and took the first route up I saw."

"I'm seeing you like to make things hard for yourself," she said. She was laughing at him again. He liked when she laughed at him in that affectionate way.

Half an hour later they found the creek among lodgepole pines and cottonwoods. They filtered the water and filled their containers. Then they took off their clothes. She showed no shyness about becoming naked with him. She took his hand and led him into a deep pool in the creek. He knew there was no use in trying to hide his arousal. He thought she pretended not to see. The water came up to his navel. They washed each other's backs, and submerged themselves fully to scrub their heads. The cold began to creep into his bones, but he would have stayed in there with her as long as she wanted. Again she took him by the hand and led him onto the bank where they dried off quickly and got dressed.

They had lunch, then spent the early part of the afternoon sitting on some comfortable boulders and talking about the whirlwind that would come to visit. To see a whirlwind was why she had invited him, and why he had made the journey. Or at least part of why he had made it. Mainly he wanted to lay his eyes on her again, and hope. It had been difficult to get enough time off from his IT position to make this trip. He had to believe that she knew how he felt, that he was in love, and that he only resisted expressions of his feelings because he knew that was what she wanted, what her adherence to Whirlwindism required.

She told him the whirlwind would likely arrive sometime later in the afternoon. The conditions had to be right. For whirlwinds of that species and type, high windy locations with conflicting currents and fluctuating temperatures were best. She said she would act as a kind of psychological vacuum as they had taught her, and that would induce the advantageous conditions. Whirlwinds rarely speak to humans, she told him, but it was possible that this one would because they trusted her.

"But you," she said, "will also have to be trustworthy."

"How do I do that?" he asked.

"You empty your mind of all negative thoughts and images. You must become an inward vacuum. A receiver instead of a transmitter. If you're projecting, it won't speak to us."

"By projecting do you mean talking?"

"Maybe, in part, it depends on how you speak. But mainly I mean fear, anger, wanting something, any kind of ulterior or exterior motives. Defensiveness."

"I might not be aware of all of that when I'm doing it. It just happens."

"I know," she said. "I never told you this would be easy."

"No, you didn't," he said. "But is it even possible?"

"Trust me," she said. "It's possible."

Frank's friends, Charlie and Tom, had decided after long deliberation that she was luring him into some kind of kinky religious cult. They're dumbasses, Frank thought, and today would reveal it. If some guy showed up calling himself Whirlwind and spouting religious doctrine, it would be a sad day, and Whirlwindism would be just another meaningless belief system conjured out of the human desperation for meaning and certainty. He didn't know what was going to happen, but he believed in her. He was excited to share it with her, whatever it turned out to be.

As the afternoon wore on, the winds increased, shifting direction suddenly as if someone had flipped a switch. Sometimes the conflicting winds swirled the limbs of a nearby juniper tree full of thick, green needles as if it were being stirred by a giant, invisible spoon. She was so still that Frank thought she had become part of the boulder. Her stillness inspired him to clear his own mind to see if it were possible to be empty of all thoughts. To be a vacuum. After a while, he felt the stillness enter him like the subtle warmth of a shot of good whiskey. He was no longer trying to make it happen, it was just happening, and he relaxed.

Soon the air started twisting into a column like a double helix. As it strengthened and picked up dust and sand and pieces of bark, twigs and needles from the trees, it slowly took form. Like a man, Frank thought, made of wind and debris standing up in front of him. The visible aspect was maybe fifteen feet tall. Frank wasn't exactly sure why it was like a man because it was basically cylindrical, had no persistent features, but still it felt like the presence of a man, just a lot more potent. The nearby trees were bowing and shaking. The air felt charged with electricity. The force of it was strong at first and Frank thought he might be knocked flat and not be able to get back up. But as the whirlwind's form became more self-contained, more defined, the outward force diminished and was tolerable. The whirlwind's inward force seemed to increase, creating a subtle, audible hum. The trees quieted down. Frank didn't want to move, but he couldn't resist turning his head slowly so that he could see her. She had held the same relaxed position. Her eyes were fixed on the whirlwind. As Frank shifted his gaze back to it, he suddenly had the sensation in his own body that eyes like dim shadows had emerged in the whirlwind where eyes on a human would be. And then the voice broke onto the strained air.

"Good to see you."

The words were articulated clearly, but the voice was unlike any human one Frank had heard. It quavered and scraped like two pieces of sandpaper rubbed together mixed with that hum. Still, its pitch was in the human range.

"Good to see you too," she said.

Frank felt the whirlwind turn to him, and a pressure arose in his chest and head. Too much of this, Frank thought, and I will explode. The whirlwind kept its attention on Frank for a moment, then returned it to her and the pressure eased. "You have come to ask questions," it said.

"Yes," she said. "I and my friend. But I'd like to start with a comment. You are beautiful."

"For whirlwinds," it said, "everything is beautiful. No ugliness exists for us."

"I understand," she said. "Thank you for joining us here."

"I had no choice," it said. "And neither did you."

"So in your world there is no such thing as choice?"

"Our worlds are the same, and there is no choice anywhere."

"Are you saying that I didn't choose to be here?" Frank heard the words breaking out of him. Where did that come from, he thought.

Again, Frank felt the force of the whirlwind's attention. "You think you choose, and you believe your thoughts. That is one of the differences between us. You have thoughts that say, I am this, I am that. Behind those thoughts, there is nothing there. Thoughts thinking they are an 'I' that is a something—we have none of that."

"How do you know our language?" Frank asked.

"I don't know your language," it said. "Not in the way you know language. I don't really know anything in that sense, since I have no brain and therefore no mind. My kind of knowing is instantaneous and unconditioned."

"Is it possible that what is true for you is not true for us?"

"Isn't that clear? I don't speak the truth. Words arise in me and are spoken. There is no one here to claim the speaking of truth. It isn't for a whirlwind to deny the possibilities, or to affirm them."

Frank felt his mind splitting into fragments and then spinning. It was as if the whirlwind had gotten inside of him and was whipping his mind like a big pot of mashed potatoes. He was heading toward blacking out if he wasn't careful, but he didn't seem to have any control. He was aware of falling back onto the boulder. His mind ran away and jumped over the edge of the butte, soaring like a hawk on that ocean of air, and a sweetness filled the empty space that the mind left behind. He could've stayed right there forever as far as he was concerned because that space was bliss. He vaguely heard her voice and the voice of the whirlwind in the background for a while. And though his eyes were closed, he saw the whirlwind stagger to the edge of the Butte like a drunken clown where the air dismantled it.

When he woke up, his head was in her lap and she was stroking his temple.

"Hello there," she said, and smiled. "You did good."

As it grew dark, they sat beside her small fire. She prepared stew for them on her stove. They drank lots of water. Frank was quiet. He just didn't want to talk, to break the silence that had descended into him. He looked at her, at the stars, and the juniper trees nearby bronzed by the firelight. After food, she brought out a small plastic bottle of whiskey. She carefully poured each of them a finger or so into cups. They sipped slowly and made it last. And then they finally talked about what had happened.

"You told me once," he said, "that you had been inside a whirlwind and it had carried you along."

"Yes," she said, "it's happened a few times."

"That's what I want," he said. "I want to be inside of a whirlwind. I want to see what they see."

"Be careful what you ask for," she said, taking the last sip of whiskey in her cup.

Lying in his tent that night, his mind was still clear and open, no thinking, but a keen awareness of the world around him, especially the night sounds of wind and debris hitting the side of his tent. Just simply being was great pleasure. After a while, thoughts began slowly to return. The emptiness of the whirlwind is contagious, he thought. Then he thought about her lying in her sleeping bag in her tent only a few feet from where he was lying. And his longing returned. He suffered there in silence. Once, he thought he heard her voice, but he couldn't be sure. He thought he heard the zipper of her tent, but it was only the wind.

She was not able to sleep that night. She'd spent an hour taking notes on the conversation she'd had with the whirlwind. Her second book was going to be better than the first. She just knew it. The whirlwinds were opening more and more to her. It was interesting to her that she had experienced her first whirlwind as being much more like a human with eyes and a mouth. She believed that her human mind at that time had to project human qualities onto the whirlwind in order to deal with the encounter. But now, she saw them as they were, an entanglement of energy and consciousness entering the human mindscape. It has form, but it is much closer to the formless than we are, she thought.

And then there was this man Frank. What was she going to do about him? With her husband it had become sex on demand. He expected to get it whenever he wanted it. When she resisted, he pouted, which made her resist more. And when she gave herself to him, it was neither fun nor pleasurable. It wasn't that he didn't know what he was doing. He was skilled. She remembered now for the first time in years that the girlfriend who had introduced him to her had called him "Mister Fabulous." But he was a performance, all about ego. He didn't get lost in her, he got lost in performing. She didn't feel anything for him anymore. His touch had become repulsive. Then she met a whirlwind. When she left her husband, and especially when she entered into the sexless orientation of Whirlwindism, she believed that she would never again have an intimate physical relationship with a man, or a woman for that matter. Friendship, yes. Sex, no.

She was surprised that she had let this Frank into her life. She could tell he wanted her, but when she told him that sex was out of the question, he took it in stride. He still wanted to be with her. When she began to talk to him about Whirlwindism, he didn't treat her like she was crazy, which had been the response of her family and friends. He listened to her, he asked questions. And when she had given him this opportunity, he had jumped at it. He had driven across the country and hiked for two days over rough country to get to her.

And when they had bathed together earlier that day, she liked that he pretended not to notice that she pretended not to look. She had looked alright. She liked his body, she liked his beautiful erection that he could not control. Just thinking about it brought feelings into her body that she hadn't felt in years.

"Damn," she said to herself, hoping he had not heard it. He wasn't much more than ten feet from her.

She slipped out of her sleeping bag and pulled her moccasins on. She thought about putting on her jeans. She was wearing only her long-sleeved flannel shirt for warmth and her panties. But she decided she wouldn't be out in the night air for more than a moment. She unzipped her tent and zipped it back quickly. Did he hear the sound of the zipper?

She unzipped his tent, zipped it back down, crept into the darkness, slid into his open sleeping bag, swung her left leg over his body. No words yet. His breath quickened, as did hers. Her hand explored and found his hard-on. "Oh God," he said, and groaned. They undressed each other quickly, and then she was on top of him. "Yes," she was thinking. Did she say it out loud? "I want this, all of this." Soon he was on top of her. This was what she wanted, this passionate entanglement. He was whispering in her ear. She wasn't sure what he was saying. Outside in the darkness all around them, she heard the crying of the whirlwinds.

The Observer Is the Observed

The Seventeenth Rescuer

I stepped out my front door for an evening walk. Before I had taken twenty steps, I saw a woman across the street strolling in the opposite direction, carrying a substantial black purse that hung from her shoulder. A young man ran up to her from behind and grabbed the bag. But the woman had a good grip on it and held on. It quickly became a tug of war. For a moment I just stood and watched in wonder, unable to ignite myself into action. The young man was simply pulling the woman down the street with him, but then he stopped and knocked her down with one punch to the face. The woman let go of her purse and the young man ran.

By this time I was in action and had a good angle on the runner. I tackled him and we rolled into a front yard. But the guy was young, quick, and agile, and he scrambled up to his feet with me still lying in the grass. I grabbed his foot and ripped his sneaker off as he broke loose and disappeared between houses. I jumped up and ran to the woman who was still lying on the sidewalk. She managed to sit up as I approached her.

"Are you okay?" I asked.

"I think so," she said. She held her cheek where the man had struck her. She looked up at me and started crying.

"He's gone, you're safe now," I said.

"No," she said, "he got everything I have. My money, my credit cards, my cell phone, my car keys . . . everything."

"Can you stand up?" I asked.

"I believe I can," she said.

I helped her get to her feet. She was a bit wobbly. Nicely dressed, wearing a handsome leather vest. Middle class, I'd say, like me.

"I can't believe this would happen in a nice neighborhood like this," she said.

"Me either," I said. "I live just across the street. You can clean yourself up and make some phone calls, if you want."

She nodded and let me guide her to my door and then into my house. I led her to the couch where she sat down, pulled out a handkerchief and proceeded to cry some more. I poured her a glass of water and brought it to her.

"Thank you," she said, drank a sip or two, then set the glass down on the table.

"Can I get something else for you?"

She shook her head. "No, you are being very kind."

"What about using my phone. You need to call in those stolen credit cards as soon as possible."

She smiled. She wore no makeup, but her face was striking nevertheless, surrounded by shoulder-length, well cared for, brown hair. "That won't be necessary," she said.

"What do you mean?" I said, "that guy will be charging things right away."

"No, he won't," she said.

"Why not?" I asked.

"Because there are no credit cards in the bag."

"But you said . . ."

"I know what I said. But I was lying." She smiled sweetly.

I took a moment to absorb her words. Her dark eyes were friendly. "But why would you do that?" I asked.

"Because I wanted to get into your house and talk to you."

A bolt of fear shot through me. "I have nothing of value in this place," I said.

"No, no, I don't want to steal from you."

I was totally confused now, and a little frightened too. I had been the victim of a couple of scams before, and I was determined not to let it happen again. "So, why me?" I asked.

"We didn't choose you. Not you in particular. You just happened to be the one walking down the street."

I sat down on the couch a respectful distance from the woman and looked into her eyes. She gazed happily back into mine.

"So who is that young man?" I asked.

"Oh, that's my son. He's still around here somewhere."

I looked out the window and sure enough that young man was standing across the street with the black bag pressed against his chest. He was just staring at the house. "I see him," I said.

"Yes, he's a good boy, he does as he's told," she said.

"But the boy hit you," I said, "I saw him."

"Yes," she said, "we have to make it look real, or it doesn't work."

"But he's your son," I said.

"It's alright," she said, "it gives him a chance to get his anger out. There will be no repressed anger at me when he grows up."

I thought her psychology was naïve, but I didn't want to go there, so said nothing.

"So there is nothing in the bag," I said.

"Oh no, absolutely nothing. Nada, as my grandfather used to say. I carry everything I need in this handy vest. It has fifteen pockets. I bought it online."

I looked at her vest again and could see that it indeed had many pockets. There were probably many more on the inside. My fear had subsided somewhat, but I still couldn't get my head around the situation.

"This is very strange," I said.

"Yes, I know," she said.

"So, I think you should go now."

"Oh, please don't say that," she said.

Her face contracted into anguish. Was she just acting? Her lovely face was very mobile.

"But what do you want from me?"

"Absolutely nothing, except what you are already giving me."

What was I giving her? I thought. A glass of water? "Which is . . ." I started.

Her face flipped from anguish to joy and she smiled again. "Your attention," she said. But then her face flipped back to anguish. "And now you want to take that away from me."

I thought about it. "But it's mine," I said, "I have the right to give it or to take it away. Everybody has that right."

Her face relaxed into a neutral phase. "Of course," she said, "you have the right. I'm asking for your attention, as a favor to an old friend."

"What do you mean? I've never seen you before in my life."

"True, but our conversation so far, in my world, means that we are old friends."

"In my world, that makes no sense," I said.

"I know, I know," she said. "It's because I never speak to anyone. Not anyone. So when I do speak to someone, it feels to me as if I've known them forever."

"I don't care," I said, "I want my privacy. I don't want you here."

"Just give me your attention for a few minutes, and I'll explain everything. Please, it will mean so much to me and my son."

I looked into her eyes again. Her gaze was so convincing I found myself torn between kicking her out and letting her stay. I looked at my watch. "Okay," I said, "you have ten minutes. No more and no less. After that, if you don't leave, I will be forced to call the police."

"That's fair," she said.

I looked out the window. The young man had sat down cross-legged on the sidewalk across the street, still watching my house keenly. I set my alarm function for ten minutes and pressed the start. I looked back at the woman. "Okay, you can begin," I said.

She turned to face me more directly. Her eyes were always very direct, probing, almost intrusive, as if she were trying to locate some sort of foothold inside of me, or maybe hypnotize me. But her eyes were so beautiful that it was difficult for me to look away. The contracting knot of fear in my stomach kept me alert, even as I drifted into her eyes.

"When I was a little girl," she began, "I was a perfectly normal and happy child. I grew up in a good family. I was loved and treated well. I met a fine young man at church, we fell in love, and got married. We had two children, a son and a daughter. Everything was fine until I began to have strange symptoms." She paused.

"Don't stop," I said, "remember you have only ten minutes. Eight minutes now."

"Alright," she said. "It first occurred at the dinner table. I found that I wasn't able to speak to my husband or my children. They were talking away, and I could find no place to jump in. And then when they stopped for a moment to eat, I discovered I had nothing at all to say. For a while, they didn't seem to notice, but when I was unable to speak to them in the morning, or any other time of day, that began to create problems."

"You were silent," I said.

"Yes, absolutely speechless. At the time, I had a part-time job as a cashier in a grocery store, but as I was unable to speak to customers or to my fellow workers, they soon let me go. The loss of income was painful. This went on for a long time. I discovered that my speaking apparatus simply had a mind of its own. My lips had no interest in moving. My tongue lay still as an alligator in a swamp."

I admit, her alligator metaphor concerned me. But I pressed on. "Was this silence accompanied by any feelings on your part?" I asked.

"Oh yes," she said. "It was a case of the most acute shyness you can imagine. If the opportunity or the urge to speak arose in me, the pain of the shyness would uncoil like a serpent in my stomach and chest, and I just couldn't get the words out. Believe me, I went to doctors, five of them in all, and they all said they could find nothing wrong with me. That made my torment even worse. Still, they were perfectly happy to prescribe medications that would have clouded my mind, changed my personality. I refused. If you've ever experienced severe shyness, you know how painful it can be. I was living with that all the time. Plus the guilt over not being able to communicate with my husband and my kids, except by writing, and that gets old. I lost all of my friends, and my family really was torn apart by my disorder, or whatever it is. After three years of the doctors all saying there was nothing wrong with me, my husband finally filed for divorce. We had not slept in the same room for quite a while anyway. He kept saying he needed to hear my voice. But I wasn't even sure I still had a voice. I wanted so much to speak to him. Can you imagine the pain of that?"

"No," I said, keeping an eye on my watch.

"After the divorce went through, my husband and my daughter moved out of the house and are living together in a nearby town. But my son loves me and wanted to stay with me to see if he could help me somehow. And he has made so much difference. We have both learned sign language. And every day we write a letter to each other. Can you believe that?"

"Yes," I said.

"But he's the one who discovered the breakthrough. One day when I was walking back home from a nearby store, a young man grabbed my bag and tried to run away with it. I don't know why exactly, but I fought him with everything I had. You should have seen me. I was fierce. But the fellow was on the verge of overpowering me when two other young men, one of them just a boy, came to my rescue. They got my bag from the attacker and chased him away. Then they were so kind to me, just as you were today. They took me into a little restaurant that was nearby and bought me a soda and made sure I was okay. The amazing part of it is that I was suddenly talking a blue streak to these two fellows. I called my son on my cell and he shouted to hear my voice. He said he was on his way to escort me the rest of the way home. In the meantime, I was talking and talking, telling these men everything about my life. The words were pouring out of me, and it felt so good, such relief. My son arrived, thanked the two men, and as we walked home together, my son was stunned to hear me talking to him for the first time in three years or more. All the pain that had kept me so bottled up was gone. When we got home, we talked for hours. We cried and cried and celebrated. I fell into my bed that night exhausted and very happy. But when I woke up in the morning, the painful shyness had returned. As much as I wanted to speak to my son at breakfast, I couldn't." She paused.

I looked at my watch. It was inside a minute before the alarm would go off. I pressed the cancel button. The woman saw me do it. When I looked up, she was smiling brightly. If I didn't know any better, I'd say her eyes were full of love. That was very disconcerting. I looked away. "So what was the breakthrough you referred to?" I asked.

"It was my son's idea. He said that my speech had been triggered by an attack or a rescue, or both. I knew right away that it was the rescue that did it. Something inside me surrendered to the guys who rescued me. I trusted them. I felt it at the time, but it hadn't registered until my son asked me about it. So he suggested that we stage an attack on me to lure someone into rescuing me, as an experiment. And so began our adventure. You are the seventeenth rescuer. Even though the effect of the rescue lasts only a few hours, the relief of talking and sharing my feelings is so great that it has kept me sane and my health has improved. Once a month, my son and I go out and stage another attack. It has become a regular part of my existence. My life will never be normal, but at least it is bearable now, as long as I can find rescuers like you."

"And that's it," I said.

"That's it," she said.

"Now what," I said.

"Now I go home. And my son and I have a party."

I looked into those amazing eyes for a minute. I glanced out of the window, and the young man was now standing on my lawn, not thirty feet away. Our eyes met. His gaze was extremely intense. That knot of fear tightened in my stomach again. The boy took another step toward the window. I looked away.

"Don't worry about him," the woman said, "he does whatever his mother tells him to do."

"I see," I said.

"Yes," she said, "you know how it is with mothers and sons."

I thought about my own mother, her beautiful eyes, her powers of persuasion. I thought about my years of living alone since she died.

The woman stood up. "Well, Mr. Hawkins, thank you very much for your attention."

"How do you know my name?" I asked.

She looked at me for a moment. "It was on your mailbox," she said.

It was my turn to look hard at her. I tried to intensify *my* eyes. "Was anything you just told me true?" I asked.

Her face contracted into anguish, then relaxed back into a smile. "Not a word," she said and laughed. "Not a single one." She turned and walked to the front door. I followed close behind. I saw the boy's sneaker on the hall table where I had left it. The woman opened the door and the boy was standing there, waiting. I swear he had the fiercest eyes I've ever seen, and they were trained on me. I held his sneaker out to him.

"I believe this is yours," I said.

He snatched it so quickly it was as if the sneaker had leaped into his hand. That brought the first smile to his face. But it didn't last long. His mother started walking, and he followed. I sensed an immense silence surrounding him, holding in check an equally immense rage within. She turned around to look back at me with that famous smile.

"The seventeenth rescuer will always have a special place of honor," she said. "You haven't seen the last of us. The rescuers are our family."

Then she turned and walked away. The boy stayed close to her, but he kept looking back at me with those terrifying eyes. Then it dawned on me that they weren't terrifying, they were terri*fied*. Maybe he was the one who really needed a rescuer. Or maybe he was the one who was the real boss between them.

When the woman and boy were a block away, and I was sure they weren't turning around and heading back, I walked over to my mailbox. My name wasn't anywhere on it. I was angry at myself for not knowing for sure if my name was on the box. Damn. If only I had known for sure at the instant the information was relevant, it might have made all the difference.

Just then my next door neighbor stepped out of his door and jogged over to me in his khaki shorts and baseball cap. He reached out his hand and out of habit I took it in a hearty handshake. "I just want you to know we saw what you did," he said. His grin was so broad I thought it might jump right off his face. I noticed his wife on their front stoop smiling and waving at me.

"What did I do?" I asked.

"You know what you did," he said, beaming, our hands bobbing up and down between us.

"Well, thank you," I said, "I didn't think anyone had noticed."

"We saw it all," he said, finally letting my hand go. "We're very proud to be your neighbor."

"And I'm proud to be yours," I said.

He nodded happily and headed back to his house.

I walked back inside my house, sat down on my couch. I felt somewhat lost. What would I do with my life, now that I was the seventeenth rescuer? What privileges and duties would I incur? I couldn't stop thinking about that woman, her eyes, her last words to me. I had to admit that I wanted to make her talk again. In fact, if I were honest, I wanted to be the only one who could make her talk. I would have to rescue her again and again and again. First of all, I would have to find her. A wave of gratitude swept over me. For the first time in many years, I had found a purpose in life, and I knew what I had to do.

Charlie's Regret

This morning I sent my Golden Retriever Charlie out for the paper. She ran out eagerly as usual, but the paper wasn't there at the end of my walkway. Charlie turned and looked at me as if to say, "What do I do now?" Then she quickly applied her nose to the ground and started working in circles. The circles became wider. She came into view and went out of view. From time to time she stopped and looked at me, to make sure I was still waiting. I held her cookie reward in my hand. No paper, no cookie. She knew the rules. Her circles became wider, and she disappeared for minutes on end. I didn't worry about her too much in this sleepy neighborhood. But I was getting tired of waiting on her. At last she came into view carrying a rolled up newspaper. It was covered with damp leaves, so I stepped outside the door.

"Good girl," I said as she approached.

She handed me the paper and I gave her the cookie. She gobbled it up in seconds. I brushed the leaves off the paper and brought it into the house. I wondered if maybe it belonged to one of my neighbors. On the other hand, what had happened to *my* paper? This paper felt a little odd in my hand, perhaps a little thicker in the middle than the usual Tuesday paper. Then I unrolled it on my dining room table.

In the center of it, resting in the midst of the front-page story, was a big toe. Human. No animal has a toe like that. Careful not to touch it, I sat down at the table and studied the toe from every angle. The nail was closely trimmed. A man's toe I guessed, from the size of it, neatly severed from the foot. The cut was very clean, surgical, beautifully cauterized to stop the bleeding. I looked over at Charlie. Tired from her run, she lay contentedly on the couch, but her eyes were watching me.

"Where on earth did you get this paper?" I asked.

But she didn't move or speak. I thought she was looking at me differently, as if she might have seen something she would rather not have seen. I decided to call my friend Mack. He had been a doctor for years until he decided to be a writer who worked at home. I dialed his number.

"What!" he said.

"It's me, Conrad," I said.

"I know who it is, whaddya want? I'm writing."

"Sorry," I said, "but I need your help."

"What kind of help?" he said.

"Charlie brought back a paper that has a big toe wrapped in it," I said.

"What?!" he said.

"A big human toe," I repeated.

"I'll be right over," he said and hung up.

He lived only a block away and was in my house within minutes. I led him into the dining room, but something had changed. The big toe was still there, but now it was lying on A2, the "Nation & World" page. Specifically, it was lying on a story titled "New Governors Face Natural Disasters."

"So this is the mysterious toe," Mack said. When he noticed that my face had turned white, he said, "What's wrong?"

"The toe has turned the page," I said.

"What?" he said. For a writer, he seemed to have very limited comprehension skills.

"You heard me," I said. "He was reading the front page when I was last in the room."

"He?" Mack said. "And what do you mean he was reading? Have you lost your mind?"

"My mind is right where it's always been," I said.

"Well, I have to call the cops, you know that don't you?"

"But why?" I said, realizing that somehow I had become attached to the thing.

"Because this toe was recently removed, and someone is in a lot of pain," Mack said. Reason had always been his strong suit, but it was also annoying as hell.

"Just let me think a minute," I said.

"There could be foul play involved," he said.

He pulled his cell phone out of his pocket, but before he could dial I tackled him. He was caught off guard, fell backwards, and hit his head on the floor, knocking him out cold. I dragged him awkwardly down to the basement into the storage room that was basically underground with no windows and only the one door that was very sturdy. I locked it.

When I got back upstairs, the toe had turned another page. He was now reading a story about a local elementary school continued from page A1. He clearly had eclectic interests. I sat with him for a couple of hours while he read every word of the paper. I read with him. I never knew so much was going on in my town.

The first time I saw him turn a page, I was amazed at his agility. He could turn a page more efficiently than most hands. He had a nine-inch vertical leap. Mack woke up after a while and banged on the door, shouted for me to let him out. But that room was so underground and so closed off that no one who wasn't inside the house would ever hear him. The toe and I could barely hear him ourselves. The shouting made Charlie a little uncomfortable at first, but she got used to it.

I knew that I wouldn't have much time. Eventually some friend of Mack's would report him missing. Or someone would come into the house and hear him calling for help. I put a novel I had recently finished reading onto the table. I broke the spine so it would lie flat when open. The toe crawled onto it and began reading the author's introduction. I knew that would keep him busy for a while. Either I was going crazy, or this was the smartest and most independent big toe I had ever known.

I took off my right shoe and sock and looked at my own big toe. It grinned back at me sheepishly. "You have a lot of explaining to do," I said, then put my sock and shoe back on.

I had taken all of my money out of stocks years ago. Everything was in interest-bearing cash accounts. I bought a ticket for Colombia. It would be cheaper to live there anyway. And if anybody came after me, I could move from there to Costa Rica to Mexico to Nicaragua. I had heard that lots of Americans moved to Granada because it was so much cheaper to live. A day later, the toe and I were on a plane. I had told Mack through the door where I had stored boxes of nutrition bars and bottled water in his room. He would be alright for a while. And when I got to Colombia, I would call to let authorities know where he was. I won't repeat the things Mack said to me through that door. He would get over it.

I was excited about my new life with my new friend. He seemed to be excited too. I had begun to hear his tiny voice. At first, I couldn't understand what he was saying. But the more I listened, the better I heard it, until I got to where I was just hearing it in my ear all the time.

I remember my father telling me one time, "Son, my big toe is smarter, right now, than you will ever be." And he meant it. He talked to my mother like that too. His brilliance and the stupidity of others was a foregone conclusion. He made everyone feel small around him. But I never had any idea how true his words were, until this big toe came into my life.

"Ralph," the big toe said, "my name is Ralph."

I trimmed Ralph's nail and that seemed to make him feel better. He had been through a lot.

Unfortunately I had to leave Charlie behind. She was too big to travel in the plane's cabin with us. Plus Colombia wouldn't allow me to bring in a dog. Besides, she and Ralph didn't seem to get along very well. Every time Ralph tried to play with her, she would growl. And I didn't want Charlie to do something I knew she would regret.

The Observer Who Can't Be Observed

I was in a remembering mood. I decided I wanted to see The Breezeway Court Motel one more time. It was a small, light-blue, ten-room motel on the beach road in Jacksonville Beach, Florida. Six hundred miles from where I now live. My father owned it for many years when I was a kid. As a family, we spent weeks there every summer. My brother and I felt like we owned the place, not just the motel but the beach and the whole damn town. All of it was our playground. My father sold The Breezeway a long time ago, and I hadn't been back since I was a teen. Need I say I'm a much older guy now, not that it matters.

I was retired and had enough money to survive until the end, and I could do what I wanted to do. So I packed my car, tossed my Jack Russell, Leon, into the back seat, and headed off. Took two days to get there. The evening we arrived I didn't even look for The Breezeway. I was tired and hungry. I found a dog-friendly motel, played with Leon in the parking lot, had dinner at a nearby burger joint, and went to bed.

The next morning, Leon and I started early. I was going on memory, but everything had changed. The streets, of course, were still there, but the buildings had been replaced by newer, taller ones or refurbished completely. The old amusement park with the giant roller coaster was gone. Only a remnant of the old boardwalk remained. And where was the pavilion? When I was a kid, my brother Will and I were allowed to roam this downtown area, go on the amusement park rides, and play the games in the penny arcade. But it was all gone. Now, it was a place for adults with bars and restaurants and clubs. The beach was still there, of course, so that was something. But the small mom-and-pop motels that had lined the beach road had all been replaced by high-rise hotels or modern homes.

There was no chance The Breezeway would still be there after all those years, but damn if it wasn't. I spotted it almost right away. It was on a corner—I had forgotten that—still light blue, surrounded by new two- and three-story homes. It had the shape of a three-sided rectangle, with arms open toward the street. The courtyard, once a green, manicured lawn, was now a cement parking lot. The motel sign was long gone. I parked my car, and Leon and I walked all around the building, taking photos.

No doubt that this was the place. My father had paid a woman to live in one of the units and manage the motel when we weren't there. The building still had the breezeways at each of the two corners—the armpits so to speak. You could look from one side of the motel through those breezeways all the way to the other side. My brother and I played in those when we were kids. Of course, we played everywhere, including across the street where the open access led down to the beach.

Not long after my father sold this place, my brother turned eighteen. He was drafted and fought in Vietnam for two years. I was lucky, drew a good number in the lottery, and never went to Nam. When Will came back, he never was the same. He killed himself in 1983. On the other side of the country, California, as far from family as he could get, he hanged himself in a run-down old motel he'd been living in. May the Lord have mercy on him. That was thirty-five years ago. I always wished I could talk with him one more time. But he never did listen to me. I had been a counselor for many years, I knew a few things about trauma, but he just wouldn't listen.

I stood on the sidewalk and studied the old building. It looked a little worn and beaten, but it was still a fundamentally solid structure. Several cars were parked in the lot. Clearly it was no longer a motel. It must have been renovated into small apartments at some point. A young man came out of one of the doors on the back row and strolled to a Toyota truck with a shell over the bed. He pulled down the tailgate and fiddled with something inside. I walked over to him.

"Excuse me," I said.

He turned to look at me. He had a thick but well-trimmed mustache, short hair, and his jeans and shirt fit him loosely. This was midday on a Monday, so I figured he was the type who worked from home. Computers maybe. I thought I recognized him, but I couldn't imagine where or when I'd known him. We just looked at each other for a moment. I'd say he was in his midtwenties. It occurred to me that he was feeling some old connection with me as well. But he would have been born years after my family had left The Breezeway.

"Can I help you?" he asked, finally.

"I don't know," I said. "I used to come here when I was a kid. This place was The Breezeway Court Motel. My father owned it."

"Is that right?" he said.

"Yeah," I said, "I just wanted to see it again. I'm really surprised it's still here."

"I bet," the young man said, "It's been these small apartments as long as I can remember. An old lady owns the place. She lives up the beach a ways."

"Do you have her address?"

"I think so," he said. "I pay my rent to an agency, so I'm not sure."

"My brother and I had a lot of fun here growing up. When you get old, you become nostalgic, I guess."

"Hey," he said, "you want to see one of the apartments? Mine's right over there. It's a little messy, but I don't mind showing you around. That might trigger some memories."

I glanced down at Leon, and he glanced up at me. He seemed to be saying that it would be okay. I looked around and for the moment there wasn't a soul walking up the sidewalk, not a single car in sight on the road. The sky was clear blue with a few white clouds dimming the sun. I heard seagulls calling in the distance, and the sound of breaking waves.

I looked at the young man. "Sure," I said, "that would be great."

"Okay," he said. He turned back to his truck. I noticed he had a piece of machinery in his hands.

"What's that?" I asked.

"This?" He held the object up between us.

"Yeah, that," I said.

"It's a machine part," he said. It was a beautiful thing made of brushed metal with odd convolutions and curves. I had been around machines a lot in my time, but I had never seen anything that looked quite like that.

"May I," I said, reaching out to him.

"Sure," he said. He handed it to me gingerly. It was exceptionally light, fitting well in the palm of my hand. It had no moving parts that I could see. Smooth to the touch, it was the kind of thing one might rub for good luck. I rubbed it a few times.

"What kind of machine does this fit into?" I said.

He took the object out of my hands. "A hyper-collaborator," he said.

"So, it collaborates . . . things?" I said.

"Sort of," he said, "but not so much things."

"Unh hunh," I said.

"I've got one in my apartment. I could show it to you."

I looked down at Leon. He looked at me and shrugged his shoulders.

"Okay," I said, "I'd like to see the apartment, and the hyper . . . collaborator."

He slipped the part into his pocket and led me to his door, which wasn't locked. He just pushed it right open. I noticed his windows were shut with tightly pulled curtains. Looking through the door deep into the room, I could see a table and a lamp. I saw a chair and part of a couch. In the middle of the room stood an object on four sturdy, steel legs. It was about as tall as a ten-year-old boy, made of that same brushed metal as the part he'd shown me.

"Come on in," the young man said with a wave of his hand.

Leon had tensed up and was creeping cautiously with his flank pressed against the side of my calf. The young man was inside holding the door open for us and we walked in past him. My eyes connected with his again and I knew that I knew him from somewhere. The instant the door clicked shut behind us, the room went black.

"Just a minute," the young man said, so I just stood there waiting. I expected a light to come on, but it didn't. It was pitch black in the room. On second thought, those windows of his must have been painted black. A minute or so went by.

"Young man," I said, but there was no reply. I strained my ears to hear, but there were no sounds coming from deeper in the room. "Young man," I said, "this isn't funny. Not at all."

But again, there was no reply, no sound. Until . . . I heard a very low hum. It was a warm sound, not intrusive at all. Then a low but strong purple haze emanated from the other side of the room. It was coming off that object, that machine, a purple vibration that my eyes could feel more than see. The young man must have inserted the missing part. I reached back until I touched the door. It was reassuring to know the exit was still there. But the knob wouldn't turn. And the door was solid as stone, shut as securely as one of those institutional doors meant to prevent any kind of breach. Not a shred of light came in through the windows. The purple haze increased until it was more blinding than revealing. Suddenly the leash I was holding in my right hand went slack. Leon was loose.

"Leon!" I called, but he was gone. How had that happened? I pulled the leash up and felt the end. The carabiner was intact. Who or what had let him loose? It was not like him to leave my side, especially in a tense situation. I wasn't sure what kind of situation this was.

"Leon?" I called again. Not a sound, except for that welcoming low hum.

But I didn't feel welcome. Just scared shitless. My eyes adjusted some, and the purple light from the machine was just enough that I could make out the couch to my left.

"Have a seat," the young man said, though I could not lay my eyes on him. I carefully made my way over to the couch. I sat down. What else could I do? Everything in the room glowed with that vibrant purple light. The longer I sat there, the clearer my mind became. Or so I believed. Thoughts, ideas, concepts, worries, flitted across my mind like butterflies. I was just observing them, not getting caught up in them. They disappeared quickly, and slowly my mind became still. The purple vibration began to take various forms before me, but they remained amorphous, never quite crystallizing. I felt that they were human forms, but I wasn't sure.

I must have fallen asleep. Time passed. When I woke up, the purple haze had lifted like a fog. A small lamp on a table lit the room dimly with yellow light. The machine was no longer there. A man was sitting on a couch across the room from me. Even in the dim light, there was no mistaking who he was. My brother. But how could that be? I had flown to California and had gone with our father to identify the body. He was dead, long buried in a cemetery in our hometown in South Carolina. We had shipped his body all the way across the country.

We just sat there looking at each other. Leon trotted out from the back of the apartment and jumped up on the couch next to my brother.

"Leon!" I called. He turned his head toward me, but he didn't run to me as usual. Instead, he nestled against my brother's side.

"Leon!" I yelled in my I-mean-it voice, but he was happy where he was.

Suddenly I was weeping. I had never cried like this in my life. It went on for a while, until I cried myself out. I didn't even know what I was crying for. Was it my brother, or Leon? Why wouldn't Leon come to me?

"Hey there, Jack," my brother said to me.

"Will," I said. Tears started streaming down my face again. I was going to dehydrate if I kept this up. I never cried like this. The tears were burning my face.

"What are you doing here?" I said as best I could, "You're supposed to be dead."

"The problem is, you don't know a thing about death," he said.

"As much as the next man," I said.

"Which is nothing," he said.

"I know what I know," I said.

"You always knew more than everybody else," he said. "That was the core of the problem."

"What problem?" I said.

"Always trying to straighten me out, like you had a clue what was happening to me."

"You would never listen to me. If you had only listened to me, you might be alive today."

"Like that's what I wanted. You should have listened to *me*."

"But you were talking crazy . . ."

"Like when I said, 'I am the observer who cannot be observed?'"

"Yeah, like that."

"But that's what I am. Do you want to hear about it or not?"

"No," I said. He just looked at me. "Okay, yes," I said.

"It happened in Nam," he said. "I was in a situation I couldn't escape. I was in a room. A peasant family, seven of them, mother and father and grandma plus a bunch of kids, all sitting on the floor with their backs against the wall. Their hands were tied behind their backs. They were gagged. I tried everything to get out of it."

"Out of what?" I asked.

"You don't want to know what it was, believe me. My mind snapped. I became pure observation. After that, nothing mattered anymore. Everything was only the observed. That's the truth."

"That's *your* truth," I said.

"Do you want me to lie to you?" he asked.

I thought about that. Did I want him to lie to me? This could not be my real brother, I thought. But there he was, still wearing his army fatigues like he always did when he wasn't at work. It was his face, his eyes, even the unique way he held and moved his hands in space like he was caressing the air. Leon had curled up on his lap, and Will was absentmindedly stroking his chest. Leon seemed to be in a trance. I felt like I was in a trance too. How could I get out of here?

"But Will," I said, "reason defeats you. I am observing you."

"Only for the moment," he said. "I'm doing you a favor. After this, you will have to become the observer who can't be observed for yourself. It's the only way."

"But why would anyone want to be such a thing?" I asked.

The next instant, a bright, overhead light came on. Will and Leon disappeared. The original young man walked into the room. That feeling of having a connection with him had vanished. He was a stranger to me now.

"Okay," he said, "that's enough. What did you think of the hyper-collaborator?"

My eyes were slowly adjusting to the new light. The young man was still a blur. All I could think about was Leon.

"Where is my dog?" I said.

"What?" he said.

"My dog, Leon, I came in here with him."

"I didn't see no dog," he said.

I stood up. My legs were shaky. Rage poured through me. "I'll find him myself," I said, and I started toward the back of the apartment where there must have been a small bedroom, bathroom, kitchen—all shrouded in darkness at the moment. But the young man basically tackled me. We fought for a while, rolling around on the floor, but I was old and he was young and strong for a wiry sort of guy. Pretty soon he got me up and shoved me out the front door where I promptly fell down again.

"Some people don't deserve to see!" he shouted. Then he slammed the door shut.

I lay on the concrete for a time, looking at the blue sky above the houses across the street. My knees and elbows were throbbing with pain, from the falls I had taken. Finally I pulled myself up. I tried the door to the apartment, but it was locked tight. I walked to the right, passed a couple more apartment doors, and slipped into the breezeway where some chairs were lined up against the wall. I sat down in the shadows and started crying again. Why was I crying all the time?

I turned my head to the left and looked all the way through to the other breezeway. Will and Leon were sitting there in a chair. Leon looked so happy there, sitting up proudly in Will's lap. "Leon!" I shouted. He looked at me, but he didn't move.

"It isn't fair, is it?" Will said, his voice traveling clearly to me though he had spoken softly.

"Leon belongs to me," I said.

"That's you alright, thinking that fairness is how the universe works. Thinking that people and dogs belong to you. That's what I saw when my mind snapped. Nothing belonged to me anymore. I could no longer see myself observing. Even I didn't belong to myself. I was observation itself. The me part was gone. And from there, fairness has nothing to do with anything. People, dogs, whole villages. What is, is."

Will and Leon disappeared. My mind snapped open. I was a funnel with some kind of energy pouring through me, a kind of hyper-collaborator. It poured and poured. Suddenly, Leon was sitting beside my right foot, looking up at me. There was worry in his eyes. I felt so relieved to see him, but at the same time, something was different. How to explain this.

I saw Leon for the first time, just as he was, not as my pal or my possession. He was an amazing creature: flesh and bone and blood and light. He saw me see it. I knew that this small animal, though a companion, did not belong to me. Never had, and never would. I put the leash in my pocket. Nothing was mine, not even my memories, not even my brother. I was so exhausted I could barely walk. I looked at the other breezeway one more time, but no one was there. I knew in that moment that my brother, the observer who can't be observed, was gone from view forever. On the other hand, he was also inside of me forever.

The young man's Toyota truck was still parked in the lot, but I didn't want to get anywhere near it. Leon and I found my car parked on the street where I'd left it. I managed to drive it cautiously to the motel. My hands could barely hold the wheel, they were shaking so badly. I slept for two days, getting up just often enough to let Leon have a go at the bushes and to drop some dry food in his bowl.

Two days later, I loaded the car. Leon jumped into the shotgun seat as always. He loved watching the world go by outside his window. I wondered if he also were the observer who can't be observed. I didn't bother to drive past The Breezeway Court Motel. Like all memories, it no longer existed for me as a real place. I didn't bother to look up the old woman who owned the apartments. She was even less than a memory, a dream of some illusory future.

That's the way it is for the observer who can't be observed.

We took our time getting back home. Three days. We sat very still in our little capsule, as the world passed us by.

The Spell

"What the hell do you think you're doing?" he said.

"Nothing," I said, "I'm just here."

"You call that 'here'?" he said sharply.

I couldn't tell where his voice was coming from. And he was right: "here" wasn't clear at all. But I carried on. "Yes," I said, "as best I can tell, I'm here."

"Well, that used to be fine," he said, "just being here, but it's not enough anymore."

I spotted a tiny black dot in an upper corner of the room.

"What are you staring at?!" he said. It was one of those powerful, miniature cameras. "Well, answer me!" he shouted.

"Nothing!" I shouted back. Words felt like upside-down chairs coming out of my mouth.

"Sit down!" he said.

I didn't even realize I was standing. Was I standing? There was no place to sit. A hand came into view, like the head of a crocodile. I half expected it to turn and look at me. Where was it going? All the way out to the end of an arm, reaching. For what?

"What are you reaching for?" he said.

"I'm not reaching for anything," I said.

"Well then, who is reaching?" he asked.

That was a good question. I wished he would stop asking questions. I wished he would stop talking. Only a moment ago, there had been silence, nothing, I realized, for a long, long time but silence. It felt like forever.

"I see you're thinking now," he said.

"Is that what it is?" I said.

"Yes," he said, "reaching and thinking. That's the way it always starts."

"The way what starts?" I said.

"You'll find out," he said, "just keep reaching and thinking like that."

The hand suddenly touched a wall. The palm flattened against it. Yes, it was *my* palm, *my* hand, and the end of *my* arm. I located an elbow. The wall was white, like the rest of the room—floor and ceiling too—a bright white, so much so it wasn't like seeing at all. My eyes felt full, too full. As I pressed against the wall, it began to turn blue. Just that one wall . . . became a rich, mesmerizing blue, vibrating. Near my hand, a framed photo appeared. A woman looking out at me. A blue shift full of light. Long blonde hair. Knowing blue eyes. Smile. Hand reaching out as if to cast a spell. A white house and a giant oak in the background.

Other photos and drawings and paintings appeared on the wall. One wall turned brown, another green, another yellow. All of them filling up with hims and hers and landscapes and rooms and houses. In the yellow wall was a window. From out there, a woman approached. Then she stood there on the grass and smiled. Behind her was a white house and a giant oak. She reached out with her hand and cast a spell. Her mouth moved and her voice came through the speaker. "You're beautiful," she said.

Something else woke up and I knew I was naked. Feet. Knees. Penis. Belly. Chest. Where were the words coming from? Not the words from the wall, but the ones in my . . . ? Where were these words located? These words right here? Something had slipped out of view. The something in which these words appeared and disappeared. All of the places and faces on the walls. All of those voices and eyes gathered around me.

"Who are you," she said. I looked at her outside the window. She was closer now, her face just beyond the glass. Her hand reached through, but the window didn't break.

"What are you?" she said.

"Nothing," I said.

Her hand kept reaching through. Her fingers, growing closer, were trembling.

"You are nothing," she said. Her fingers were touching my . . . I couldn't find it. What were they touching?

"You are everything," she said.

Her fingers were touching more and more of the nothing, more and more of everything.

"I am . . ." I said, but then the words stopped. Her fingers were all I could see. They touched me everywhere all at once. They smelled like roses.

"You are here," she said. "You are here."

The Inward City

I had lost sight of myself in recent days. Every time I looked for myself, I was too far ahead or too far behind to be seen. Or I was around some corner, and when I got there, I had disappeared. I poured over the card catalogue in my local, ancient library until I finally found a book entitled simply *Stalking the Self* by one Oscar Dilby who died in 1847 having never written another book. I studied this tome for a month. It was not a bad companion as books go, the cover somewhat worn, the spine almost broken, the pages beginning to loosen from the gutter, the style a little stilted maybe, but the concepts and practices were unlike anything else I'd seen. Then, on a Monday to start the week right, I began.

My default vector of energy flowed outward: thinking, wishing, dreaming, talking, doing things, projecting beliefs onto other people. The technique I had read up on was to stop that outward flow, turn around, and look back up the vector in an inward direction. Surely my self would be in there somewhere. I was out of work at the time, so I was free to pursue myself, for a while at least.

I sat down on my couch with a cup of coffee, made myself comfortable, and I turned around, metaphorically speaking, and looked inward. It took a little focus and energy, but after a couple of hours the world suddenly put on brakes and came to a stop. I began to take a stroll inward. The inward city wasn't much different than the outward one, not at first anyway. After all, I was still on a part of the vector that had been formed outwardly.

The Cavalier Store was still the same as I passed it. I stopped and looked inside and a few old guys were drinking beer and gazing up at the television over the bar where a football game was in progress. A couple of guys were shooting pool at the one table. I kept walking. I peeked over the red brick wall of the liberal arts college and saw numerous young women in bikinis lying on beach towels on the lawn catching some rays. It was September, that strange time when the college football teams were squaring off and the college girls were still out sunning in their bikinis. Up at the campus I could see students and professors walking between buildings, going to their classes. I passed Rivermont Pizza but couldn't see in the blackened windows. I knew students and other kinds of people were in there eating pizza and drinking beer. I passed the tea shop, the burger joint, the lawyer's office, the flower shop, the athletic shoe store, the gourmet sandwich shop. But no matter where I looked, I couldn't catch sight of myself, except as a reflection in the windows, and I knew that wasn't me.

"Who am I?" I asked myself.

A thousand answers appeared in my view, but I quickly saw that none of them were accurate. For example, I'm not a loser. I'm not an ex-IT guy. I'm not a flake. I'm not a genius. I'm not a loner. I'm not an asshole. I'm not a saint. I'm not anybody's friend. I have friends, I am friendly, but that's not what I am. I know I'm not because something is seeing that. If something is seeing it, then the thing seen can't be me, I reasoned. I must be the thing that is seeing, and not the things it sees.

This realization didn't stop all the forms from appearing before me. But after what seemed like hours, nothing I saw or heard or felt or thought was me. I wasn't even my own body because I could see it. But I couldn't see who it was who was seeing it.

"Okay," I thought, "*what* am I?"

But the word "what" didn't seem to make much difference.

I kept walking through the inward city observing each object and crossing it off my list. I realized that after all of this effort I hadn't had even a glimpse of myself. It was as if my self had left the inward world altogether, unless I was the one seeing. But I couldn't see who or what that was. Very frustrating.

It dawned on me that I had totally forgotten that I was actually sitting on my couch at home. My small dog jumped up beside me and lay against my thigh. That feeling of him going to sleep against my thigh was reassuring to me, sort of like an anchor out there in the outward world. I relaxed and kept walking inward. The sun was sinking on the horizon and it was getting dark inside.

What a strange realization, that there is also an inward sun, rising and falling. I was determined to catch up with myself and have a little conversation. I wanted my self to stay close by so that I could always rein it in if I needed to. Too often I lost control of myself, did things I regretted, and I wanted that to stop. That didn't seem like too much to ask of myself.

"Seriously, self, stay close to me," I wanted to say to it, if I could ever find it again. It seemed like I used to know myself very well. We were old friends, took trips together, made love to the same women, compared notes. I missed him.

Anyway, it was getting dark in the inward city and objects and people were becoming harder to distinguish. The streetlights in the inward city weren't as effective as they were in the outward city. Maybe I should file a complaint at the inward City Hall, I thought. It was dark now, inwardly. Too late to find anyone still working at the inward City Hall.

I kept walking, strolling really. I was taking it all in, and the all that I saw I knew wasn't me. Or if it was, there was still some separate seer who was seeing it. Very strange. This seer felt like it was slightly behind me and was looking through my brain and my eyes the way I look through my glasses. I felt that it was perfectly objective, had no judgments and took no actions concerning whatever it saw.

I, on the other hand, appeared to react to everything. I tried suddenly turning around, but no matter what direction I turned, I couldn't see the seer, just more stuff that wasn't the seer and wasn't me. In the dimness of the streetlights, the world became fuzzy. I didn't seem to be in a city anymore, but was in the suburbs. I saw lawns, lights burning in windows, silhouettes.

At one house, a kid was standing on the front stoop. He waved at me and I waved back.

"It's dinner time," he said to me.

He signaled me over with his hand. As I got closer I realized I was looking at myself—a much younger version of myself. He led me into the house and a strange anxiety came over me. The little boy took my hand, looked at me, and said, "Tell me about it." We entered the dining room and they were all there: my father, my mother, my sister, and my brother.

"We're waiting on you," my mother said.

"Yeah," my sister said, "like one pig waits on another." She dove into the mound of mac and cheese on her plate.

I sat down on the vacant chair, scooted up to the table, and saw all the turkey and fixings. It was Thanksgiving Day. The little boy sat in my lap. We were one and the same. The others at the table, my one time family, all had haunted eyes. That's the only way I know to describe it. Everything was fine, we all had a good time, but everyone was haunted.

I stayed in that house for what seemed like years. All the shame and guilt and victory and defeat and happiness and sadness and even fear roosted in my body and in my mind like vultures in the canopy of a tree. I wanted to get out of that house.

One day I opened the front door and walked out onto the stoop. I saw a man walking by and I waved at him. He came to me and I could see that he was myself, but he too was haunted. I tried to lead him into the house, but he refused, saying "been there, done that." Instead, he took my hand and led me with him.

I became confused. Which I was I? At that thought, I was suddenly the man. I was back on the street. I remembered the boy, but I knew that I wasn't him. He wasn't the me I was looking for. He was memory. Since I could see the memory, it wasn't me. That had become the one principle I could rely on in my inward vector. If I could see it, it had to be outside of me. And yet it was inside of me too. Even the inside had become a kind of outside.

I kept walking and was soon moving out of the suburbs onto a dirt road that became a path leading into woods. I understood that the inward city was ancient and vast and it contained within its limits many forests. Soon I was surrounded by tall trees. The moon was full and high in the sky, so even though it was dark I could see reasonably well. I have never been so alone. It felt as if I were walking against a strong headwind, but I could see no wind in the trees. So it wasn't really wind, more like some kind of energy current pushing me away. I leaned into it and kept going.

Something large zipped by in front of me, right to left across the trail. Then another one, and another one. I was afraid, but I was also determined to continue on my path. One of them came very close and took a bite out of me. I looked down at my body but there was no wound, and yet I knew it had bitten me and taken part of me away. Energy, it had taken energy. I was suddenly tired. Another one took a bite out of me, and I could barely stand. Another one stalled, floating in the trail right in front of me, its face a big grin like the Cheshire cat, its eyes two spinning spirals. I fell into those eyes right into a dream about playing baseball with friends of mine. It went on for hours. I was the dunce who dropped a fly ball and cost my team the game. What an idiot.

When I woke up, I was lying on the trail with a root for my pillow. I was exhausted. Flying beasts circled all around me like vultures. I felt my dog asleep against my right thigh, and I knew I could just go home back into the outward vector if I wanted to. It would be like getting on a raft in a river. If I relaxed, I could just flow right back out to where I had been, looking for myself. My dog moved a little against my leg, but I wasn't back at the couch with him. I was still on the trail in the woods with beasts circling all around me.

I managed to stand and the beasts tightened the circle around me. They took several more bites out of me and I had to go back down on one knee. I caught the eyes of one of them and went right into a thought about my girl-friend that led down a narrow trail of betrayals and ecstasies. Time started to pass, but I stopped myself, withdrew from the eyes of the beast, and it flew away. A little bit of energy returned to me. I saw what I had to do. With each beast, I caught its eyes and held my ground. I simply looked at the beast but didn't enter it. It was hard sometimes, because the beasts were often beautiful and seductive and millennia deep. I regained some of my strength and I was able to proceed. I had a way now to deal with the beasts.

It was slow going for a while, but they began to keep their distance. I could look at them with more confidence now. I knew them to be thoughts, dreams, wishes, hopes, ideas, concepts, and most importantly, beliefs. Every one of them wanted my attention and my energy. But none of them was me, and so I just kept going. The headwind became weaker and I could walk almost normally.

After a while, I came to a clearing. The sun was rising. In the distance, a great gray wall rose to the sky. I walked for a few miles until I stood right in front of it. It was at least a thousand feet high and disappeared over the horizon in both directions. Its surface was smooth and had no handholds or footholds for climbing. I tried, but I was like a spider trapped in a wet bathtub. For days I walked in both directions, I constructed scaffolding, but no matter how high I got, the wall seemed to just grow taller. The wall was pulling me like a magnet. Maybe it wasn't the wall, but was whatever was behind the wall.

One night, I pressed my back against the wall and looked back in the direction I had come. The wall was sucking me into itself. Either I would become wall, or I would walk back through the inward city and back out into the outward city, or I would pass backwards through the wall into a place I had no ideas for. But I knew it wasn't a place. In any case, whatever was going to happen was not in my control. I had begun by looking for my illusive self, and had found a wall that I knew wasn't me. In front of me, I could see the inward and the outward like two great cities of light observed from an orbiting satellite. Everything was there, within my view.

I allowed my body, or whatever it was, to be held tight against the wall. It felt alive behind me, pulsing with energy and potential. It was looking through my brain and through my eyes out into the inward and outward vectors. But it couldn't be the wall that was doing that. Surely, at my essence, I am not a wall. Besides, I could turn and see the wall, and if I could see it, it wasn't me. I had a felt sense of my presence, and yet I still couldn't find myself. Something behind that wall, out of my sight, was me. That's what I decided. And I knew the moment I saw it, it wouldn't be me. It could not be seen. Could it be known in some way?

I felt my dog stir against my leg, and since I could go no further, I let go of the inward vector, and found myself sitting on my couch. My little dog rolled onto its back and asked for a belly rub. Why not, I thought, I could use a belly rub myself. My dog groaned in ecstasy under my hand. It was growing dark outside my window. Streetlights flickered on. A neighbor walked past. He appeared to be haunted by the ghost of himself. But no, it wasn't a ghost. What was it?

Years have passed. Now that I know the way, I often return to that wall. I lean against it. I fall into it the way a breathless body drifts downward into the vast body of water. Both the inward and outward cities fade from my mind and heart. I surface into a vast, empty space, perfectly alone, but not lonely. It feels like home. Then, to my amazement, both the inward and outward cities slide toward me and come fully back into view. Everything is the same, and yet can never be the same. I am part of it and yet could never again be a part of it, even if I wanted to.

I return to my home. A cold wind is shaking the canopies of trees outside my window. My dog groans again, and I scratch his belly.

Yoke

I did something I shouldn't have done. I threw a rock at Wally and hit him in the head. He'd been throwing rocks at me because him and me and the other boys had been arguing about Jesus. He was for and I was against. Not really against, just not for. He called me a heathen and started throwing. I threw back, to defend myself. I took one on the arm and I threw the next one really hard and he took it right on the forehead. He fell on his butt. He put his hand on his head where the blood was already trickling out and down onto his face. He stood up quick so I knew he wasn't hurt bad.

He and the boys started chasing me. "Assholes!" I shouted. That made them even madder. I didn't care. I knew the streets but they knew them too and I couldn't lose them. I stayed to the neighborhoods and back alleys at first where there were plenty of loose rocks in case I needed them. I was faster than them, I beat them in races all the time, but their Jesus anger gave them extra energy and they were catching up. I cut down a side street and made it out to Main. The old man who did landscaping for the town slowly plodded up the street in his horse-drawn wagon with the cars whizzing past him. There were stories about this man—that he ate the flesh of children, that he conjured demons from the bodies of animals—and I was afraid of him. Still, if the boys caught me, they would beat me up. It had happened before. I knew I could take any of them one-on-one, but they would gang up. So I clambered onto the back of the old man's wagon.

He felt the jolt and turned to look at me. His eyes were calm and shiny, face covered in a scruffy white beard. He looked at the boys chasing me. He turned to face forward again, but he continued to allow the horse to go at the same slow pace. The boys caught up with us, but they were afraid of the old man too, even more afraid than I. They followed for a while shouting the worst names they could conjure, but when we crossed the town limits, they stopped and then turned back. The old man spoke in a low, loving voice to the huge, ancient, black horse who just kept walking with his head held low and his sleepy eyes. Shovels and rakes and other tools rattled in the wagon bed, along with bags of seed and fertile soil. I leaned back against a bag and fell asleep.

When I woke, we were heading slowly down a rutted dirt road beside a big field planted with grass for hay. A thick and musky smell filled the air. The wind played with the tops of pines and oaks. The old man towered above me in the driver's seat, wearing a tattered, brown coat and a floppy hat, casting his long shadow over me. His hands held the reins but kept them slack, allowing the old horse to walk at his own pace. I wanted to jump out of the wagon and run home, but I didn't know where I was. We couldn't be far from town. But I was scared and I stayed put. We entered some thick woods, and soon arrived at a meadow with a small, weather-beaten old cabin in the middle.

The old man climbed down and stood beside the wagon. He looked at me. His skin was very brown from the sun, and his eyes were even browner. His face was lean and muscular as if he'd been chewing on something all his life. Sparse white hair spilled out from beneath his hat. He walked around to the end of the wagon and pulled the gate down. He picked up a bag of seed and motioned for me to get the next one. It was heavy, but I managed to pick it up, hugging it against my chest. I didn't give the slightest thought to disobeying him. We put the bags into a storage shed near the house.

He motioned for me to follow him to the front of the wagon. The horse's head was the size of an oak stump, but his eyes were gentle. He played with the loose bit clinking against his teeth, sliding his tongue around it, long strings of slobber falling to the ground. He stomped his back foot impatiently. The old man loosened a couple of straps and buckles and freed the horse from its yoke. He undid the horse's "diaper" and flung the dung onto a mountainous pile. The horse and the man walked side by side over to a small paddock, the old man opened a gate, and the horse walked in. The old man grabbed a brush off a post and brushed the horse for a few minutes. The horse liked it, making funny ecstasy faces, bowing his back slightly like a dog. Then the man came back out of the paddock. The horse went down on his front knees, buckled his back legs, fell on his left side and rolled. He snorted and farted loudly in what seemed to be great pleasure. He stood back up and shook himself all over.

"Don't know why I bother brushing him," the old man said. The horse began to graze in a far corner of the paddock where there was still a little bit of grass.

The old man said, "Hold out your hands."

I did, and he dropped the tack and yoke over my forearms. It was heavy and warm, covered in horse sweat and hair.

The old man nodded to the shed. "Hang it," he said, pointing to hooks on the outer wall, and I hung it as best I could.

He used an old sponge dipped in a water bucket to wipe the tack off. Half way through he handed the sponge to me and studied me until the yoke was clean. He led me to the house just as the sun was going down. It was dark and cool inside. He lit a gas lamp and the flame sputtered and caught. He brought out food: apples and tomatoes and some kind of meat already cooked, rabbit I think.

We ate in silence. Our eyes would meet, and he would ask or answer questions just with his eyes. I realized I was doing the same. I knew when he wanted the salt. He knew when I wanted the knife. When we were done, I helped him clean the plates using water he poured into a basin from one of three buckets that stood in a row. He led me out to the front porch. The moon was almost full and felt like a spotlight landing right on us. He pointed to a small outbuilding, and I nodded my head. Inside, he led me to a room not much bigger than a closet. A made-up mattress lay on the floor. Light poured in through a small window. As I lay down, the old man pulled the door shut.

I slept good for a while. I woke up without knowing why. Cicadas and crickets owned the night. But then I heard the outer door open. Then the inner door to my room. The old man stooped over, picked me up from the mattress, and stood me up on my bare feet still half asleep. He gave me a glass of something to drink. It was very bitter. It seemed like time passed. Then he picked me up again and carried me outside to a table under the stars. He lay me down on it gently, and I realized that I couldn't move. I felt the mental signals, but my body remained still as a corpse. His eyes were friendly, but I was very afraid. The old man produced a large butcher knife, both sharp and serrated. Now I was screaming inside my head, though neither my throat nor mouth were moving. No one could hear me out in these woods anyway. First, he cut off my left hand. I shifted my eyes down enough to see him sawing, to see my hand separate. Then he cut off my right hand. I stopped screaming because it dawned on me that I felt no pain, though I could feel the biting of the serrated blade inside my flesh and bone. He gathered my hands and they crawled on him like a pair of big spiders. He dropped them into a bucket with a thunk. He did the same with my arms. Now I was just watching it happen. At some point, I drifted above my body, what was left of it, like a puff of smoke. From above, I watched the old man dismember me. Next it was my feet, then my legs. He threw them into various large buckets nearby. At last he cut off my head. He hoisted my torso and hung it on a large hook. It swung in the air, blood draining into a bucket. Then I was looking into the eyes of my head, which was still alive all by itself. Who or what did I see within those eyes. What eyes was I looking out of? I felt that I was both inside my head and floating before it, seeing in both directions at once. Then the old man grabbed my head by the hair and threw it into a pond. The fish attacked it, roughening the surface of the water for several minutes. When they were done, I could feel my skull drift down to the deepest muddy floor of the pond among others. My body was gone, but somehow I was still here. It dawned on me that whatever I am, I am not my body. The old man wiped my blood off the blade with my old shirt. He looked at me and laughed. And that was the last I remember.

At dawn the old man woke me and gave me chores for the day: put out fresh water in the horse's washtub, pull weeds in the garden, gather wood for the fireplace. He would not allow me to speak. I didn't particularly want to anyway. He hitched up the horse and headed for town. Later, I fell asleep on the porch. I dreamed of the old man, like a great heavy cloud, planting flowers and trees on the town's public grounds, tending the ones he'd planted in past years. I dreamed of the pieces of my body feeding those plants. I became this new life, holding on to the dark earth below, reaching up for the air and light above.

When he returned late that afternoon, there were more chores to do. I stayed with him for three days. On the fourth day, he said, "Go home." I climbed up on the wagon, but he shook his head. He shooed me with his hands.

"Walk," he said. I nodded. The old horse hung his great long face over the paddock fence. I went over and scratched between his ears. His eyes told me he liked that. I suddenly knew that I loved this old horse, wanted to be his friend, but there was no time for that now.

I walked out of the meadow and found the two-track through the woods. I took my time on the dirt road alongside the hay fields where the grass was going to seed, the wind brushing through the heads. I finally found the highway, and in an hour or so I walked back into town.

And then it began to happen. Everybody I met was transparent. I could see things moving inside them, like fetuses that wanted to be born but never would be. I knew what they wanted and why they wanted it. When I got home, my parents hugged me and cried. I could tell they wanted to be mad at me, but they were too happy to see me for that. I don't think they believed my story about being lost in the woods, but they accepted it. In a couple of days, I went back to school. I avoided the boys, and they avoided me. I knew they were curious and would start asking me questions in a few days. I would tell them about being dismembered. I knew they would never reveal what happened to me because they were afraid of that old man. And now their fear would be even greater.

I figured I would get back to playing their games soon enough. But not yet. I was preoccupied. I could see what was happening inside of everyone. I could see every yoke they wore, every lie they had swallowed. Most important, I could see my own yoke, my own lies. That made me feel, for the first time, that I am not alone. For the first time, that I have no fear. For the first time, I knew that we are all in this together.

The Silence

I was sitting on the couch in the silence of my old house when the telephone rang. "Hello?" I said.

"Hello, sir, my name is Jennifer, and I'm calling from the President's office." Her voice sounded highly competent, friendly, happy.

"What President? I quit the Moose Lodge ten years ago because of that rotten president, or Head Moose, whatever he was called."

"The POTUS, sir."

"No, that's not what it's called . . ."

"The President of the United States, sir."

I let that settle in for a minute. "Are you Jerry's girlfriend?" I asked.

"No sir, I do know a couple of Jerries, but they are not your Jerry."

"Come on Jerry, I know you're listening. The jig is up. This one isn't even very original," I said.

"The President would like to speak with you sir, if that's okay with you."

"Yeah, sure, put that rascal on," I said.

A moment passed, the phone made a clicking sound, and a man spoke. "Mr. Paterson?" the voice said.

"That's right," I said, "where's Jerry?"

"I don't know Jerry, but I do need to speak with you."

"Okay," I said, "speak."

"First of all, how are you doing today?"

"Fine, just fine. I was sitting here enjoying the silence of my old house. It's a warm day outside, but my house is cool, perfect really. The limbs of the cherry tree were bobbing in a breeze outside my window. My dog was snoring on the carpet, sometimes paddling her feet like she was chasing a dream in her rabbit."

"Did you mean to say . . ."

"I said what I meant to say, Mr. President," I said. "Also, my breath was silent, but I could feel it moving inside of me. I had an itch on my left cheek, but I didn't scratch it. I was keeping an eye on it, like a fire breaking out in the forest of my body. I just kept watching it until the fire went out. Let's see, what else?"

"That's enough," he said, "I just was asking how you are. I think I get the picture now."

"No you don't, you don't get the picture at all. You weren't really interested in how I was doing, were you?"

"I guess that's true. I was just being polite, asking how you are. I expected a short, routine answer from you," he said.

"Well, how are *you*?" I asked.

"Fine, thank you. See how that works? Now we can get on with the real purpose of my call," he said.

"You mean there's a reason for this call? Why would the President, any president, call me? I have no expertise. I possess just enough to get by. I have no family or friends. I am completely alone, even when I go out among people, to a ballgame for example, I sit shoulder to shoulder with other human beings eating my hotdog and drinking my beer without knowing or interacting with a single person, except to buy the food, of course."

"I don't believe that," he said.

"Okay, you're right, I say 'hi' or 'excuse me,' but that's all."

"Do you feel safe, Mr. Paterson?" the President asked.

"Safe?" I said.

"Yes, secure," he said.

"I'm ready to die, if that's what you mean," I said.

"Yes, that's precisely what I mean."

"I have no reason to live," I said, "except for the silence of my house, the breeziness of my yard, the happiness of my dog."

"That's why I have called," he said.

"It's quite a lot, now that I think about it," I said.

"Don't think about it, Mr. Paterson," he said.

"I guess that's another reason: the rummaging of my thoughts in the attic of my brain like a swarm of old junk pickers," I said.

"Keep thinking like that, and you will ruin everything," he said.

"I like the sound of that," I said, "Let's ruin everything together, Mr. President."

"You misunderstand my reason for calling, sir. Your country needs you," he said.

"Needs? What do you mean by 'need,' Mr. President?"

He hung up.

I held the phone to my ear for a moment listening to the whispery silence. Then, like the President, I hung up. A calm came over me. Gratitude. I walked back to my couch and sat down. The limbs of my cherry tree swung back and forth in the wind outside my window.

The Belt

It stretched down the length of the closet door like an unrolled scroll. The boy laid it across his palms, the gold buckle clinking slightly. It had belonged to his father before he went off to the war from which he didn't return. Two of those who did had visited the house and told the boy that his father died bravely in battle. They described some of the fighting for him, the hand to hand, how brutal it was.

His father used to wear the belt when he wasn't working as a carpenter building the new houses in their rural county, or repairing the old ones. He'd worn it when they went to town to buy supplies, when they hiked down to the river to fish, when they attended church on Sundays, though he never repeated the words of the Apostles' Creed or the Lord's Prayer, nor did he sing the hymns from the worn hymnals, though the boy's mother made up for it by singing loud enough for all three of them.

When the preacher called for sinners to repent and walk down the aisle to salvation, the boy's mother slid her elbow into his father's side, but he remained so still and erect in the pew that the boy thought his father had left his body and flown to some ancient mission out in the forest that they sometimes explored together. At these moments, the boy would study his father's lean face, the creases around the mouth and closed eyes, the scoops and knolls of the bone structure under the skin, and the boy thought then what an amazing and strange landscape a human face is. At night he sometimes had dreams that were journeys over the continent of his father's face. On the inside of the belt, his father had burned a message in his own code. His father had been like that, mysterious, seeming to keep some private knowledge to himself. He carried himself as a man who knows things. Not like how to roof a house—though he knew that and many other such skills—but something he carried within him that words couldn't touch.

The boy tried the belt on, but it was way too large for him, the long tongue of its excess hanging down. Still, it felt right on his body. He packed his backpack and crept out of the house and away from his mother and stepfather watching television in the den, believing the belt would lead him somehow to an adventure beyond his dull summer vacation. He soon found the woods his father had loved half a mile from the house and followed a doe and two young bucks into the dark edge. He tucked his father's belt inside his pants so it wouldn't catch on thorns. After picking his way through for a mile or so, he found a trail, and decided to go wherever it led him. When he took off his shoes and socks, waded across a knee-deep creek, and mounted the opposite bank, he felt that he'd passed into a different world where constant readiness was required. He carefully put his socks and shoes back on, tying the laces into double knots, looking around alertly as if the very air might consume him. He had enough food in his pack for three days, a pocketknife his stepfather had reluctantly given him for his birthday, a spoon he'd stolen from a kitchen drawer, and a small flashlight with a pack of spare batteries.

Much later, when he rediscovered the belt in an old chest of drawers as a middle-aged man, it was too small, the tip of the tongue barely slipping through the buckle at his waist, the last hole far short of the prong. He'd not realized he'd become physically a bigger man than his father. He laid the belt out on his dresser, disappointed, wondering what to do with it. For one thing, it was still beautiful, the leather for most of its length so dark it reminded him of the darkest chocolate. Sewn into the front of the belt, surrounding the buckle, was leather of a lighter shade in the shape of narrow, serrated leaves, penetrating the darker scroll. And then, burned into the rough inside hide of the belt, were thirty-seven symbols, indecipherable as letters or numbers. The man marveled at his father's imagination that could create so many unique forms. He hung the belt behind all of his others out of sight so his wife wouldn't see it and ask questions. But one day, when she was devoting herself to the many details of cleaning in the house, she did find it, and so he sat her down that night and told her the story of the belt. He would have given the belt to his own son, but he had died of complications at birth, and his wife could have no more children.

On the first day in the woods, the boy came upon a bear in a great patch of berries. A large male, he rocked back on his haunches and looked at the boy for a moment without fear or ill intention, then ambled off, a huge black cloud disintegrating into the forest. The boy gorged himself on blueberries, listening to the bear's slow progress through the underbrush. One day he saw a female red wolf digging in pine straw. She stared at him with the steady fire of her eyes, then trotted off, head slung low, tongue flopping from the side of her mouth. The boy went to the spot and found a footprint there, much larger than his own, a man's, the tread of a boot sole recorded like a fossil in the hard clay. Could it be his father's? No, the weather would have washed it away a long time ago. Another day through a gap in the canopy the boy saw an eagle soaring high in the sky. The eagle landed in the top of a nearby sycamore, male or female the boy couldn't tell. The boy felt that the bird was watching him as he passed beneath. He kept looking back to catch sight of the eagle among the highest leaves, the fierce clench of its head, the cool witnessing of its black eye. The forest was full of watching and listening. The boy spent one whole day carving each of the thirty-seven symbols of his father's belt into a different tree. At last they meant something to him in the woods, though he couldn't say exactly what it was, as if the unknowable nature of his father would linger there forever. Or at least as long as those trees remained.

At night he ate his peanut butter sandwiches and oatmeal cookies, drank creek water from his canteen, and let the darkness come to him. The forest canopy held back the light of stars and moon, and the darkness was almost complete. He turned his flashlight on, and the trunks of trees stood around him like giant horses sleeping on their feet. Would they ever wake up? Would they stretch their legs and walk? Were they protecting him, or oblivious to him? He turned out the flashlight and listened to the creaking of limbs in the breeze sounding like the voices of whales he'd heard in a documentary on TV. He listened to the calls of owls hunting, sometimes heard the *whup-whup-whup* of their wings among the limbs over his head.

One night there was a storm, and though it was summer and the weather mild, the boy shivered in the heavy rain. When lightning struck a nearby tree, the flash of light and explosion of thunder were so strong they transported him into a silent, deep place inside himself, where he sat so still in the pew next to his father he thought he would never move again, hypersensitive though to the congregation around him, the slightest adjustments of their bodies, a cough, a subtle amen, the words coming from the pulpit like wind chimes, or the knocking of a tree on the window. Then, he suddenly felt the current pouring through his body, an intensity that stretched the boundaries of every cell, and yet he was aware of no pain. He withdrew into the dark place inside like repelling down into a well. He became less and less of himself going down until he curled up at the bottom like smoke, and then not even that. If time passed, it was none of his concern. If there was light at the top of the well, it didn't enter his eyes. If somewhere his mother and stepfather were worried about him, he didn't care. They would just have to get over it. The darkness and silence and emptiness descended on him with a weight unlike anything he'd ever known. But this weight felt good, felt like a warm, heavy blanket covering everything. The boy rested. He would have been happy if it lasted forever. The thirty-seven symbols of his father's belt slowly appeared like glowing embers in the wall of the well around him. He had no mind left with which to interpret their meanings. They just existed, the alphabet maybe of a language that had never formed. He had plenty of time, so he studied each one as if it held the secret of the universe. Without words, how does meaning arise, and yet he felt it and knew it. And when he knew that he knew it, each symbol crawled slowly up the wall of the well until it disappeared somewhere up there in the night sky. And then, slowly, the boy felt himself become a cold body curled up on the dusty floor of a dried up well. A crow's call drew him up the tunnel of the well and deposited him in a bright, clear morning. He lay on the pine straw floor of the woods. His eyes were dry and covered with the crust of the deepest sleep he'd ever known. He was still drenched from the rain but no longer cold, and his body hummed with a relic of the current.

One day the boy stumbled out of the trees into the sunlight of a dirt road. A farmer in a pickup truck gave the boy a ride home, only a few miles away after all. His mother despaired of his thinness, hugged him and cried and didn't let go of him once for a whole week. The first chance he got, his stepfather whipped the boy with his father's belt and made him vow never to hurt his mother like that again. The boy bears the marks on his scrawny old legs to this day, the remnants of his father's code catching fire on his skin and swelling into his whole body when lightning comes close.

The boy who became a man and now an old man sometimes thought he could hear those symbols crawling out of the woods and toward the house in the dry leaves of fall. Over the years, he whittled each of the symbols into freestanding forms, which he would have given to his son, but which now lay randomly about the house, saying and not saying whatever it was his father knew and that he knew but could not speak. He could feel it when he sat on the porch with his wife in the evening after work. When he lay down in bed those first moments before falling asleep, he felt it. There were days when he felt it constantly, that presence for which he had no name, because he knew it wasn't his father, but rather the understanding of his father, that lived in the still continent of his face.

The Shadow of Shadows

The phone rang. I let the machine pick up, but whoever it was left no message. Since my divorce more than two years before, my life had become a deep well of loneliness that I had fallen into and had accepted as my fate. I had long ago discovered the fact that no call would ever again be her. And I no longer felt any great urgency to answer the phone, whether it was my landline or my cell.

A moment later, the same thing happened. The phone rang four times and then my answering machine picked up. No message left.

"Somebody who wants my money," I thought, and kept reading. I was sitting in my favorite reading chair in the den. If the caller were someone who really wanted to talk to me, they would have left a message.

A moment later, the phone rang again. This time I laid my book down on the arm of my chair, got up, and crossed the room to the phone. I was going to give this intrusive caller a piece of my mind. I picked it up on the third ring.

"Hello," I said.

"Look out your window," a male voice said.

Right away I didn't like his pushy attitude. "What for?" I asked.

"The Shadow," he said.

I started to hang up, but I was curious. "Do you mean like Lamont Cranston from the thirties?"

The man laughed. "No," he said, "not in the slightest."

"Whose shadow?" I asked.

"I am the Shadow *beyond* shadows. Look out your window," he said.

"Which one?"

"The big one, in your living room."

I walked into the living room and stood in front of the big window. An old man was standing in my front yard. He wore a fedora, a yellow bow tie, a speckled jacket, and a bright blue pair of pants. He waved at me and smiled.

"Go outside and talk to the man," the man in my phone said. He hung up.

The man outside continued to smile and to signal with his hand for me to join him. My little dog climbed up to the back of the couch, sat down, and watched the man in the yard. Though an avid barker at strangers, she didn't make a sound.

"Okay," I thought. I grabbed my cap and, to be safe, my keys. I stepped outside on my stoop and pulled the door shut behind me. The old man was there. He smiled brightly, but seemed shy. I looked around my neighborhood, but no one else was out. It was cold and breezy, the trees bowing and sighing. I walked over to the man cautiously. He took his hat off and pressed it to his chest. His hair was curly and longish around the edges but very sparse on top. His grin was big.

"How can I help you?" I asked.

"Oh," he said, "there's nothing you can do to help me."

"Then what do you want?"

"Absolutely nothing."

"Who was the man on the phone?" I asked.

"Nobody."

"What am I supposed to do next?" I asked.

"Only you can say," he said.

He pressed his fedora to his chest as if he were humbling himself to me.

"Do you want to come inside?"

"Oh, no," he said, "there's no such thing as inside for me anymore."

I chewed on that for a moment, but it had no taste.

"Do you have any questions?"

He shook his head eagerly. "No questions."

I thought for a moment. "Answers?" I asked.

"Far from it."

"Okay," I said, "I'm going back inside."

He nodded, almost excitedly. "Yes, back inside," he said.

"Goodbye," I said.

"Goodbye," he said.

I turned and headed toward my door. I could feel his eyes on my back. I stopped and looked back at him. "Shouldn't you be going now?" I asked, but it was more an assertion than a question.

"Not my decision," he said, turning his hat in both hands like it was a steering wheel.

"Well, whose is it?" I asked.

"Can't say," he said.

"Okay, I guess that's that."

"Yes," he said, "it is." He nodded and grinned as if encouraging me on.

I turned, walked to the house, unlocked my door and crept back inside. When I got back to my living room and looked out the window, the man was nowhere in sight. My dog was asleep on the back of my couch. I stroked her head and neck, and she groaned and rolled over on her back. I checked my phone, but the caller's number had not been preserved.

I sat back down in my chair in the den, picked up my book, but I couldn't concentrate to read. What if it had all been a ploy to get me out of the house? I jumped up and explored every inch of every room, checked all of the doors and windows to the outside, but no one had entered and nothing was missing. I sat back down in my chair.

My mind went blank. All my thoughts lay down like my dog and went to sleep. For all of that day and all of that evening, my mind was perfectly empty and clear. I tried to read a novel, but my mind wouldn't hold any thoughts or judgments. The story lost its flavor. The story of my own life—

growing up poor in the South, spending five years in the army, going to college then law school and becoming a lawyer, getting married and getting divorced—all of it lost its flavor, its power to define me. I had become something else, or maybe nothing at all, just a conglomeration of senses operating in service to an undefined observer who just kept seeing and feeling.

Fortunately I was on a sabbatical from teaching in the law school, and I didn't have to do anything for several months if I didn't want to. This condition, if that's what it was, persisted for weeks. This clarity of mind accompanied by the loss of identity with the old story of my life left me somewhat less interested in the human-created world. But my loneliness became a more simple and painless aloneness. I felt like a man standing in someone's yard without any idea about who I am or what I'm supposed to be doing, but also at the same time without any concern for those matters.

For a year or more, I totally forgot about the phone call from the Shadow of Shadows. I forgot about the pointless man in my yard. I eventually regained my personal story, went back to work teaching, and fell back into the shadow of loneliness that my life had become.

One day, a memory of the man sprang into my mind like a piece of a dream coming back. It was the weekend and I was relaxing at home when his image started putting itself together behind my eyes one feature at a time. I walked to the living room, and sure enough the man was standing fully formed in my yard pressing his hat to his chest. I threw on my coat and ran outside. He watched my approach with curiosity.

"You came back," I said.

He shook his head. "No."

"But you're here."

"I'm always here."

"But I haven't seen you."

"Depends on what you mean by 'see,'" he said.

"I don't want to play this game again."

"Good. I don't play games," he said.

"Please come inside and let's talk. I'll make you a cup of tea."

"I have nothing to say," he said.

"I don't understand," I said.

"Who is it that would understand, or not understand?"

That was the first question he had asked me. I looked and looked for the understander inside myself, but I couldn't find him. "I don't know," I said, with an irritation I didn't care for.

He nodded and smiled. We stood on the lawn looking at each other for a moment. His soft blue eyes were calm, alert, kind. Suddenly I was looking through his eyes at me: a man in his fifties in a heavy old jacket, hands in the pockets for warmth, sparse white hair swirling in a kind of whirlwind on the top of his head, brow furrowed, eyebrows angled up toward the center, eyes holding puzzled sadness. Why was he puzzled? Why was he sad? Something that felt like "me" kept sliding back and forth between us to look first out of one set of eyes and then out of the other, or dangled in the open space between us feeling as though the two were one. Time passed. Suddenly I came fully back into my old self. Something had happened, was happening, but it had no reference point in the life I was living.

"Okay," I said, "I'm going back inside."

He nodded. "Back inside," he said.

I turned, walked back into my house, and went to the big window in my living room. The man was gone.

I sat down in the nearest chair and started to cry. I felt that I was free falling in a vast space. I had no place to land. I was alone.

The next day I taught my classes as usual. I returned to my normal life, but I was never a person again. Even now, I'm not a person. What am I? Maybe I'm the shadow of a shadow. Maybe I'm the end of all questions and answers. If you see me standing in your yard, turning my hat like a steering wheel, I hope you will come to say hello.

The Secret Life of Henry Rose

For the third day in a row, a helicopter is circling my house. The first time I noticed, I was out in my back yard refilling my birdfeeder. It flew so low it nicked the tops of my pine trees. The birds didn't return for hours. The little downy woodpecker, one of my favorites, has never returned. I called City Hall and complained. At first, they said it had nothing to do with them. But when I insisted, they finally said they would look into it.

I have never married, and unlike my neighbors who have jobs in town, I work from my house and have the neighborhood to myself during the day. I made a bunch of money when I was young in the real estate business I inherited from my father. I don't really have to work at all if I don't want to. Mainly I write for blogs and certain online journals. Sometimes I take a break and just stroll among the empty houses. All of the dogs know me by now. I carry little treats for them, so they are always happy to see me. I have taken the time to train a few of them: no, sit, lie down, shake hands, speak, heel. If my neighbors have noticed any difference in their dogs, they've never said anything to me. They probably think they have trained the dog themselves.

The second time I saw the helicopter it was hovering in the street outside my window, just barely fitting in the opening between all the electrical and phone wires. One false move and the blades would snag. Transformers would blow in a shower of sparks and wreckage would break into the street and yards. Plus the pilot could easily be killed or badly wounded. Looking out my window, I was gazing directly into the eyes of the pilot. He was wearing headphones and dark glasses. He just kept looking at me for a minute. Then he gave me a little salute with his right hand and rose out of view. By the time I got outside, he had disappeared into the sky. For another minute or so, I could still hear his engine and the whirlwind rhythm of his blades.

I ran back inside and called City Hall. They said they had checked out my earlier complaint and confirmed that there had been no helicopter flights in my part of town. When I told them that I had looked the pilot right in the eye, I heard someone in the background laugh. The person I was speaking to covered her mouthpiece for a moment. I didn't wait for her to uncover and speak. I just hung up. I now knew they would not help me. Some rogue helicopter pilot was doing very dangerous things, and they didn't care.

I went back outside. My neighbor's empty garbage can had been knocked into the street by the force of the helicopter wind. That made me feel better. I wasn't imagining things.

Armed with that evidence, I watched for my neighbor, Carl the plumber, to return home from work. When his car pulled in, I jogged over and caught him at his front door with the keys in his hand.

"Carl," I yelled to him.

He turned and smiled. "Hey there, Henry. What's up?"

"Have you heard anything about the helicopters?" I asked.

He frowned. "What helicopters?"

"The ones that have been buzzing our neighborhood," I said.

He shook his head. "Don't know nothing about that."

"Yeah," I said, "they've been flying really low, like right down to the level of the street."

"No kidding," he said.

"Yeah," I said, "I called the cops, but they don't know anything about it."

"Well, that's good enough for me," Carl said.

"No, Carl," I said, "this could be a real problem. I mean, today the copter blew your garbage can into the street. I brought it back for you."

"Thanks," Carl said. "Look, Henry, I'm tired, I need to get a shower, some food, spend a little time with the wife, you know how it is."

"Yeah, I know," I said, "but I just thought you ought to know."

"Thanks pal," he said.

"So what do you think we should do about it?" I asked.

He got a sad expression on his face and just looked at me. He was a former Marine. He'd been a professional boxer for a while after he got back from the Middle East. He still had muscles to burn. I figured he'd be a good guy to know in a pinch.

"Henry," he said, "this don't have anything to do with those men in the sewers you were seeing, does it?"

"No," I said, "those guys haven't showed up in a long time. This is totally different. A lot more dangerous."

"Why's that?" Carl asked.

"Well, for one thing, those blades could cause a lot of damage."

"Okay," Carl said. "Okay, Henry, I'm really tired, man."

"Yeah, I know," I said. I could tell he'd had a hard day. His hands were almost black. His shirt and pants were stained with various dark liquids. "But I just thought you ought to know."

"Thanks Henry. I know. Okay?"

"Okay," I said.

"And one more thing," he said.

"What's that?"

He waived those big, filthy hands in front of his chest. "I need . . . you know . . ." He was searching hard for the right words. Carl wasn't a very talkative guy.

"What do you need, Carl?" I asked.

"I need . . . you know . . . for you to . . . you know . . . to stay away." He immediately stepped through his door and closed it.

I stood on his porch for a minute or so staring at his American flag. I wondered what exactly he was trying to tell me. Stay away from what? I puzzled over that the rest of that evening.

The third time I noticed the helicopter it was just earlier today. I was walking around the block, getting a little exercise. I heard the helicopter coming from the distance. As usual it was flying right above the tops of the trees. When the pilot caught sight of me, he hovered right over the top of my head. Naturally, there wasn't a single person around to see any of this. I'd been thinking about what Carl had said. I think I finally figured out he was trying to tell me something, to tell me not to talk to him anymore. The more I played it back in my head, the more sure I was about it. And I have to tell you, it hurt. I really respected Carl. But somebody got to him. Money, you know? In America, that's what talks. And threats on his family, on his own self. Carl is a brave man, but he can only serve his country so much, he can only take so much pressure, before he knuckles under. I can't say I blame him. It's okay for me. I don't have a wife and kids. I don't have anything to lose, anything to keep me from doing what's necessary. I had a stint in the army when I was young myself. I never saw combat, but I can tell you crawling on your belly with live ammo flying over your head teaches you how to handle yourself. After that, I wasn't scared of anything.

So when the helicopter landed in the street right in front of me, I was ready for whatever was about to happen. That same pilot with the headphones and the shiny dark glasses was looking right at me through the windshield. A man in a blue suit with a red tie jumped out the other side and started walking toward me. Wind from the blades folded his jacket back against his arms. I could see the pistol holstered against his side. Orange hair flew around on his head. He was wearing dark glasses too. I figured I'd better get me a pair of those if I was going to stay in this business.

This fellow walked like he meant to do something. He stopped right in front of me. A little smile crept onto his face. Then he reached his hand out to me.

"Mr. Rose," he said, "it's great to finally meet you."

I figured I'd better play things in the middle until I knew what was happening, so I took his hand and shook it. Then he paid me the respect of taking off his glasses and meeting me eye to eye.

"I want to personally thank you for your service to the country," he said.

"Thank you, sir," I said. What else could I say? False modesty doesn't count for anything in this world. I was just glad to realize that the helicopters were friendlies. I should've known. "What particular service are you referring to, sir?" I asked.

"Your reports to the Pentagon on those sewer-men has led to a clandestine nationwide search. And I'm glad to report to you it's been very productive. Very productive indeed."

I have to admit I could feel the tears welling up. "I'm really glad to hear it," I said. "So, are they Russians?"

The smile fell off his face. He put his glasses back on and looked around for a moment. "I'm afraid I'm not at liberty to say," he said, "but just let me say that the enemies of America, the whole bunch of them, and you know who they are, have banded together."

"My God," I said, "and the sewers give them access to every neighborhood in the country."

"Yes," he said, "our enemies have taken to the sewers. But don't worry, Mr. Rose, thanks to people like you, we have it under control. I do have to warn you, though. The ones that remain are heading this way. They know who tipped us off. So you need to be vigilant. And I recommend that you arm yourself."

"I am armed," I said. I felt for my pistol in its holster under my arm. "I'm prepared for anything they can do."

"Excellent," he said. He gave me a little salute. I saluted him in return. He turned and walked back toward the helicopter.

"Will I see you again?" I shouted over the sound of the whipping blades.

He stopped and looked back at me. "Not likely," he shouted, "the battle calls me to many places." He looked around to make sure no one was observing, and then he climbed into the copter. He gave the pilot a wind-up signal, and the great machine began to lift off. It drifted straight up, paused for a second, then headed east fast and low over the trees. They disappeared, and soon the sound of the engine and the blades faded away.

Now I'm standing in the middle of the street in my sleepy neighborhood. The silent aftermath of my encounter is as heavy as truth. All of the houses around me doze like old dogs. Even if the Carls of the world have been bought or frightened into submission, I know my duty.

I walk slowly and purposefully back to my house, sensing that the enemy may be observing me. I keep a close eye on the culverts. The last time I saw one of the sewer-men, he slithered out of the gutter like a lizard. He made himself skinny to fit through the opening, then filled back out when he stood up. The enemy have invented amazing, if disgusting, new technology. He was so filthy I couldn't tell what his true color was. It could've been black or tan or red or yellow or brown. When he saw me watching him, he ran into the patch of woods at the end of the street and disappeared. I would've been at a great disadvantage if I'd followed him. That was a month ago. He could still be there, for all I know.

Keeva of Lomasaya

Keeva

When I was a kid, I could buy, sell, and trade anything for a profit. It was a knack I had from the first moment I sensed what it meant to possess something, even before I could talk. Grasping one of my mother's diamond earrings with that oblivious strength of an infant, or one of my father's gold-plated pens, I would not willingly let go without first collecting something valuable in trade: a lengthy ride around the house on the old man's shoulders; a trip to the market where I would be chauffeured among the gleaming aisles in a grocery cart.

With speech, my bartering skills increased a hundredfold. I have always had a taste for exact language and the will to persist against overwhelming odds. When I was seven, after three days of intense negotiations, I sold a box of threadbare socks I had collected or stolen from family members to a friend of mine as ammunition against his nagging sister. He would ambush her and her boyfriend necking on the couch, pelting them on the run with those socks rolled up into tight balls. He had his fun and I had those crisp dollar bills to fatten my wallet.

By the time I was a young man I fancied myself an entrepreneur. I had attended the business school of my state university and graduated with honors. Eager to prove myself, I was willing to travel the world over for my clients in search of opportunities that would one day lead me to my own independent business. One such journey took me to the small land-locked country of Fallada, which was mostly wilderness—great forests and ancient, snow-capped mountains. The capital and only city in Fallada was Lomasaya, located deep in the interior. According to the maps and guidebooks I had studied, it was surrounded by a wide band of farmland, and then another even wider band of dense forest—like an atom with its rings. The roads leading out of Lomasaya all ended abruptly at the interior edge of that forest—that is, all except one. Here and there, faint trails entered the woods. Deer, bears, coyotes, wolves, even mountain lions would occasionally appear at the edge, but hunters posted at the perimeter kept them at bay. Only one main road led from the outer world across the wilderness and farmland into Lomasaya. In many ways it was an ordinary city, with the luxuries and conveniences that had become commonplace in developed countries. In the photos I had seen, richly carved gargoyles peered from the buildings like a fierce but silent audience to all that went on in that strange place.

I travelled there against the advice of my father, who had heard many stories about the dangers of that mostly wilderness nation. Apparently, some who visited never returned. Even my father's closest friend, a man known for his own adventures around the world, tried to talk me out of it. The Lomasayan merchants and traders were reputed to be fierce, interested only in the most baroque, rococo or otherwise ornate objects of the outside world. And Fallada itself was among the least explored and least understood of nations. But I was not to be dissuaded. Their own arts and crafts were unique and beautiful and highly prized around the world. I stood to make a lot of money that would stake me in later ventures. I would travel there as the agent of a number of European and Asian traders.

A week before I was to leave, my father and his friend, Jack, who was also a good friend of mine, took me out to dinner at one of the finest restaurants in the city. The two of them, especially together, were great company, and we talked about many things that night. After the plates and wine glasses had been removed and all three of us were sipping a glass of excellent whiskey, a silence descended over the table, and I saw a shift of tone in my father's eyes.

"Son," he said.

"Yes, Father?"

He took another sip of his whiskey. "About this trip to Fallada . . ."

"Everything is arranged, Father, you don't need to worry about it."

"I'm not worried about the arrangements," he said with a bit of irritation in his voice, "I'm worried about the whole damn thing."

"We've been through all of this before," I said.

"You'd better listen to your father," said Jack. "He knows what he's talking about."

I had been ambushed, plied with good food, wine, and whiskey, and now I would have to withstand the slings and arrows.

"Have I told you about Falladan women?" my father asked.

I looked at him surprised. My father never spoke about women in any but the most respectful of ways. And I could feel him moving toward a less than generous tone.

"No," I said, "I believe the women of Fallada is just about the one subject you have yet to broach."

"This is no laughing matter," he said.

"I'm not laughing, Father. What do you have to say?"

"I know of two cases of men who traveled to Fallada returning with women they wished to make their wives."

"So?" I said.

"In both cases it didn't turn out so well."

"I knew you were going to say that."

"It seems that Falladan women are very beautiful. They are highly skilled in the art of making love . . ."

"You are making me want to go even more than before!"

"If you would allow me to finish . . ."

"Please, go ahead," I said, happy with myself.

"In both cases, within a year the women went virtually insane."

"Virtually?" I said.

"Yes," he said, ignoring my sarcasm. "They couldn't tolerate the stresses of our culture."

"What form did this insanity take?"

"I'm getting there," he said. "They became allergic to the touch of their husbands, for one."

"That may be more of a mark against the men . . ."

"Shut up for minute," my father said, "and let me complete my thought."

My father never spoke so bluntly to me as this, and he certainly had caught my attention.

"They attempted suicide," he said. "One of them took enough poison to kill an alligator, but somehow she survived. They finally decided to ship her back to Fallada where, I'm told, she fulfilled her mission. The other one attempted to shoot herself in the head. But her husband had not told her that he kept only blanks in his pistol. Still, she believed that she had shot herself, and she fell down into a coma as if she were indeed dead. That was five years ago. She remains in a coma to this day."

My father clearly thought this final bit of information would be the last nail in the coffin of my plans. All I could say was, "Very strange."

"Indeed," my father said. "Falladan women will be the most significant danger you face there. There is a book about their women who have come to live in our country. It will wake you up a bit, I believe. I have located a copy and I placed it on your bed this afternoon. I suggest you take a look at it."

"I promise I will," I said, wanting to laugh. I hid my smirk behind my whiskey glass.

"One more thing," he said.

"Oh my God," I said, "Can't it wait until tomorrow?"

"No, it can't." My father mashed his cigarette out on an ashtray. "Many of the men from our country who go to Fallada . . . never return."

"Well maybe Fallada is a great place to live," I said.

"Maybe," he said, "but the problem seems to be that they simply disappear there."

"Disappear?" I said.

"That's right," he said. "No trace of them there or anywhere else. That's why nobody sends their reps to Fallada anymore. That's why I implore you not to go. You are my only son."

I thought he was going to cry. I had never seen my father in such a state before. But I had no intention of allowing him to use his emotions to convince me not to go to Fallada. I was certain of my abilities to navigate the city of Lomasaya without concern.

"You'd better listen to your father," Jack said, beginning to show the effects of his second glass of whiskey. "Oh wait, I think I said that already." He smiled.

"Okay," I said, "I'll think about it."

"That's all I ask," my father said.

And the evening ended on that note.

Looking back on it now, I wish I had taken my father and his friend a little more seriously. I have to admit that Fallada was my first, and most profound, defeat. I wasn't conquered by the superior negotiating skills of their merchants. In fact, though they were alert and not to be taken advantage of, I found them to be quite reasonable. I was able to generate substantial profits for myself and my distant clients within the first week of my stay. No, that wasn't the problem. It was some kind of psychic malaise that forced me to retreat, resulting, I believe, from my prolonged exposure to the society of Lomasaya, the culture of that strangest of cities—and my prolonged exposure to a woman named Keeva.

My father insisted on driving me the three days journey to the border of Fallada. I told him he didn't need to do that, that I could easily rent a car and drive myself. But he wanted to talk. Wanted to remember our times together. It was as if he worried that this may well be the last time he would ever lay eyes on me. I tried to convince him that he need not worry. We talked a lot, but there were also many long silences. Much of our love and respect for each other were communicated in those wordless spaces. We parted as the best of friends.

At the border station, I was met by two agents of the city of Lomasaya. The man, who introduced himself as Hanglar, was white-skinned, tall, muscular, and wore formal clothing, including a large-collared shirt and a tie. His dark hair was long and pulled tightly back in a ponytail. He sported a close-cropped beard and a pair of jovial eyes. The woman laid her long, slender hand in mine and introduced herself as Keeva. I noticed her fingernails were painted an unusual shade of blue. She was dark-skinned with classical bone structure, tallish, slender, and wore colorful clothing that displayed the traditional tastes of the people of that region. Indeed, as I had read, Fallada was populated exclusively by descendants of those who originally settled it perhaps several thousand years ago. But the city of Lomasaya had developed to some degree under the influence of other cultures. It was at first difficult to grasp that these two very different people were apparently of the same race.

We climbed into an old, beautiful Rolls-Royce and drove on a very fine stone road slowly through the wilderness. We spotted elk and deer and even a moose cow and her calf crossing the road ahead of us, which is why we continued to travel cautiously. Keeva told me they sometimes encountered bears or mountain lions on the road. She and Hanglar conveyed that the preservation of the wilderness with all of its native animals and natural wonders was a key feature of Falladan philosophy and practice. I later discovered that was only partially true at best. They basically left the wilderness to itself. The country consisted of the outer belt of protective wilderness, the inner belt of sustaining agriculture, and the cultural center of the city.

After a hundred miles or so, the wilderness gave way to agriculture. We stopped at another Falladan station and got out of the car. Keeva and Hanglar escorted me the rest of the way, ten miles or so, into the city via a man-drawn cart. A three-man team, to be exact, shirtless, lean and carved by muscle. Their collaboration was exemplary, reaching a top speed of twelve miles an hour. We proceeded through vast fields of wheat, corn, and cotton. Irrigation appeared to be achieved with a labyrinthine system of channels, canals, and giant sprinklers that crawled slowly across the fields like praying mantises. After nearly an hour, the runners slowed down to enter the city streets.

When I saw that there were no cars on the streets, I asked Keeva, who sat next to me in the cart, about that. Her skill with my language was limited but still very good. She managed to communicate to me that there were only a handful of motorized vehicles in the city—all of them electric—reserved for emergency use only.

"What about horse-drawn carriages?" I asked.

She said that in order to maintain a high degree of cleanliness, no domestic animals such as dogs, cats, and horses were allowed in the city limits of Lomasaya. Horses and mules were used on the farms outside the city to help with work. Cattle, chickens, and pigs were raised for meat. But the only animals to be found within the city were squirrels and birds, the kind that could live wild mostly in the trees and on the rooftops. Rats had been eradicated many decades ago. I noted that the city was bustling. No building that I could see was taller than twelve stories, and those appeared to be rare. Not a scrap of trash could be observed on the streets. When we crested a hill, I could see that the city stretched out for many miles in every direction. A hopeful excitement rose up in me at that moment.

Within the first hour of my stay, I wanted to ask a thousand questions, but I held back. I was essentially an intruder, and I didn't want to jeopardize my business opportunities by asking ridiculous questions. So I was patient and kept my eyes and ears open. Certainly I had read all of the available books and articles on Fallada, including the one about Falladan women that my father had given me, but nothing could have prepared me for what I found there.

We stopped in front of a large, handsome but also ornate, five-story building—a huge square with a highly landscaped courtyard in the interior. Keeva stepped out of the cart and extended her hand to me. Hanglar said his goodbyes and was carried away in the cart. Keeva smiled and said she had been assigned to me as my assistant for the duration of my stay. It would be difficult for me to state here just how beautiful Keeva was. I suspected that she may be some sort of test for me, and I was determined at that moment to maintain my physical, emotional, and psychological distance. I hate to admit it, but the book my father had given me was having some influence.

Keeva escorted me into the building and into a quiet, smooth elevator that took us to the third floor almost instantly. Out of a window I saw what appeared to be a moving walkway transporting several people across the courtyard at the fourth floor level. Keeva tapped me on the shoulder, smiled at my gawking, and handed me a key. My flat was small, but it was very comfortable with a well-stocked kitchen and a balcony with an excellent view of the street below and even a few cloudy mountaintops in the distance. Keeva helped me with my luggage, and when I was fairly settled, she said she would return the next morning to take me to my office, which was only a short walk. I stood on my balcony and watched as she exited the building and crossed the street. She suddenly stopped, turned, caught my eye, and waved. I returned the wave. Then she disappeared in the crowd.

With plenty of daylight remaining, I decided to go for a walk, making sure I took notes to help me find my way back to my building. The city seemed to go on forever. On the street, I could not help but notice that the children ran loose like herds of domestic cattle owned by everyone. My observations told me that adults fed them at random with what they had in their pockets, according to their inclinations, and there were kiosks on certain corners where the government made food available to them, usually fresh fruit, vegetables, and nuts. Also clothing laid out on shelves. I returned to my flat with many more questions than answers. No one I spoke to knew my language, and so all of my inquiries had been frustrating. I discovered that I was exhausted by travel, and I went to bed early.

The next morning, Keeva arrived at seven thirty, and we strolled through the streets for no more than fifteen minutes. She was happy to answer my questions about the children. The weak, sick, or injured were cared for only if they found their way to facilities established for that purpose. As the children grew older, they were presented with a variety of choices: they could enter the city's educational system; they could take low-level jobs in the maintenance of the city; they could work on the farms outside of the city; or, they could disappear into the wilderness.

Keeva told me that children who wanted to live among the city's adults were not denied. When they reached the age of eight, and again at twelve, they were given an opportunity to leave the streets and enter the homes and institutions of the city. But only those who wanted selection were selected. In fact, no form of persuasion existed on either side. I can vouch for this myself, as I witnessed the process daily for many months. The one notion held sacred by all was the freedom of choice. Eventually, and without consultation, each child made the choice, and that was that.

Keeva led me to a small building in the business district. She produced a key and swung the door open to a very inviting space, complete with two desks, couches and chairs, excellent lighting, and small quarters in the back where one could withdraw to rest and take nourishment. She showed me a large desk that she said was mine. Then she sat down at a somewhat smaller desk that would be hers. She told me that my first potential clients would be arriving soon. She would make appointments for me and would be my translator and notetaker. Was there anything she couldn't do?

That first week, she showed up at my office early every morning. She had contacts with artisans and dealers all over the city. Very soon, I had several appointments a day, and my business dealings got off to an excellent start. No landline telephones or cell phones were allowed in Lomasaya. The few that existed were reserved for the government's contact with the outside world. Due to my circumstances, I was allowed the use of a satellite phone in a nearby government office for the purpose of contacting my foreign clients. In general, local use of phones was against the law, punishable by expulsion. Couriers carried messages back and forth by foot or by bicycle. In this way, everyone was always gainfully employed. When I pressed Keeva on the lack of sophisticated communications systems in

Lomasaya, she laughed and said the people didn't miss what they had never experienced firsthand. She personally liked the slower life and deeper relationships that were afforded by face-to-face communication.

Let me add here that computers were absolutely banned by both the national and the city government, which were closely affiliated and occupied the same buildings in the government's expansive quarters at the city's center. Because of this ban, Falladans had no access to the world economy facilitated by the internet. I, and maybe a few other outsiders temporarily ensconced in Lomasaya, were their only conduit to the global economy.

I noticed very soon that there were no infants in the homes of the people, and the youngest among the children that roamed the streets were three or four. When I asked her about this, Keeva said she would show me.

One morning when she had made sure I had no appointments, she took my hand and smiled. This was so provocative that I was unable to calm my pulse for quite some time, though I was practiced in the art of controlled breathing. I shouldn't hold back any facts whose dearth may, in the end, be misleading: though Keeva bore the general characteristics of her people, she was beautiful almost beyond imagination. Tall and slender, her hair was long, black and luxurious; her eyes were dark, deep, and steady. Her clothing was colorful, but she wore no makeup. Honestly, any description is pointless in its ineptitude. She could look at me for extended periods of time without blinking. This was disconcerting at first, but I soon became accustomed to the fact that she was attentive to me. I came to expect her to be looking at me whenever I turned her way. As an experiment, I sometimes held her gaze for minutes on end while speaking with her. Though this activity did not faze her in the least, I would find my eyes watering and my gut filling with some indefinable shame, and I would look away, get back to my work. Her face was expressionless, and yet some content was emanating from her eyes that I could not decipher. So when she smiled, it was like a significant change in the weather. And her hand, a beautiful object in its own right, most certainly *took* mine, and in that moment gained control of me. She led me through the streets of

Lomasaya. I noticed for perhaps the first time that most pedestrians were holding hands with someone as they walked. Perhaps one in ten walked alone, weaving among the couples. With Keeva holding my hand, I felt comfortable. She was including me, making me part of it. My attraction for Keeva was fast becoming a kind of anguish. It took every ounce of my concentration to be in her presence and not simply stare at her.

I had certainly noticed before, but was now confirming on this walk, that the people of Lomasaya appeared to have every color of skin I could imagine—from black to white and everything between. In one sense, they looked like the people in any cosmopolitan city of the world where all races engaged with each other, but I had read and had been told they were all of the same unique race. When I asked Keeva about this, she just shrugged her shoulders. It wasn't something that she, or they, gave much thought to.

We came upon a huge public structure, a great maze of a building covered with thousands of grotesque gargoyles. It turned out to be one of several government nurseries. Highly trained nurses, both men and women, carefully tended the babies and infants. They were treated with warmth and affection, but the nurses rotated each day, so that the baby was never able to form a close attachment to any particular person. Still, the gentle handling of the babies was duplicated precisely by each of the nurses.

I was surprised to find myself enthusiastically welcomed at the nursery, and I returned several times, with and without Keeva, in an effort to make sense of what I was seeing. Adults who were fulfilling their required, one-week stint of nursery service supervised the entire operation. Keeva would interrupt them at times and introduce me to them. Their primary function was to observe and, when necessary, offer counsel to the nurses. They made certain that the treatment given to infants was absolutely consistent. These supervisors were always friendly to me and allowed me complete access to both the building and the proceedings. Keeva whispered something to one of the attendants, and he soon handed me one of the infants who squirmed in my arms like a wild puppy with boundless energy. Keeva took her from me, and the child quickly calmed down. Keeva carried her with us as we walked and both of them were happy, the child's eyes bright and quick with curiosity.

I enjoyed my excursions into the nurseries, but with each visit it became harder for me to remain in the building for any length of time. The place was frighteningly homogeneous. It wasn't just the institutional sameness of the walls and rooms; it was the voices and mannerisms of the nurses and the corresponding murmurs of the babies. From every direction came the same encouraging tones, the same techniques of positive reinforcement. Only people with a great affinity for babies could be employed as nurses, and their training was rigorous. Even on that first visit, after I had spent an hour in that atmosphere of designed cheerfulness, all the voices melded, and the whole building started to hum in a way that resonated with my skull, a maddening vibration that caused my mind to boil. It was difficult for me to remain calm as Keeva and I walked out the door. Holding my hand, she could feel the tension in me, and gave me a sidelong, puzzled glance that cut like a knife through my heart.

The babies themselves thrived in that atmosphere of the nurseries. They gave every appearance of good health and happiness. They remained there until they were able to walk on their own and had begun to develop the rudiments of sensible speech.

Every day around noon groups of children gathered at the nursery. On more than one occasion, Keeva and I stood nearby, hand in hand, and watched the event. And almost every day at least one nurse would emerge from the building with a squirming three-year-old in his arms. The child was simply handed to the nearest children and carried off into the streets with great shouts of celebration. I was of course shocked by all of this, but my anxiety subsided as I began to realize that the older children were actually conscientious about their parental duties. Keeva told me that when she had been a child on the streets, she was often one of the ones who took care of the new infants when they arrived.

I'm sure the transition period was difficult for the little ones, but their survival rate appeared to be high. They were carried around a great deal, and were always shielded from whatever danger might be present. But little danger existed in this city. And within a few days they could be seen running about wildly in the streets as if they'd always been there. I decided that the danger that foreigners often felt in Lomasaya was an illusion created by the sheer strangeness of the culture.

Another factor that eased my concern was the faces of the children. This was a handsome race of people that had inhabited this corner of the planet for thousands of years. Many of them, those who still lived in the old ways, were now relegated to the surrounding wilderness or worked in the fields of the farm belt to produce the city's food. It was not known how many of them still survived in the wilderness, for once there, they never returned, and city dwellers were forbidden entry to the wilderness. There was a tall nobility about the Lomasayan frame, but skin complexion and color were as varied as the autumn leaves. It wasn't their beauty, however, that moved me to an instinctive feeling of trust. Almost all of them, the children I mean, had a mixture of gentleness and good humor about them, a surface calmness in the eyes no matter what they might be doing. I am by no means a scientist or a psychologist, but I have always believed myself a perceptive observer of human behavior, though you must, of course, judge the value of my words for yourself. But I have never in all my travels seen such energetic, healthy children. And I cannot adequately explain why these strange methods should be so successful. By our criteria the younger children lived in appalling circumstances, with almost nothing in the way of clothing or shelter, and next to nothing indeed in the way of adult supervision. And yet they not only survived, but thrived. When I expressed my concerns to Keeva, she just laughed and said that she was a product of the streets and she had turned out okay.

"Do you want me to be different than I am?" she asked playfully.

"Of course not."

"Then watch how you assess our ways," she said, with an edgier flash in her eye.

There were of course some positive factors that aided in the children's success. For one thing, the streets were kept almost flawlessly free of refuge and filth by a large corps of maintenance personnel who were as vigilant in their service as the children were in their play. And the weather itself in the lowland of the city was mild year round. Also there were many natural springs in the surrounding area that provided the children an abundance of fresh, clean water. Within the city itself there were sculptured fountains fed by these springs in which the children could swim and bathe. Sitting on the wall of one of those fountains one day, Keeva reached back and splashed the back of my head, but was up and walking away before I could retaliate. More than most of the adults I met, Keeva maintained the children's spirit of play. While the children might appear dirty by our standards, they were essentially clean. Very little disease could be found among them, though broken bones and deep bruises resulting from their extravagant antics were frequent.

The children tended to divide themselves into many loosely formed groups. Leadership was informal and noncoercive as far as I could tell. One's relationship to the ultimate choice was everything, and they made the choice one way or the other by the age of twelve. After that there was no turning back. About two-thirds of the children chose to live in the adult world of Lomasaya and the farm belt. The others drifted into the Falladan forest and were never seen again. The children who reached the age of twelve without making a decision were routinely rounded up and taken to the wilderness border where they were forced to cross. Children had to decide whether to be civilized or wild. Keeva told me that for her personally it had been a very difficult decision. She had waited until the very day of her twelfth birthday to choose to be an adult of Lomasaya. And after she made her choice and scratched her mark on the papers, she was forlorn for months, even with the comfort and protection of her assigned "parents."

But before she made that decision, she was quite free and ran about half naked in the streets and had not a thought in her head nor a care in the world. I could understand why it was so hard for her to leave that life. I was astonished to see that many of the children attempted to breed soon after reaching puberty and were too often seen coupling in the alleys. Keeva told me these were teenagers who had stayed beyond their twelfth birthday without registering but who had managed to escape the round-ups and had not yet left the city for the wilderness. Girls of this group who became pregnant were allowed to deliver their babies in the same hospitals used by the adult women. In any case, these holdovers rarely reached the age of fourteen before they had joined the outward migration into the forest. Their date of birth was tattooed on a shoulder of every child during their first year, and the cold fact of the law could not be escaped.

Keeva told me how afraid but also excited she was on that first day when authorities delivered her to her assigned family, a middle-aged couple who had already raised one child. They were kind but she was trembling and already missed her friends on the street. But then the rigorous regimen of the educational system soon consumed her life. Within that first year, she discovered she wanted to be an artist and never looked back. Art saved her from her despair.

We were discussing these matters one day at the office between appointments. Keeva told me that she had greatly limited her sexual activity since officially choosing to become a member of the Lomasayan society at twelve. She was concerned about becoming pregnant because she didn't want to interrupt her active life. Likewise, she had avoided bonding with another person and entering into a household with them because she didn't want to be assigned a child to rear.

"What do you have against children?" I asked her.

"Nothing. I love children," she said. "I'm just not ready for those responsibilities."

But there was a slight faltering in her voice when she spoke these words, as if she were camouflaging a truth, keeping it both from herself and from me.

"What do you want?" I asked. I knew I was prying, but I couldn't keep the words from shooting out of my mouth.

She abruptly turned away from the work of her hands and glared at me. The blades of her eyes when she was perturbed were the sharpest I have ever witnessed. If she had extended that stare for another moment, I might well have dropped dead then and there. But she didn't. She stood up and pushed the chair away.

"I have some errands to run," she said. She strode out of the office and disappeared.

Of course, I immediately regretted asking the question. I sat there alone in my office. Soon, my next appointment showed up. But without Keeva to translate, no real business could be conducted. When my client left, I considered what Keeva had told me about child-rearing in Lomas-aya. Once a child committed himself to the adult world, he was kept apart from the children that ran wild in the streets. In residential areas of the city, houses were built around communal yards that were walled in. One of the buildings that opened onto this communal yard was the school. There was at least one teacher for every ten children. A large part of the population went into the profession of teaching. Keeva told me she had considered it, but she was an ambitious artist and decided to give her time and energy to that pursuit which was generously supported by the government.

Everything these people built or made was considered to be art. There was no end to their concern for detail, perspective, spatial relationship and the like. The study of aesthetics with all of its theoretical and practical ramifications was the core of their approach to education. In their work, individuality and inclusivity were somehow conjoined with an extreme sense of structure and conformity. I was learning that almost everything about this culture was paradoxical in one way or another.

When I was there, all of the arts were caught up in the lush complexities of detail and ornateness that we associate with the Baroque and Rococo. Those few artists who worked against the grain in a more minimalist approach were a welcome relief to me. Keeva was such an artist.

Each day, Keeva set aside an hour or two to take me by the hand and guide me on long walks in the city to show me the architecture and the galleries. Sometimes we sat near the extraordinary fountain in the park and just watched people. She invited me to ask questions, and so continued her instruction of me in the ways of the Lomasayans. I was cautious, but I could not help but notice the warmth of her hand in mine, of her thigh pressed tightly against mine, as we talked and laughed and observed the people. It felt almost as though she were grooming me for some role I might have to play, but when I kiddingly expressed this view, she just laughed and pushed me away. Her laughter was profound. Like most Lomasayans, her bearing was calm and relaxed to the point of appearing stoic. For the longest time, her face would remain absolutely relaxed and expressionless. But when something struck her as humorous, her face came alive and was richly seductive. The Lomasayan sense of humor, she said, derived from the games of their free children.

She told me that the education of the "eight-year-olds" was a great deal more formal than that of the "twelve-year-olds." They became the masters of their language and studied higher mathematics, philosophy, literature, history, and law.

"Are you sorry you didn't choose to register when you were eight instead?"

"Not at all," she said. "I loved those years in the street. It was the most freedom I've ever known."

"And the wilderness would be even more freedom. Are you sorry you chose the city when you turned twelve?"

Her eyes flashed. "Why are you digging into me like this?"

"I'm not digging. I just want to know more about you, understand you."

"I have no regrets," she said. "And you will never understand me."

She shifted the subject quickly and said that those of low ambition or ability from both groups were channeled into various battalions of the lower-skilled work force, such as the interior and exterior maintenance crews, construction laborers, messenger-carriers, and the like. But there was really no low-level work in this society. Every form of work was honored and carried with it a sense of prideful achievement and a salary conducive to comfort. She insisted that neither unemployment nor poverty existed in Lomasaya. Every city has its other side of the tracks, I thought. I just hadn't found it yet.

Most interestingly, adults with their assigned children at their sides went about the business of their lives in the streets as if the free children were invisible. Keeva said the most unsettling sight for outsiders was the juxtaposition of the civilized children and the younger wild ones.

These circumstances created the most unusual aspect of the Lomasay-an culture. While the adults were ignoring them, the wild children were absolutely fascinated by the adults. Children gathered in small groups at street corners, at the entrances to stores and government buildings, any place they might find adults going about their business. For long periods of time children would lounge in a colorful pile of bodies, small ones wrapped in the arms of older ones, watching in complete silence, studying the nuances of adult speech and movement, the way they dressed and shaped their hair. Then the children would slowly begin to move and laugh among themselves. Keeva's eyes always brightened when she saw this happening. I sometimes felt that the children were the true rulers of this culture and that watching the adults was their own special form of entertainment. But they went much farther than just watching. They were masters of imitation and mockery. They loved to follow an adult around in the street, mimicking his or her every step and gesture: the stiff, slow shuffle of an old woman; the arrogant, careless strides of a politician; the slim, glittering elegance of an actress; the self-conscious spiffiness of a student. If two or three adults were together, then two or three children would take them on as a challenge, deepening their voices into serious pronouncements, sticking out their bellies and gesturing with their hands. Their imitations employed the exaggerated elements of caricature. I was myself the victim of their antics many times. Some little boy would come skittering up beside me, synchronizing his step with mine. Then the strange contortions would begin: a gangly, slew-footed shuffle, puffed-out lower lip the result of a slight underbite, nervous hands searching for a place to rest. Surely these were complete fabrications, as I had been an athlete when younger and had a strong, agile way of moving through space.

Keeva enjoyed these antics of the children to no end. Sometimes, when a child appeared beside her in order to imitate and mock her, Keeva would join the kid in exaggerating her own long-strided, athletic movement. And she positively exploded into laughter at the sight of a child imitating me and would often join in. At such times, other adults in the street would have to make room for us and our wild gyrations because I soon found myself leaping about as well. I could tell by the strained expressions on their faces that the adults were not pleased.

During my stay in Lomasaya I was, of course, a guest of the adults. Communication with the ones who lived in the wilderness outside the city was forbidden. The strictness of the boundary around the city was, I admit, unnerving to me. No matter how far afield Keeva led me in our walks in the city, it still felt claustrophobic.

Out of curiosity, I attended religious services held in the city's main cathedral several times. As I recall, there was much pomp and ritual and reverence, not unlike Catholicism at its most formal, though the imagery was more atavistic, using the animal figures from their worldview. Also, in ancient times, when wilderness had been the only way of life, there arose among them a man of great character and personal power. They called him Lomasay. "We are both one and many," he would say. "Where there are many acting as one, death is defeated." As far as ethics goes, they believed the spirit guided them within the context of each situation. The people universally practiced "The Art of Convincing" as it was demonstrated by Lomasay himself and his disciples, and as it was passed down from generation to generation by the priests. The most notable effects of this openness in their philosophy could be seen in the realm of sexuality.

Keeva took great pleasure in telling me about the Lomasayan approach to Eros. Sex was a gift, she told me, like the ability to open and close one's hand. Adults, both young and old, partook of each other sexually without guilt or shame. Only coercion was forbidden, and only a certain amount of decorum, including privacy, was expected. This produced a degree of contentment among the adult masses that might otherwise have been absent. Because they had all grown up in the streets where nudity and sexual expression were not discriminated against, they experienced no fear or repression concerning the body and its functions. To the best of my knowledge no prostitutes existed in their city, no scantily clad ladies dancing on the stages of sleazy bars, no pornography. There was no market for them.

Being a young man as yet unmarried, I confess I had mixed feelings about this sexual promiscuity. In the first few weeks of my time in Lomasaya, a number of women made what I considered overtures of a sexual nature. And though I was tempted, I was also repelled, I suppose, due to my own sexually repressed upbringing. But my relationship with Keeva was different, because she carefully cultivated a real friendship between us. I enjoyed her company. I delighted in her physical presence, though I kept my attraction to myself as much as I could. I didn't want to offend her. Plus, she had made clear to me her reasons for restraint in her sexual affairs.

One day when Keeva and I were engaged with some of the children who were particularly outlandish in their antics, we found ourselves carried away by a gang of them to a neighborhood I hadn't seen before. Here, no adults were present except for Keeva and me. The buildings appeared to be warehouses with little activity. Narrow alleys were lined with many pallet beds. Small stoves containing fires stood here and there. The children played various games with balls and hoops or lay on their pallets napping. "As you can see," Keeva said, "they supervise themselves." I noted that some of the older children were teaching the younger ones how to play a game. Others were sitting with younger ones and talking to them. "The buildings on either side here remain empty," Keeva said. "They take shelter in there when it's raining or cold or hot."

"Can we take a look inside?" I asked.

"No. We are not permitted."

"This is how you grew up?"

"Yes," she said.

Children came running up to us and asked us to join their play. And we did, a game where someone threw a ball against the wall in such a way that it would come back to them and not the others. It was very difficult to be successful, even for me. I would throw the ball, it would come bounding back to me, and some athletic ten-year-old would jump in front of me and snatch it. Then it was his turn to throw, and amazingly he could find ways to make the ball return to him without being intercepted by the mob of kids between him and the wall. I forgot myself for a while and jumped around wildly in my effort to succeed at the game in the midst of raucous and infectious laughter. I stopped for a rest and saw Keeva watching me and laughing. The next thing I knew I was in a passionate embrace with her. Several of the kids gathered around us, laughing. After a moment she separated from me, her eyes alive with the nearby fires, took my hand and led me away from there with a few goodbyes to the children, a group of which followed us to the end of the alley before turning back. I don't believe I had ever seen Keeva so excited before, as she drew me swiftly through the streets without a word for perhaps half a mile. We entered one of the many buildings that contained small apartments for unattached women. She took out a key, opened one of the doors, and pulled me in behind her. Darkness. A moment later a light came on.

We were standing in a small living room/dining room, with a couch, a table, and a few chairs. A door led into a narrow kitchen, another into a small bathroom, and the last into the bedroom. The walls were covered with the most wonderful abstract paintings. As my eyes adjusted, I realized they were actually expressionistic portraits of animals and humans. I had to focus and look through my eyes in a certain way to see how confident brush strokes of many colors coalesced into a face, or a body in action, revealing, somehow, the core attitude of the subject, the heart and mind of a real being.

"Are these yours?" I asked.

"Yes."

"They're amazing."

She smiled. "Let's talk about art later."

She led me into the bedroom. She pushed me onto the bed, stood before me, and began to remove her clothes. Her movements had none of the attributes of a strip tease. She was neither rushed nor hesitant. Within a minute, she stood before me naked. I admit that my sexual experience at this time was limited, but she was stunning. My heart pounded, and my state of arousal was painful. She laughed.

"What are you waiting for?" she asked.

She grabbed my hands, stood me up, and started taking off my clothes. "Help me," she said.

It was as if I were in a trance, but I woke up enough to help her get me out of my clothes. As I did so, I noticed for the first time a tattoo on her right shoulder. I ran my fingers over it. She stopped her work for a moment and looked at me.

"My date of birth," she said. I nodded. Then she helped me get out of my shoes.

Our lovemaking seemed to me to have little in common with the sex I had experienced back home. It was slow and sweet and beautiful. She wouldn't allow me to rush anything, which produced the most agonizing pleasure. Beyond that, there was something essential about the way she made love, as if the most fundamental and vital aspect of who she was, was finding and drawing out the same in me. The rest of me, my history and my work, fell away, and only that moment—that touch, that whispered word—existed.

The Lomasayan approach to love was much different from my culture's attitudes. A man fell in love with "woman"; and a woman fell in love with "man." In each case the person took all members of the opposite sex as his or her lover, a way of life that made for a tremendous amount of personal freedom. Homosexual relationships were certainly a distinct minority, but they also appeared to function in a context of openness and were assimilated into the culture seamlessly. But for an outsider like me unaccustomed to their ways, this freedom brought on feelings of hollowness and fear. In Lomasaya any two people, regardless of sex, could form a household, a family unit, for the purpose of raising children. It had nothing to do with a division of roles and attitudes based upon sexual norms, nor did it relate to carrying on a family bloodline or heritage. There was such a custom as marriage in Lomasaya: two people swore to a vow of celibacy and joined for the purpose of raising "eight-year-olds" to the priesthood. Those who wore the robes of celibacy were off limits sexually and were held in great reverence. As I lay in bed beside the sleeping Keeva, I thought about all of these unusual conventions. I wondered what would be the future of our love, of our relationship. Did Keeva have other lovers? Did she, in fact, love me in any way I could understand and recognize?

The Lomasayans lived without conflict, but that was the greatest irony of their lives. For one of the most noticeable characteristics of the adults to an outsider was their eyes. I hadn't noticed this attribute at first, but became increasingly aware of it over time. After looking into those eyes for months, it became clear to me that it was the adults who were wild. All of them, even Keeva. I soon felt that each one of them was capable of the most unpredictable behavior at any moment, though I never witnessed or experienced the slightest discourtesy or indiscretion of any kind. But the likelihood of much worse lurked in their eyes where terror and passionate anger and fierce ill humor all met at a deeper level beneath the calm surface. That at least is how I interpreted what I saw. I began to feel that were it not for the release of energies provided by their sexual freedom, murder and chaos would be much more the norm for these people. I think this partly explains why they kept themselves so busy creating, building and organizing, and why they felt they had to maintain such rigid formality in their daily lives. I managed, to a degree, to ignore this look of wildness, finding a number of rationalizations to discount it. For example, I suspected that it was a physical characteristic of their race and was not a reflection of their internal state of mind and emotion. This theory seemed to be supported by statistics that showed the almost total nonexistence of violent crime, or any other kind of crime for that matter. Still, it was disconcerting to hear cordial tones of voice coming from a distinguished gentleman who seemed to have murder in his eyes.

Keeva's eyes somehow contained but transcended this sharpness. In them, I saw the sweetest affection toward me. Not long after we had our first sexual encounter, it became clear to me that I was in love with her. I wanted to be more certain about her feelings for me. But whenever I would broach the subject, her eyes would grow puzzled. She knew my language, but her mind couldn't extract from it exactly what I was saying. I decided to let it go. Her lovemaking and the intimacy of her friendship said everything I needed to know. I started to make plans about taking her back home with me. I wondered what my family and friends would think of her. I thought about the book my father had given me on the dangerous strangeness of Lomasayan women, but decided the author of that book did not know Keeva and could not possibly understand the greater subtleties at play.

More generally though, it was this paradox of Lomasayan demeanor, this sense of conflict and anguish beneath the surface of every courteous encounter, that produced in me an anxiety that I found difficult to escape, and a curiosity about the way of life of the wild ones in the forest. Was this what they had chosen to avoid? What had enabled them to break completely from this highly developed culture that produced them? And what kind of culture had they evolved on their own? Since the wilderness had remained intact, since other cities had never formed, I could only suppose that they were nomadic hunters and food-gatherers. Beyond this, all speculation seemed foolish. In any case, the Lomasayan fear of the wilderness rubbed off on me. The adults could never go into the wilderness to find out what was going on there. This subject was the one source of embarrassment and confusion for them, and I quickly learned to steer clear of it. The irony of this situation was that the wild ones knew what they had left behind, while the adults had no knowledge of life in the wilderness. There was something about this fact that seemed to eat away at the philosophical certainty of the adults, undercutting their fierce pride in the achievement of Lomasaya. The wilderness was two hundred miles wide in many places and completely encircled the city. Were the boundaries strictly adhered to? Did Falladans in the wilderness cross illegally into bordering countries?

In an attempt to understand more, I asked Keeva if she would direct me to any written resources that could explain. The next day on our walking excursion in the city she took me to the CFL, the Central Falladan Library. This was yet another immense government structure covered in gargoyles, as if it were attempting to protect the dreams of every Lomasayan. I noted that each gargoyle was unique, an independent creature sitting shoulder to shoulder with the gargoyles on either side. Over the next few days I spent time in this building, but very little of Falladan literature and history had been translated into my language. My reading skills in Falladan were limited. Plus, no Falladan book was more than seventy-five pages long. And a book dedicated to, say, a history of the city of Lomasaya, would invariably break into poetic psalms of praise for buildings and architects and artists and poets. Poetry trumped history in every book I consulted. Consequently I was able to piece together only the most limited outline of their past. I wish I could say that Keeva was a help to me. But she appeared to have no interest in what we, the people of my culture, call "history." Slowly I realized that even the notion of "memory" was less developed in Falladan psychology. Using my limited Falladan, I asked the head librarian if he could recommend a book on the wilderness that surrounded Lomasaya. A puzzled look came into his eyes, and then, after a moment of thought, they went altogether blank. He became very still, just staring straight ahead. I waited for a few moments, but he didn't move or say a word. It was as if the mere mention of the wilderness had flipped a switch in the librarian's brain that eliminated thought and speech. After another moment or two, I returned to my carrel, gathered my notes and materials, and left.

Later that evening, after making love, Keeva and I lay curled up comfortably together in her bed. Her eyes were closed and she appeared to be drifting off to sleep.

"Keeva, I had an interesting experience in the library today," I said.

"Hmmmm," she said.

"Yes, the librarian went into a trance right in front of me. He was still in it when I left maybe ten minutes later."

A small smile crossed her lips, and a chuckle thrummed deep in her throat. But I could tell she was drifting deeper toward sleep.

"Really," I said. But she didn't respond. "All I did was ask for information about the wilderness. And he went completely blank."

That seemed to reach her. Her eyes flickered open. Her hand came up to the side of my face. When she spoke, her breath was warm and fragrant from the Falladan vodka we had drunk after dinner.

"The unknown is the unknown," she whispered. "For that reason, there is no writing about the wilderness. We know nothing to write. You can only know it if you go there. If you go, there is no coming back. Truly, no one ever returns. Your question triggered the librarian into the realm of no thought, which occurs when the mind's pursuit reaches its logical end. Mentally, he was drifting in formless emptiness. I'm sure he returned from there shortly. But I have a question for you. Do you want to go into the wilderness?"

I shook my head. I had a spirit of adventure for the cities of the world. But wilderness had always frightened me. I had always admired those people who could strike out into backcountry with backpacks and stay there for days or even weeks on end. But sleeping on the hard ground, tolerating the cold, and encountering mountain lions and bears, did not appeal to me. Keeva was gazing into my eyes and smiling.

"I have to tell you something," she said.

"What's that?"

"I'm pregnant."

I felt a switch flip in my mind. I suspect my eyes went from puzzlement to a blank stare, very much as the librarian's eyes had.

"Well?" she said. "Don't go wandering in the realm of no thought."

"I . . . I don't know what to say, yet." The most natural question arose in me, though I tried to fend it off.

"Yes," she said, "it's yours." She drew her face closer to mine and looked steadily into my eyes.

"This is a good thing, right?" I said.

"Of course it is," she said.

"But, what am I supposed to do? I want to do whatever is right. It's just that things are so different here."

She smiled again. "You bear no responsibility for the child. You know that's how it works here. I just wanted you to know."

"But what about you? What responsibility do you have?"

"I bear the baby to term. And then it becomes a child of Lomasaya. And I'm free again." But her eyes fell away from me as she said these words. And I once again felt a current of emotion held in check within her.

The fire of shame and regret spread through my body, while at the same time I breathed a sigh of relief. The two feelings created a nervous tension right down to my bones. I started to climb out of bed, but Keeva held my face to the pillow with her hand.

"Don't leave me, please, right now," she said.

"You could go back home with me," I said. "We could set up a house and raise our child."

"You would do that for me?"

"Yes, in a heartbeat," I said. The words just jumped out of me, without thought. I felt good about that. It was the right thing.

"Falladan women do not fare well in your world. The ones who go return within a year full of sadness and regret. We have almost no suicide in Fallada, but some of those women kill themselves."

"It would be different for us," I said. "I know both worlds, and I could help you adjust. And we could raise our child."

"But we would be raising it in your world," she said. "And your world is a dark place."

"No darker than yours," I said.

"I believe it is," she said, "much darker."

A flood of defenses for my country and my home city rushed into my mind, but I held my tongue. I knew this was the right path for us, but I didn't want to rush it or force it on Keeva. I wanted to persuade her slowly, over time, so she would feel she had come to it herself. I let the subject rest. I held her close as she fell asleep, knowing that I would not likely sleep at all that night. I couldn't bear the thought of my child growing up in the wild streets of Lomasaya.

The next few months were among the best and the most difficult of my life. Business was going very well. I had established a number of lines of trade between Lomasayan artisans and artists with the outside world. Lomasayan sculpture and pottery and paintings and even such edibles as cookies were highly prized. I had talked Keeva into allowing some of her paintings to be sold and shipped. But I couldn't detect that she was using the money to make any changes in her life. I continued to slowly practice the "art of convincing" to make her understand how we could build a fine life with our child in the outside world. But we would have to leave together before she gave birth so that she could have her child in the best hospital in my country. In the beginning she would wave me off whenever I opened the topic. But gradually she would just smile and tolerate my talking, but she didn't have much to add to my words. I took this as a good sign. She was slowly changing her mind, allowing herself to imagine how it could work. I could see this happening, though I knew her pride wouldn't permit her to say it.

Our work together continued as usual. And I was making a lot of money, saving it up for the day when Keeva went home with me. I wrote my father and told him to prepare a place for us, and he wrote me back saying that I'd gone crazy just as he'd feared I would. But he acquiesced and found a small home for us near his own, which he filled with furniture and all of the necessities of a couple with a small child.

When I told Keeva about these plans one morning at breakfast, she laid the forkful of food she was raising to her mouth back into her plate.

She sighed, and shook her head slightly. Her amazing eyes changed suddenly, as if they became more of a surface than an entrance, as if she were now looking at a blurry space rather than a man.

"Why didn't you tell me you were doing this?" she said.

"I guess I wanted to surprise you."

"And you did," she said, "but some surprises aren't . . ." She hesitated.

"I thought you like surprises."

"I do, but there are some things we should work on together."

"Look, if it's because my father—"

"I'm sure his tastes are excellent."

"They are," I said.

"This has nothing to do with him."

"Don't you like the idea of a house?"

"I'm sure the house is wonderful."

"Yes, I know it is," I said.

"And I'm sure . . ." She caught herself. I waited for a moment, but she had become as still as the librarian.

"Sure of what?" I said, finally.

She slid her chair back and stood up, tossing her napkin over the half-eaten plate of food. "Sure that I'm going to be late for work." She headed across the room toward the bedroom.

"You work for me," I said.

She stopped in her tracks and turned to look at me. Those eyes. "I know whom I work for," she said. She was particularly careful to pronounce "whom." She turned and strolled into the bedroom to dress. I could feel how disciplined she was not to slam the door.

I don't want to say there was a cooling off of our relationship after that conversation, but it definitely changed. We continued to be lovers, as before, but if our lovemaking became less passionate, it nevertheless became more tender. This seemed like a natural evolution to me.

As the months passed, I didn't notice much change in Keeva's body. Of course, she often wore loose clothing as was her style, and that may have had something to do with it. As far as I could tell, when I saw her unclothed, her belly was almost as flat as it had always been. Until she reached about five months, and then the bulge became more prominent. And I knew it was really going to happen. I felt both happiness and fear. One day in her apartment she let me kiss her belly and press my ear against it.

I looked up at Keeva and said, "Did you hear it?"

"No," she said, laughing. "What?"

I made my voice small and high. "She said, 'Take me to Daddy's world.'"

Keeva quickly covered her belly and just looked at me. She stood and walked into her bedroom, but then she came right back out.

"I'm afraid to let my child be raised in your world," she said.

"I'm afraid to let her be raised in yours."

"Her? You keep saying 'her.'"

"Or him," I said.

"You don't hear anything I say," she said. And then she walked back into her bedroom and shut the door. This was her M.O. To exit, when stressed, into a more interior space. And what had she said that I was supposed to be hearing?

As she entered her sixth month, her belly became more prominent. But Keeva remained as active as always. In fact, we took a day off because I had asked her about the power supply for the city, and she wanted to show me. Lomasaya didn't seem to have any shortage of electrical power. I already knew that solar panels were imported and used liberally all over the city. Lomasayans were ingenious at integrating the panels into their architectural designs. But these panels alone were not enough to supply all of such a large city. Living in Lomasaya was like returning to the nineteenth century in the way people dressed and the way they mostly walked wherever they needed to go, rode bicycles, or hired man-carts. There were a wide variety of man-cart options. Keeva rented one for us to ride to the border of the farm territory. There, we changed to a horse-drawn cart for the ten miles to the wilderness border where electricity was generated by the power plant of a great dam. The Jujoni River flowed over huge boulders from the wilderness boundary. Keeva explained that "Jujoni" is a word in Falladan that means "sourceless." The Falladan mind was rarely occupied with wonderings about sources. They preferred to dwell in the auras of mystery. The river itself was the source of energy and much of Lomasaya's fresh water. But what was the source of the river? Since there were no state-sponsored expeditions into the wilderness, and since citizen expeditions were forbidden, they would never know. As Keeva and I inspected the dam, the reservoir above it, and the continuing river beneath it, I was struck with the technical expertise it would have required to build it.

"Forgive me for asking, Keeva, but how did Lomasayans manage to build such a massive and efficient structure?"

"Outsiders were brought in to help us solve the engineering problems. It took us twenty years of continuous work. But we accomplished it with many innovative engineering solutions. Still, it was very difficult. We salute the engineering . . . prowess . . . of your society. Still, our people are very proud of the Jujoni Dam."

"You say outsiders came. Since I've been here, I don't believe I've encountered a single one. Why is that?"

"They're here," she said, "in small numbers. We don't encourage them to gather together. We spread them out so they will learn to manage on their own in the city. And we don't allow more than a hundred at any one time."

"Are Falladans afraid of what outsiders might do if they were allowed to congregate together?"

"Outsiders are ambitious, judgmental. They begin to see ways they can make Fallada into what they want it to be. You know better than anyone how your people are. Right?"

I could tell I was supposed to acknowledge what she had said, so I nodded.

"We send them away before problems can happen, unless they are serving us well without trying to change us. You, for example, have been allowed to stay because you have adapted to us, and you haven't sought to manipulate us. You make money for yourself, yes, but you also make money for us."

We climbed several switchbacking flights of stairs up to an observation platform. It looked across to that point where the river broke through and over a field of boulders on the border between Lomasaya and the wilderness. I couldn't stop thinking about the source of that river in the mountains. Was it a glacier high up in the peaks? I would like to see such a glacier, but I knew I would never embark on that journey, even if it were allowed. While we stood there, several Falladans had come to look. They bowed down on one knee, touched the gathered fingers of their right hand to their forehead or their hearts, and entered into deep, silent prayer before standing and walking away.

"Falladans seem to worship this river," I said.

"Yes, we do, because it brings life."

"So why don't you seek the source of it?"

"You know why. Anyone who crosses the border into the wilderness is not allowed to return."

"Yes, but why?"

Her eyes grew distant with impatience. She was no longer talking to me, her lover, the father of her soon to be born child, but to an ignorant outsider. "This law is fundamental to the absolute separation of city and wilderness that defines and guarantees the survival of Falladan—and more particularly—Lomasayan culture."

I shook my head. I wanted to ask another "why" question. Why was this separation so necessary? I just couldn't understand it. Wouldn't it be even better to have a free exchange of ideas between the people in the wilderness and the city? After all, they are all brothers and sisters. But I was not about to ask. I could see that this was an issue I should let go of for the moment. But as we took our leave of the Jujoni dam and found our horse-drawn cart, which might be better described as a stagecoach, another question occurred to me. We climbed aboard, took our seats, and signaled to our driver.

"Why is it that older, adult Lomasayans don't escape to the wilderness?" I asked.

"Because there is nothing to escape *from*. They made their decision, and they love their city," she said with a sidelong glance.

"Yes, but surely there are some, maybe only a few, who are unhappy here."

She exhaled heavily. "Okay, yes, I suppose there are. But entering the wilderness as an adult is against the law. Guards are stationed at all of the trailheads. But of course it's possible to sneak across if you really want to badly enough. But once you have crossed, you may not return. Returners are treated harshly."

"But if you can sneak across, surely it's possible to sneak back again."

"Okay, it's possible. Perhaps there are a few who do it. But it would be unwise of them to talk about their adventures in open society. And if you ask 'why' I may have to punch you in the nose."

I like my nose, so I kept quiet. But I wondered if there weren't an underground subculture of adventurers in Lomasaya who kept their own counsel. Like the subconscious part of any mind, the city had to have its hidden territories. I hoped to meet someone from this shadow zone of the city.

As Keeva entered the seventh month of her pregnancy, her belly began to swell much more noticeably. She had a few days when she didn't feel well, and on those days I went to the office and attached a note to the door saying we were closed for the day. Couriers and clients would slip their messages under the door and I would catch up on things the next day. I had been in Lomasaya for almost two years, but I still didn't fully grasp their language, though I could communicate crudely. And so being in my office without my translator was very nearly pointless. Understanding my clients precisely was key to the business we conducted. Besides, I wanted to stay home with Keeva. But like pregnant mothers everywhere, Keeva didn't always want the company of her mate. Sometimes she would retreat to her studio that was in a separate room on the floor above reserved for artist studios. From experience I knew better than to intrude with my presence when she was painting. So I often went for long walks in the city.

I systematically explored districts that Keeva hadn't shown me. Many were suburbs full of communal dwellings around courtyards favored by households who were raising children. But eventually I found areas of the city where people appeared to be less a part of that highly structured culture. Here, more people were just hanging out on the street. They weren't bustling around purposefully. They were talking. Some of them carried books that appeared to be from other countries. They wore informal clothing like jeans and knitted shirts. They looked at me and my suit suspiciously as I passed them. Here, the buildings were not well defined on the outside, but they were surely the abodes of the people I saw in the streets, probably small apartments. I wouldn't say that these people were poor, but they did seem to be less affluent than those I had met before this time.

Here, I found certain establishments where people were gathering and obviously imbibing an alcoholic drink. In the more established parts of the city, alcohol was certainly available, mostly Falladan-made whiskey and gin and vodka, and people locked it away in cabinets and partook of it cautiously when the children were asleep. Here, it was out in the open, and it was some kind of homemade brew. At last I summoned enough courage to walk into one of these . . . I want to call them bars. The conversation stopped as I entered and everyone turned to look at me. I sat down at a table near the door in case I needed to get out of there fast. At first I acknowledged their stares by looking back at them, and I nodded in a friendly way. Then I kept my eyes to myself, making a close study of my hands. After a few minutes, the people turned back to their conversations. What I felt from them was more curiosity than threat. I was self-conscious about my clothing, but there wasn't much I could do about that.

At last a young man showed up at my table. He spoke, and I thought that he was asking if I wanted something to drink. I was uncertain what the words for "beer" or "whiskey" were in Falladan. So I gestured to the table next to me where the people were drinking a brownish liquid from pint-sized glasses. The young man smiled, nodded, and said "bracca." He turned and went to the bar that was located at the back of the room. Moments later he brought me one of those glasses filled to the brim with bracca and set it on the table before me. Before I had a chance to take some Falladan money from my pocket, the young man walked away. The men and women at the nearest table raised their glasses to me, and I raised mine to them. I suddenly felt a lot more comfortable in this room. I took a sip. It was room temperature, had a thick texture, and was mildly sweet. Not bad. Why hadn't Keeva shown me this part of town? I would have spent time here had I known about it. I settled in and thought about the possibility of taking Keeva home with me. I would have to be more persuasive than I'd been so far.

As I started on my third glass of bracca, two men and a woman strolled over to my table and sat down. I was surprised, but again they were not threatening in any way. They carried their glasses of bracca with them, but they gave no evidence of being drunk. Their clothes were not exactly shabby but well-worn, work clothes I'd say. Maybe they were gardeners or carpenters. Their hands, including the woman's, were calloused and looked as if they could bend bars or carve subtle images into wood if required.

One of the young men, who was about thirty I would guess, said, "How are you doing, sir?" in my language.

"Very well," I said, and that was no lie. Bracca creates a distinct sense of wellbeing.

"We're glad to hear it," he said.

I raised my glass to him, and he returned the gesture. "Thank you for speaking my language," I said. "I wish I could speak yours more fluently."

"Ours is a difficult language," he said, "filled with tributaries of inference. It takes many years to master it. You shouldn't feel bad about the level you've reached in such a short time in our country."

I had said nothing about the amount of time I'd spent in the country.

"Yes," he said, "I'm aware of who you are. We all are." He gestured around the room. "But we didn't expect to see you here."

"How and why would you know me?" I asked.

"Because there are so few from your country who remain here as long as you have. The rumors spread that an outsider has taken up residence. But you are most welcome here. We hold no grudges. We consider each man or woman as an individual."

I wondered what he was referring to with "grudges," but I decided it would be better not to go down that path. "I'm grateful," I said.

"Some of our people here are artists and they're making money from your transactions, so we are also grateful. Many of the outsiders who come are only takers. They pretend to give, but everything they offer turns to dust, or worse."

"I'm really glad to hear that what I do is helpful," I said. "I try to get the most money I can for your art because it's so beautiful." To be safe, I didn't respond to the "takers" part of his comments. Clearly these people had a history with outsiders.

We talked like this for maybe half an hour. All three of them were courteous and friendly. One was a plumber, one a carpenter, and one designed and made clothes. In this country, it meant that all of them were also artists.

Finally I asked him, "What is this drink?"

He laughed and said, "Do you really want to know?"

"Absolutely," I said.

"It's made exclusively by the women of this area and also by the women in the wilderness. There they gather roots and bark and parts of various plants, mostly a wild potato and certain berries. They mash it into a paste, and then they chew it for a while and spit it into ceramic containers made for the purpose. The enzymes in the women's saliva start the fermentation process. It is a very ancient recipe, sir, very important to us. We're honored that you like it."

I didn't betray my momentary revulsion at the fact that I was drinking women's saliva. I was even more interested by the information that it was made by women in the wilderness. "So you must have some sort of exchange with wilderness people," I said.

"Of course," he said. "We are all the same people. We have just made different choices, that's all."

"But . . ."

He held up his hand and interrupted me. "Don't pursue this line of questioning, sir. For our sakes, and for your own."

"Of course," I said. "My apologies."

We spoke together for a few more minutes, but then the three of them conferred with each other in Falladan and the man turned to me.

"We have been occupying your time long enough, sir. Someone important wishes to speak to you. Thank you for the conversation. We have enjoyed it." With that, the three of them rose and returned to the table from which they had come. Almost immediately a woman made her way toward me. It was Keeva. My heart turned over. But as she neared I realized that this woman wasn't pregnant, and Keeva most definitely was. Then I saw a subtle difference in the way she carried herself and in the way she wore her long hair. This woman tied it so that it ran in a black river down her back. She smiled at me suspiciously as she sat down at my table. I nodded to her. I noted that she did not have a drink in her hand. She simply looked at me for a long moment. I had become accustomed to this behavior from Falladans, especially the women.

It took me a moment to believe that I wasn't looking into Keeva's eyes, but then I began to note subtle differences in attitude and expectation there. And I had the distinct feeling that she saw me seeing those differences.

"Much can be learned just from looking, isn't that so?" were her first words to me.

"Yes," I said. "That's one of many things I have learned from your people."

"You speak with consideration, but are you a truly considerate man?" she asked.

"I'd like to think I am," I said.

She gestured to the young man at the bar and he came to the table bearing a ceramic pitcher. He poured my glass full again. The woman nodded at him appreciatively, and he went away.

"I am Keeva's sister," she said when she turned back to me. "I made the poor decision to be absorbed into society at the age of eight. She wisely waited until the age of twelve. Once she was in, it became very difficult for us to see each other. They made sure we were raised in different parts of the city. But now in adulthood we have become friends again."

"She never told me she had a sister. People don't speak about brothers and sisters here."

"That's because it's considered nonessential information by the government, but for some of us it remains relatively important. There is more going on in Lomasaya than you can imagine from the position you hold here."

"I'm beginning to see that."

"Are you?"

That stopped me. Clearly she felt that I wasn't seeing very much. "Keeva has shown me only a limited part of the city," I said. "I now realize it was only the parts she wanted an outsider to see."

"And that's as it should be. Don't you agree?"

"I don't know."

"It's quite a surprise to find you here, in this establishment."

"I like it here, quite a lot."

"You are industrious, I admire that, but there must, at some point, come an end to it."

"You mean I'm forbidden to enter this part of the city?"

"I mean you will not be taking my beloved sister to your country," she said in a somewhat stronger voice. People at the nearby tables turned to watch and listen. "You may come and go as you please, you may enjoy our food and drink, you may speak to whomever you wish . . . but there are some privileges you do not have."

I had not expected this turn in our discussion. I wasn't sure how to proceed. "I'm not forcing her," I said.

"You are forcing her to make a decision," she said. "Has she not been forced to make enough decisions already?"

I didn't know what she was referring to. What decisions? To be absorbed by the culture at the age of twelve? To be an artist? What other decisions had she made?

"I don't know . . ."

"This is the problem," she said, "you know nothing, but you think you know everything."

"I want my . . . mate . . . and my child . . . to be . . ."

"She is not your mate, you fool. And that baby will never be your child. Here, there are no husbands and wives. There are no fathers and mothers. There is no ownership of people."

"It's not like that," I said, "I'm not like that. I'm not talking about ownership. I'm talking about love."

She stood up and pushed her chair back. "We have seen what happens to our beloved sisters who are taken to your country by men like you in the name of love."

"I'm not like them," I protested.

"Don't you know they all say that? It always turns out the same."

I didn't know what to say. I wanted somehow to turn the conversation and keep her engaged, to convince her that I was different. "What is your name?" I asked.

"What?!" she shouted. "You aren't listening to anything I say. You don't need to know my name."

Then she turned and walked briskly away. Her long hair swung as she pushed through the door to the street. The people at the other tables all turned away from me, muttering to each other. I sat there for a few minutes more, trying to understand what had just happened. I stayed long enough to finish my glass of bracca. I did not want them to think I had been intimidated. When I left, darkness was coming on, and I wasn't as stable on my feet as usual.

It was a three-mile walk back to Keeva's apartment. Darkness descended on the city. I passed from the dingier but somehow more interesting district of the city back into the more upwardly mobile sector. The cool air and my steady pace slowly sobered me up. I began to feel some urgency about getting back to Keeva. I ran into her apartment building, ran down the hall to her door, and stopped. The door had been left slightly ajar. I pushed it open. The main room was dim. I turned on the overhead light that cast a yellowish film over the scene. The room was largely as I had left it hours before. Two cups leftover from morning coffee were still on the table. The bathroom door was open. I could see in, and Keeva wasn't there. The bedroom door was closed. I pushed it open. The room was dark. I could see just enough to know that something was different. I turned on the light. At first glance Keeva did not appear to be in the room. Second and third glances were no better. "Keeva," I said, but not to call her. I knew she wasn't there. Some of her clothes were missing from the closet and from drawers. Other clothes were half pulled out in disarray. She, or someone, had been in a hurry. Wherever she had gone, wherever she had been taken, she didn't need many clothes. Or else they would come back for the rest when they were certain I would not be here. A sickness crept over my heart and mind, my whole being. I stumbled out to the table and sat down, holding my face in my hands. Why had I left her for so long? What did it say about me that I wasn't here to protect her? Maybe she had left of her own free will. Things had not been as good lately, that was for certain. I let my eyes pass over her paintings on the wall. Each of them was full of fire, earth, and water. Each of them gave off the sense of watching, eyes barely suggested but present enough. Then I remembered her studio on the floor above. I ran up the stairs. Again, the door had been left ajar. Inside, all of her paintings had been removed. Strangely, her supplies appeared to be fully intact. One painting remained on the easel. Knowing her work, I would have said it was complete. The brush strokes were perhaps more forceful than her usual. Sharp eyes and an angular form lurked beneath the surface. I went back to the apartment. What was I not seeing? For the first time I noticed a piece of paper on the table onto which something had been scribbled. I sat down and slid it toward me. "Please take the paintings. They are portraits of you." It was not her handwriting. How could I know if it was telling me her wishes? And her paintings were not about me at all.

I looked back up at the paintings on the walls of this room. Seven of them in all, eight counting the one left upstairs. I remembered that the paintings I had first seen in this room on that day when we first made love had slowly been replaced over time. Her older paintings were sold or hung in galleries or stored. The newer ones showed up here. That half-representative expressionistic style remained, however. Like her others, these were portraits of a kind. I got up, wiped some tears from my face, and took a slow tour of the paintings. Sure enough, some personage was being subtly unveiled. It would never have occurred to me that they represented me. Whenever I had asked her about the subject of her paintings, she'd always said she made something up, or they were self-portraits, or they portrayed some animal. It suddenly dawned on me that none of those descriptions necessarily excluded me. The mate you choose is a portrait of you. We do make up things about our mates; we don't see them accurately. And our mates are animals. Keeva's brush strokes were confident and strong. Beneath the surfaces of paint, the remote contours of a face or body emerged, the transmission of an emotion. At a glance, these paintings appeared to be similar. With a deeper look, I saw how different each was. There was a violent underpinning in some of them. An angular cloud of controlling pressure. I saw it, again and again. And all I could do was to sit back down and weep.

Over the next two months, I searched for Keeva. I found and spoke with everyone I had ever seen her with. There weren't that many. None of her friends knew what had happened to her. I wondered would they tell me even if they knew. I thought about her sister and the people in that bar. Of course, I had gone to the police that night and reported her as missing. But in the Lomasayan culture the word "missing" when applied to people didn't have the same heaviness that it did in my home culture. They said they would investigate, but I never saw any evidence of that.

In any case, I thought I knew what had happened to her. I returned to the district and to the bar where I had met Keeva's sister. I spoke to everyone there, but they just shrugged their shoulders, acting as though they didn't understand my language. I caught the eye of the young man I had spoken to at length on my previous visit, but he disappeared immediately. Keeva's sister was nowhere to be seen. People acted as if they had never heard of such a person. Of course, in a city the size of Lomasaya, she could easily hide from me. Still, I explored more and more of the city in the hopes of finding out anything I could. I had basically closed my office. All of my clients had taken their business elsewhere. We'd had a good run. I had no complaints. I needed all of my time to search for Keeva. I bought a bicycle so that I could cover more ground. I was organized, marking off sections of the city on maps as I explored them. At some point, I realized that I wasn't really looking for Keeva anymore. I no longer believed that I would ever find her unless she wanted to be found. Which, I suspected, she didn't. I was spending my time in a way she might have approved of. I was coming to know her beloved city.

Month eight of her pregnancy passed, and I was entering her ninth month without her. I became more depressed, but also more determined to set foot in every last corner of Lomasaya. There weren't many places left on my maps that weren't crossed off. I kept asking officials and her friends about her, but they started to avoid me when they saw me coming. I wasn't sleeping much. I had transported the paintings in her apartment and studio back to my own place. I'd removed the trivial landscapes that had been on the walls and hung Keeva's. I spent hours studying them, trying to understand what she had seen in me that had forced her to leave. I wouldn't let myself believe that the darkness she saw was true. She had been influenced by the opinions of others. Her nameless sister perhaps.

For a while, I had been trying to reach Hanglar, the other agent of the city who had met me at the border of Fallada on that first day and who had met me for lunch on a few occasions. He and Keeva had appeared to have a friendly relationship. But I hadn't been able to catch him. The messages I'd sent by courier had never received a response. I had gone directly to his office several times in an attempt to catch him in a free moment, but he always had someone else with him when I was there. On a couple of occasions I waited virtually all day for him, but he never showed himself outside his locked office door. His assistant just shrugged her shoulders. I had decided he was prepared to remain locked behind that door for weeks, if that's what it took.

Finally, the last day of the ninth month came and went. I began to go to the hospitals and nurseries daily hoping to catch her there while she was in labor or recovering. But there were so many women giving birth. And there were five hospital/nurseries spread out around the city. And the nursery workers did not keep records of the women who gave birth and then reentered their routine lives. Anonymity was the whole idea. Each child belonged to everyone. There were no fathers and mothers. It was driving me crazy to think that my son or daughter had been born and there was no way for me to know which baby I saw in the nursery might be her, or him.

I was stunned when I received a message by courier from Hanglar. He apologized for not being able to meet with me sooner. He said we could meet the next day for lunch at a restaurant we both had frequented in the days when I was still working in my office. When he saw me approaching his table, I could tell that he was concerned about my appearance. I had lost a lot of weight. I wasn't taking much care with how I looked. He gestured to the chair across from him, and I sat down. After the usual pleasantries, I turned the conversation to the only thing that mattered to me anymore.

"Tell me what you know about Keeva," I said. "I'm so worried about her and my child."

He shook his head and looked at me sadly. "My friend," he said, "your suffering is exactly what our culture is designed to avoid. I thought you'd know that by now."

"But it's just so wrong," I said. "I want my wife and daughter."

"No, it's so right. Don't you see? There are no wives and daughters in Lomasaya. Therefore, there is no suffering over wives and daughters, or husbands and sons for that matter." He poured me a glass of Lomasayan wine. "Relax for just a little while. Drink some wine. Eat a good meal. You need to let go of this burden for at least an hour. You'll feel better for it."

I tried to honor Hanglar's prescription. I sipped the wine. I ate a bit of food. But I couldn't for even a moment shift the weight I felt on my shoulders or the burning embers I felt in my gut. When we had completed our meal, Hanglar sat back in his chair and took stock of me.

"You're going to be okay," he said. He leaned forward with his arms on the table. "You have to understand, Keeva is okay."

"Have you seen her?"

"Calm down," he said. "No, I haven't seen her. And I haven't heard anything from her or about her. But this is the way things often work here. I know she is safe."

"And the baby?" I said.

"He or she is safe too."

"And what about me?"

"You also are safe. And free."

But I didn't want to be free. How do you say that to a free man? How do you explain it? I wasn't even sure I could explain it to myself.

"Listen," he said, "It is said that if you win the approval of a Lomasayan woman, you are considered to be a true human being. You have been so honored. No Lomasayan woman can give you more."

I considered what Hanglar had told me. And maybe I could have been convinced if my mind had cooperated. All I could think about was Keeva and my child. My searches in the nurseries were certainly incomplete and likely misleading. It's possible I had laid eyes on my child and would never know. But somehow I was convinced that Keeva had never entered one of the nurseries. She knew I would search for her there. If my hypothesis was correct, then where had she given birth? Keeva had told me that anyone who crosses into the wilderness never returns. But the young man I met in the bar assured me that there was movement back and forth, that there were transactions, cultural exchanges. Who was I to believe?

At the midpoint of the tenth month, I made a decision. I packed a small backpack with food and water. I studied the map for the dead end of a road at the wilderness border that I thought might not be guarded. I admit, my reasoning wasn't clear. I rode my bicycle the nearly thirty miles out to that point of the border. I passed through fertile farmland with great houses and barns, through miles and miles of vineyards, groves of fruit-bearing and nut-bearing trees. Many people worked hard. The only traffic I encountered was horse-drawn farm carts and carriages.

Finally I approached the forest edge, where the last cultivated field ended. The wheat was high and windswept. A path led into the woods where the road ended. The mountains rose majestically until they climbed above the tree line to snowy caps. I also noted two guards posted on each side of the trailhead. I'd hoped this remote location would be unwatched. They were lounging on the ground eating their lunch. I saw canteens, a small cooler, sandwiches. They saw me coming, but they didn't appear to be concerned. There was no way I could ride my bicycle up the steep incline that climbed to the trail entrance. I stopped and let my bike fall to the ground. The two guards were relaxed and chewing and merely nodded at me. I nodded back. I realized I could catch them off guard, so to speak. I had been a sprinter when I was young. I knew I had a fair chance of making it. I went for it, running as hard as I could. I hit the steep slope at full speed and managed to scramble up it to the trail. The forest was thick, the trees tall. The sharp scent of fir and lodgepole pine. A coolness in the air. I slipped and fell on the uneven, root-ridden ground. I could see up the trail just a little way. It was dark in there. The trail turned soon into a switch back heading up, and disappeared. Each of the two young guards grabbed me by one of my legs. I held on to a root, and one of them smashed my hand with something that I couldn't see, and I had to let go. They dragged me back down the slope. One of the young men, a boy really, sat on me. I was still in my prime back then, still pretty strong, and I unseated him and scrambled back up the slope. This time when they caught me, the lights went out.

I would have been happy if they had stayed out. But I woke up in a hospital bed back in Lomasaya. My head was hurting so much that I almost forgot all of my other problems. Almost. A female nurse came into view. She was smiling.

"There you are," she said in my language.

She fooled around with a bandage on the back of my head. My hand had also been treated and was bandaged. A doctor appeared shortly thereafter. He told me I had a concussion, but that I would recover in a few days well enough to proceed with my life if I took it easy for a while. There were precautions I would have to take. And I had some explaining to do to the Lomasayan police. I thought it was they who had some explaining to do. But they didn't see it that way.

I spent the rest of the tenth month recovering and making unwanted plans for my return to my home country. The police had made it clear it was time to leave. They allowed me to use a phone to talk to my father. I caught him up as best I could without making myself look too bad. I knew there was an "I told you so" lurking in the background of his voice, but for the time being all he said was "Come home as soon as you can."

On the last evening of my time in Lomasaya, I packed up Keeva's eight paintings, pretty much all I had left of her, her artistic renditions of my psyche. To this day those paintings hang in my home. I keep their origins to myself, telling my wife and kids I bought them on one of my adventures. I still sit down in front of one or the other of them, sometimes for hours, and try to ferret out what she was seeing and why she was seeing it that way. Those paintings are worth quite a bit of money these days, but

I will never part with them. On that last evening, I prepared them for shipping to my home the next morning.

Then I rode my bicycle out to an overlook at the top of a ridge that gave a magnificent view of the forest and mountains not so far away—a spot that many Lomasayan couples visited on beautiful evenings to gaze at the wilderness they would never know intimately. It was indeed a gorgeous night. A cool breeze made sweaters a requirement. Some people stood with binoculars to see what they could see. But it was getting dark. Some of the couples had laid blankets down on the grass and snuggled up together. Why had Keeva and I never come here? It would have made a great memory. The sky was clear and full of stars. All of us gazed and gazed at the distant hills and mountains that made the circle of our horizon. Out there, everywhere we looked, we could see the flickering of many small fires.

EPILOGUE

Unmistakable

for Roger and Daisy

One morning while watching herself dress in the vanity mirror, slowly buttoning the green sweater she had worn every day for the last two weeks, Mrs. Roberta Waters realized she had not spoken to anyone in months. Maybe she would lose the ability to speak, to communicate, altogether. She had read of people isolated in monasteries or in prison for many years whose vocal chords ceased to have the "muscle memory" to produce human speech. Right then and there, she decided she would get a dog, someone she could talk to, and maybe, behind all of her doors and walls, someone she could play with.

Roberta had lived alone for five years. Her husband had fought cancer for more than a year, then died quietly in his hospital room one night after several days in a coma. She had been holding his hand bruised from all the needles when his exhalation lasted longer than usual, and then he never inhaled. How could it be so simple? She had loved her husband, and after the first wave of grief, a deeper but less apparent mourning settled in, and she became increasingly reclusive, having her groceries delivered, going outside only to work in the garden in her back yard surrounded by a six-foot privacy fence she had helped her husband build more than ten years ago.

And so she broke her silence and called her neighbor, Mr. Holloway. Her voice cracked—was it with emotion?—when she asked him to help her get her car started, her husband's Oldsmobile which she hadn't driven in at least two years, or was it three? She wasn't even sure if her license had expired, or even where in the house she had put it. Mr. Holloway was as gruff as she remembered, calling up the grumpy, sturdy image of him she'd caught from time to time outside her window as he worked on his immaculate property. "Property." That's a word her husband would have used.

"Why does a woman like you need to be driving a car?" Mr. Holloway asked.

She was so surprised by the tone of his question that she could not come up with an answer right away. She opened her mouth, but the hollowness she felt deep inside made an empty cave right out to the edges of her lips.

"Are you there, Mrs. Waters?" he asked.

"That's . . . a very good question," she said. She opened her mouth again to ask him what he meant by "a woman like you," but he filled the empty space too quickly.

"I'll be over in ten minutes," he said, and hung up.

He made a great production of how inconvenienced he was, mumbling in his curmudgeonly way with a sort of half grimace. She had not laid eyes on the Oldsmobile in . . . she couldn't remember how long. Still in great condition, except that she hadn't driven it in two years, it had been nearly the sole province of her husband. Mr. Holloway put the car in neutral and rolled it out of the garage into the driveway, no mean feat for a man his age, his athletic shoes white as lilies in the morning sun. He pulled his Honda next to the Olds, unearthed jumper cables from his trunk that held, she noticed, boxes of empty plastic bottles, tin cans, glass bottles, and newspapers. As she watched him attach the cable, she realized she needed to do something. She found the key stored away in its little side pocket in her purse, climbed in behind the wheel, and turned her engine over until it finally caught. She thanked her neighbor, but he wouldn't let her leave until he'd checked the air in her tires. They were obviously low. So she got back out of the car and left it idling—it needed to do that anyway, he said—and watched him roll his electric pump from his driveway to hers, plug it into an outlet in her garage, and proceed to bring her tires up to the manufacturer's recommended pressure. She noted that Mr. Holloway's hands moved effi-ciently over the equipment, the way her own hands knew the territory of her soil, the flowers and vegetables of her gardens.

She slowly backed the car down the driveway, stopping abruptly every ten feet to be certain she wasn't cutting onto her lawn, or worse, onto Mr. Holloway's. As she bounced from her driveway into the street and paused to shift into drive, she saw Mr. Holloway still standing in his driveway observing her. Was he shaking his head slightly? She'd never much liked his eyes, the way a slight puffiness beneath them made them almost rect-angular and narrow. Was that a small smile or a smirk moving across his lips? Had she lost the ability to read a face too? She wasn't sure that was a skill she cared to cultivate.

She crept over the town's busy streets, stopping even at green lights to look in both directions as the cars behind her blew their horns. At the city pound it took her no more than fifteen minutes to select her puppy, a mixed breed. The dog had the thick, blond coat of a yellow lab and the slightly square jaw and straight beard of a terrier—a lanky energetic crea-ture with lovely, luminous, curious eyes. Roberta's heart pounded with pleasure and excitement as she drove home. At first, the dog on the front seat beside her wanted to see everything outside the windows. Roberta was certain the dog would leap from the car if the window had been down. After a few moments, the dog lay with its head in her lap, those intelligent eyes looking up at her. Back home, she made a bed of blankets and old pillows in the bathroom. It was strange that first night, having another living creature in the house, crying and scratching on the bathroom door. She was relieved a few weeks later when the dog was soundly housebroken and began to sleep in the bed beside her. And she was pleased when the dog's name came to her spontaneously: Daisy.

Daisy became her constant companion over the next year, bounding around the back yard like a child as Roberta tended her garden, lying at her feet as she washed the dinner dishes, or sitting up with its head in her lap as she gazed out the window sipping her coffee. And while Roberta did not cease her mourning, she now at least had someone to share the day, someone to speak to reassuringly and to take care of. And Daisy kept up her side of the conversation too, barking it seemed at every gust of wind, at every leaf that flew, and every opening and closing of a car door in the neighborhood. There were no other sounds in her quiet life that Roberta thought so important that she would deny Daisy her happiness for their sakes. Daisy's gleeful barking was evidence to Roberta that she was a good mistress, that her dog was happy and healthy. Roberta called a local home improvement store and hired a young man to come to the house and install a doggy portal in the kitchen door that opened onto the backyard. Now Daisy could bound in and out of the house as she pleased, barking to her heart's content.

Roberta was very upset when she discovered one morning that Daisy had escaped from the back yard somehow, simply disappeared. As much as she loved the animal, she knew that to the world her dog would be considered wild and unruly. She braced herself and went out into the neighborhood to search. At first she stood within the borders of her yard yelling the dog's name, Daisy, as loud as she dared, using a range of her voice she had not called upon in years. Mr. Holloway came out into his yard scowling at her as if she had lost her mind.

"What are you doing?!" he asked.

"Daisy has run away," she said, trying not to sound as panicked as she felt.

"Count your blessings," he said. "Maybe you didn't realize that your dog was a real nuisance to me, always barking outside my window when I'm trying to work. And now here you are, screaming your lungs out."

Roberta didn't know what to say. As far back as she could remember, John Holloway had lived alone. When her husband was alive, Mr. Holloway would stand within the protection of his front porch and watch them as they came and went. She had always felt he was studying her from the narrow openings of his venetian blinds, and when she complained to her husband, he shrugged it off, saying the man was harmless, a successful and respected entrepreneur. She could not match Mr. Holloway's intense gaze even now as he spoke to her.

"Besides, people like us," he said, "are meant to live alone. It's hard enough to take care of oneself these days, don't you think?"

What did he mean by "people like us" she wondered.

"And anyway," he continued, "I think I saw your dog get into a car. It's probably many miles away by now, maybe in another town. Why someone would want a strange dog I'll never know." He retreated to his porch, turning once to glance at her, and then he disappeared into his house.

She was disturbed by the man's news, but she could not bring herself to believe it. She realized that she had not uttered a word in response to his tirade. But what would she have said anyway? She took a deep breath, stepped onto the sidewalk, and made her way into the neighborhood, calling and calling, wondering how strange it must be to these neighbors to see her, an unfamiliar middle-aged woman, walking down their sidewalks calling out the name of a flower. Maybe they wished she would at least vary her call, moving on to other flowers and even trees. She wondered why such silly ideas had started coming into her head lately. She stopped to describe her dog to anyone she met, but no one had seen Daisy.

On the second day of her search, she encountered a man watering his lawn. He was stout with kind eyes, and while he had not seen her dog, he managed to make her smile and even laugh once as he described his ineptitude in growing flowers. "When I saw you coming toward me," he said, "I thought you were the flower police coming to get me for my atrocities." The way he gestured around the yard recounting his tales of unintended flower abuse made her laugh and laugh. He was agile as a bear, an old one perhaps. She felt something she had not felt in years, a resonance, a point of connection between herself and someone, this kind man. She could not believe it was her own voice asking him if he would like to join her for dinner at her house that evening, and being a bachelor he immediately accepted. Roberta could not fathom this sudden boldness on her part, but she determined that she would go through with her engagement, was indeed grateful to feel this attraction to another person after so many years, this Mister Harrison—she said his name aloud—this Walter. Walking the several blocks back to her house, for moments at a time she forgot about Daisy. What had happened to Daisy? Was she alive? What was she doing right then? What would she have thought of Walter, an amiable but unknown man, invading her house?

Walter arrived right on time that evening, having walked the easy trek from his house. He wore a coat and tie and had combed his hair back into a shiny blade. He brought her flowers and presented them to her in a courtly manner. "Not my own, of course," he said laughing, "but stolen from my neighbor's yard." But Roberta felt a sadness from the start that only deepened as the evening wore on over dinner and a glass of white wine. She could not bear his thick, puffy hands as they twisted and broke the bread, could not bear the way particles of pasta stuck in the corners of his mouth as he talked continuously about his failures as a gardener, his days on the road as an insurance salesman. He was a very sweet man, but she felt tired from the moment he walked into her house, and she found herself guiding him to the front door, noticing the sun was not yet down on this long, summer day. Walter was clearly unhappy to be sent away so early, said he hoped they could share another meal together soon. She stood on her porch and watched him retreat sadly down the sidewalk until he turned the corner and headed down his own street.

For a moment, she thought she heard the unmistakable sound of Daisy's bark. She strained her ear to determine the direction. There it was again, barely audible, and she moved out into her front yard, the grass freshly cut by some young man she sent a check to in the mail. It was such a small sound, but she was sure it was Daisy's bark far off in the distance. Overlaying the deep, grainy "woof" was a squeak that she had never heard from another dog. It had never occurred to her until this moment that a dog's bark was as distinctive as the voice of a human being. She didn't think she had ever listened to anything so intently before. She understood at some level that she may be imagining things. People often hear what they hope to hear. She began to make her way down this old neighborhood, its sidewalk cracked by the roots of great oaks that lined the street. There it was again, small, but not distant as she had thought at first. She turned to look at her neighbor's house, the man who had started her car, Mr. John Holloway. She took one step into his yard, and now she heard the bark again. Odd that it was singular, unlike the staccato string of pearls Daisy usually unleashed. She wasn't one to turn up unannounced at someone's front door, but this time she couldn't stop herself. She walked across his manicured lawn among the beds of red, white and yellow flowers, and up onto his front porch as clean as a living room table. He did all the yard work and house repairs himself, she remembered that. It always surprised her to see him in T-shirt and shorts pushing his mower, or wearing a tool belt with dangling hammers and wrenches. On the porch, there were two long-backed rocking chairs. The slender table between them held a pitcher of ice water and two glasses. She could not imagine what that meant. She stopped before the door and listened. Nothing. She stood there for several long moments, so still that the chickadees landing on the porch rail did not notice her. The oval window on the door was made of beautiful beveled glass, but a blue curtain prevented her from seeing in. And there it was again, Daisy. Not television, nor the radio, she was sure. She knocked on the door and waited, but John Holloway did not come. She knocked again, more loudly, and waited, but he was either deaf or so preoccupied that he didn't hear.

She didn't even bother to look around to see if anyone was watching. She turned the knob and the door opened. Not locked, as she expected a John Holloway door to be. She stepped inside the house and pushed the door shut gently behind her. Standing politely in the foyer, she called her neighbor's name, John Holloway, softly, then louder, but there was no reply. Her body grew tense with the knowledge that he could walk into the front door behind her at any moment. She stepped into a hallway and began to move slowly through the house. Neat for a man living alone. Flowers in a vase, a book open on the kitchen table beside a yellow pad with a pen lying on it. She couldn't help herself. She looked closely at the book. Its title was *The Direct-Mind Experience* by a Richard Rose. She had never heard of him. What was wrong with a good detective novel? The pad contained a paragraph written in a sharply clear hand, but she could not decipher a single word. It wasn't any language she'd ever seen before.

On the wall there were photographs of a family, no one she recognized—a young man and woman with two small children. She passed a cozy den full of afghans and books and dark paintings, and a bedroom so neatly groomed she wondered if anyone would dare to sleep in it. A guestroom maybe, but she couldn't imagine John Holloway with guests. In all the twenty years she had lived next to him, she couldn't remember a single time when some visitor's car remained overnight. It dawned on her just then that for many years, even when her beloved husband was still alive, she had been observing Mr. Holloway. She had taken note of his goings and comings, his visitors and how long they stayed. It had been, she believed, an unconscious process only now coming to light in her own mind. Was that possible? And why had she been watching him? He was strange. Not special in any way.

She called his name again. But all she heard was the sound of Daisy barking, once. Where was it coming from? She tried a door leading off the kitchen and found a stairway winding darkly down into a basement. And yes, the sound of her very own dog much louder now. She crept down the stairwell, and as her foot touched the floor she saw a faint light at the end of a large room, the light around a door slightly ajar. Daisy barked once again and she felt something in her bones she'd never felt before, a deep trembling, and she wanted to run, but she had to keep going. Why hadn't she left a note in her own house saying where she was going? She hadn't known where she was going. Too late for that now anyway. She sidled up to the door as silently as any cat. Peering into the crack, she saw John Holloway in the large, well-lit room, standing erect and gazing at something in front of him. Holloway was medium height, not slender but not thick either, and was wearing suspenders. Yes, he was one of those, a man who

260 The Sadness of Whirlwinds

wears suspenders, even in the privacy of his own basement. She flattened herself against the wall and peeked around the edge of the doorjamb. On the other side of the room, her beautiful dog sat bright-eyed, tail wagging in excitement. She gazed at Mr. Holloway as if he were the one true God. They remained transfixed like this for a moment, a powerful tension in the air between them.

Then John Holloway said, "Do not bark."

Daisy looked like she was about to explode. Her throat thrummed lowly with a wannabe bark, and John Holloway said "No" gruffly. Daisy's eyes grew wide and she became silent.

After a moment of this charged silence, John Holloway said, "Come."

Her dog bounded forth joyfully and ran to him, made a crisp stop and sat down straight in front of him.

"Good girl," he said and gave her something very small to eat. He ruffled her head. "Around," he said, and Daisy stood and walked in a tight circle around his legs and sat down smartly beside his left foot. She knew this was her Daisy, but she'd never seen her obey so well. He gave her another morsel and patted her. Daisy suddenly looked straight at Roberta where she pressed her eye against the crack. John Holloway turned his head to see what she was seeing. Roberta jerked her head away from the crack and pressed her back against the wall. "Stay," he said. Roberta imagined Daisy's attentive pose. She heard John's footsteps. She didn't breathe, didn't move. The door opened slightly farther. "Nothing there," he said, and walked back over to Daisy. Roberta pressed her eye back to the crack above one of the hinges.

"Okay," he said, and the dog turned herself loose, and the two of them began to cavort about the room. Roberta watched them for a long moment, chasing each other, leaping into the air, wrestling like a couple of wild children under a summer midnight moon, except that John Holloway moved in that room a bit like a backwoodsman from Kentucky or Tennessee, a mountain man's lanky humor, some sort of loose, make-shift clog like her grandfather used to do to the sound of banjos and fiddles. Roberta wondered if Daisy would ever really be her dog again, after all of this. She wondered what she was going to do, how she was going to be able to control her anger. She hadn't been angry about anything in many years.

At last, John Holloway called Daisy back to attention, sitting very still in front of him. They gazed at each other for a moment. Then he said, "Speak." Daisy barked once, and Mr. Holloway gave her another tiny treat that she seemed to relish. She wagged her tail furiously. Again, John Holloway asked her to speak, and she dutifully barked once, but this time he didn't reward her. She looked at him quizzically, cocking her head. She began barking, but suddenly he said, "Quiet." Daisy stopped her barking instantly. Mr. Holloway leaned down to give her a treat and pet her. As he raised back up to his full height, he suddenly turned toward the door again and his eyes met Roberta's. Roberta pulled her head away from the crack. Surely he couldn't have seen her in that narrow opening. Her heart was pounding. Fear boiled in her stomach. His eyes were like stars, she thought. They cut into her. Oh God, she thought, what am I doing here? Please help me to escape. When she thought about the long, winding course she had taken through the house, it didn't seem possible. She had to make sure that he hadn't seen her. She carefully moved her head over to the crack, allowing only her right eye to look. John Holloway was no longer looking at Roberta. He was gazing at Daisy who was gazing back at him. "Speak," he said, and Daisy began barking. "Quiet," he said, and she stopped.

Roberta decided she could wait no longer. She crept back through the dark basement, up the stairs, down the hallway from the kitchen to the front door, afraid she was making too much noise, that he would call to her before she could make her escape. She closed the door without a sound and strode across his lawn to her own house. It was dark now in the neighborhood. She saw a breeze moving the leaves of her oak. She saw the first stars coming through. She sat at her kitchen table and tried to think. The trembling in her bones had not stopped. What a silly man to wear suspenders at home, she thought. How strange to steal his neighbor's dog. Why would he be reading such a strange book? She was out of breath. She looked through the kitchen door into her living room, the comfortable disarray of her knitting left in a pile on the floor. She looked out her window, and across the alley she could see the narrow basement window, the dance of their silhouettes across the pane. She was furious at this cranky, eccentric old man who had stolen her dog. She would call the police. She dialed 911.

A young woman answered. "This is Sheila. Your name please."

"I'm Roberta Waters." She quickly added, "Mrs."

"Thank you Mrs. Waters. What is your emergency?"

Roberta's tongue was tied. What a strange metaphor, she thought. But that's exactly how she felt. Finally, she managed to say, "It's my neighbor."

"Is he hurt?"

"Oh, no, he's fine."

"Are you hurt?"

"Uh, no, not exactly."

"An intruder?"

Roberta looked around her empty kitchen, through the door into her dark dining room, dimly lit living room beyond. "No," she said.

"Well, what is the problem then?"

"My neighbor, he stole my dog. He's keeping it in his . . . basement. He's training it, the way he wants it to be. That's not right."

"In his basement."

"Yes, his basement," Roberta said, a little irritated. Did the woman not hear her the first time?

"Mrs. Waters, this line is reserved for emergencies. If you have a complaint against your neighbor, you need to call the police directly. I'm sure they'll send someone around."

"The police?" But Sheila had already hung up, so Roberta gently placed the receiver on its hook. The police, she thought. She imagined a police car parked in front of Mr. Holloway's house, two patrolmen knocking on his door. That just might set him straight. How would he explain himself? What would they do to him? What would happen to poor Daisy? Would she be returned to her? What kind of neighbor would Mr. Holloway be after that?

She pulled out her phonebook, looked up the number, took a deep breath, and dialed.

Someone picked up, but whoever it was didn't speak for a moment. Roberta heard a familiar canine squeak. "It's you, isn't it?" he asked.

She wanted to identify herself, but just said, "Uh . . ."

"What do you want, Mrs. Waters?" he asked.

Roberta hesitated. What did she want? Daisy. Yes. Revenge?

"I see you had a guest earlier this evening," the man said gruffly before she could answer his first question.

"Yes," she said.

"Well, I suppose that's alright," he said.

"Why wouldn't it be?" she said.

John Holloway was silent now and she listened for a moment at . . . at what? . . . the man's hesitancy, his confusion. She felt him stop himself. Such a subtle and agile maneuver, the way he held himself . . . back. Why was he doing that? Was he gathering and storing his energy? For what purpose? And where were these thoughts coming from? She realized that whatever he was doing affected the sound and tone of his voice when he did speak. She took another deep breath.

"Would you like to join me for dinner tomorrow evening?" she asked.

When the silence persisted, she added, "I mean . . . both of you."

Surely he knew what she meant by that. But he remained silent. She could feel his presence at the other end of the line. He was gathering the energy. For what purpose? Would he come to dinner? Would Daisy ever be her dog again? Her house was so quiet that she felt she couldn't move. She just sat there with the receiver at her ear, gathering and gathering.

BIOGRAPHICAL NOTE

Jim Peterson has published three poetry chapbooks and seven full-length collections of poetry, most recently *The Horse Who Bears Me Away* from Red Hen Press in 2020. His collection, *The Owning Stone*, won Red Hen's Benjamin Saltman Poetry Award in 1999. His poems have been published in more than eighty journals, including *Georgia Review*, *Poetry*, *Shenandoah*, *Poetry Northwest*, *Prairie Schooner*, and *South Dakota Review*. His novel, *Paper Crown*, was published by Red Hen in 2005 and is now available on Audible. His stories have appeared in such journals as *Los Angeles Review*, *South Dakota Review*, and *Laurel Review*. Several of his plays have won regional awards and have been produced in college and regional theaters; *The Shadow Adjuster* was published by Palmetto Play Service in 1997. Peterson was Coordinator of Creative Writing and Writer in Residence for many years at Randolph College in Virginia. He is currently on the faculty at the University of Nebraska Omaha's Low-Res MFA Program in Creative Writing. He lives with his charismatic corgi, Mama Kilya, in Lynchburg, Virginia.